An Arrow Through Time

An Arrow Through Time

by

Tricia Davies

Cover design

Morris Wintle & Sam Pillay

First Published by Davies the Elf, GB 2024

daviestheelf@outlook.com

Printed in Great Britain by Amazon

For all ladies who shoot longbow

An Arrow Through Time

Ahna

I need to find another way to be in my community for it seems I cannot be the mother I had expected to be. I have seen what becomes of those like me who fail to produce hunters and mothers for the future - the barren women. They are a burden. They take valuable food, furs and skins but give little back. Yes, they can forage and gather the fruits of the land but less would be needed without them anyway. All they do is provide for themselves. They do nothing for the communal future - nothing.

Just like the old people, we no longer have any need for them. But old people, who have hunted and provided, who have given birth to and raised infants, we give thanks to them. They have helped to secure the future. When they no longer need us, we leave them lying on soft moss and grasses, sheltered from the prevailing wind by stones. We leave them to take their final breaths alone as their spirit flies free.

But me, a barren woman? My future indeed looks bleak if I cannot produce infants. I may be abandoned here in the caves when it is time for the move to the green lands, where the animals roam through the warm season. Already my lover has turned away from me and now lies elsewhere. Already a child grows within his new lover. Now the coldness of the dark season has passed. The sun has returned to light the hunts and ripen the berries and fruits. She will soon give birth and be thanked and honoured. Even if she passes from us in her attempt to give birth, so long as the child lives, her memory will remain. She will be forever a part of our history.

If they abandon me here, how will I survive alone?

***

They left me here as I feared they would.

They closed the entrance to the cave with heavy stones and left me inside. They are expecting to return at the beginning of the dark season to find my bones lying here still, picked clean by whichever starving creatures can find their way in, or are already in here with me.

All around me there is nothing but darkness. I call for them to hear me, to save me, to take me along with them. Anything - I promise them anything if they will retrace their steps, take pity on me, save me from this dying alone to which they have condemned me.

Of course, I have seen abandonment before. It is the way for those who are of no value. Just as the trees drop their dead wood, so do we leave behind those who are a burden. Those without the promise of future value, such as the youngest, they carry with them.

I have seen the old in their gentle abandonment, but I have also seen barren women abandoned. Or at least the women who do not bear a child for the man they lie with, even if the same man may lie with another woman who does not bear a child, and another and another. Still, each of these women has been abandoned in this way. I have seen nothing gentle in the abandonment of these women.

I am frightened - not because I am afraid to die - we all will die. None of us know how much life we will have before we die. I am frightened of what must pass before my death. I fear the hungry days to come, I am terrified, not of the dark itself, for I see dark each time the sun goes down. No, I am in fear here in the darkness of this cave because I know I will not see the sun's return. I feel terror because I hear nothing in this echoing cavern. Yet there is so much noise. I cannot hear the trees, the birds, the wind, the water, but every movement I make reverberates to a deep booming echo far in the depths of the cave. I hear my heart beating, my pulse racing, I hear the cries of my own despair swirling wild and frantic through the cave and I am frightened.

I had pictured my dying as a soft, quiet, lying in the warm sunshine. Gentle breathing of my spirit out of my body, allowing my body to end its life and my spirit begin its journey to a new body, a new life. But here, entombed, my dying will be hard and slow. My body will cling to my spirit, knowing, trapped in this cave, there will be nowhere for my spirit to journey to. No new body, no new life.

I wait. What else can I do but wait for my own dying? Alone, I am certain the sun has gone down and returned, gone down again, returned. I am certain of this because it seems so long I have been here alone.

***

But no, I jerk upright my movements made stiff and clumsy by cold. No, I cannot wait. So much time has passed. A great hunger and an even greater thirst are upon me. It seems to me I must find a way out. There must be a way out. If the creatures who would pick my bones clean can get in there must be a way out. There has to be a way out. It is my only chance of survival. I do not want to die, not yet. How will my soul fly free if I die entombed in this cave?

I am decided. I must leave this place before my spirit leaves my body. I understand now it is not just my body they have intended to die but also my spirit. They have left me here, seemingly without an escape, because they do not want my barren spirit to fly to the body of a new-born child. They want to purge our people of my imperfections. I am not expected to escape. My soul is not expected to escape. On their return they want to find my bones clean and my soul howling through the cave in trapped desperation. I cannot let this happen. I know I have lingered too long, firstly in my hope they would return to release me, then in my despair. They are not going to release me. I am meant to die. I have lingered too long. I should have tried to escape while my strength remained good and true. I am already weakening.

Determination is upon me. I do not know what to do to affect my own release but do something quickly I must. I look around me but see nothing, just darkness. I stand unsteadily in the darkness, reach out a hand, seeking support, my fingertips stretch and stretch away from my body. I do not want to move my feet for fear of the abyss which surrounds me. I need my fingers to touch the stone of the cave. I reach out my other arm, stretching until I feel for certain my arm will leave my body. I feel thunder in my head, then it goes throughout my body, pounding louder and louder. I realise this thundering drumbeat is the sound of my heart beating as if it will burst. Just at the moment when I think to withdraw my hand, to stop my heart from bursting, one fingertip feels a tiny sensation of greater coldness. I take the smallest of steps sideways. Now all the fingertips of my hand are feeling the cold dampness of the cave wall. I hear a sound escape my throat in a deep gasp of relief. I have found the wall.

Moving slowly, always keeping one foot firmly on the ground, I feel the bumps and crevices of the cave wall. I do not know which hand to follow to reach the blocked-up entrance. I choose instinctively, running my hands along the wall and letting my feet follow in their own careful time.

I run out of wall. I am going the wrong way. The way I have been following seems to fall away into the unknown abyss, terrifying my heart into its booming and pounding once more. My ears flood with the sound. I stop. Gently, slowly, carefully, I reverse the tracks of my fingertips. I begin a slow journey back over the ground I have covered. Then I move on to new ground, testing with every step before lifting each foot from the security of its holding place.

There is no day or night passing in the enveloping darkness of this cave. I am in a place of eternity. It will keep me forever if I do not overcome it. And so I continue, one tiny step at a time, arms achingly heavy, the muscles in my shoulders burning from the work of holding up my arms. My spirit is heavy as it struggles to know if it should settle back or prepare to go. On and on, my eyes closed. When I open them there is no change, just darkness. I smell only the dampness of the cave, a smell I am so accustomed to. I pay it no mind. I have only the touch of my fingers to lead me onwards.

Onwards and onwards until I feel the fingers of my leading hand slide, almost imperceptibly around the curve of a stone. A stone not covered with the dampness of the cave walls. The stone is big. By careful exploration I am able to trace the outline of it. This has to be, must be, one of the stones they have used to block the entrance. My fingers trace more stones. This is the way out of my tomb. One of the stones will not fit perfectly, there will be a gap. There's always a gap, a crack. No wall of stones is ever a perfect fit. There must be darkness outside right now because I see nothing, but if I wait the sun will climb in the sky and light will come through the crack. Then I will find the weakness in this wall they have built.

I wait and wait. My eyes burn from the effort of staring through darkness, roaming over the wall I know is there but cannot see. I am afraid to move in case I lose my direction and have to start my search again. My whole body aches with tension. None of my muscles move for a very long time until a thin shard of light pierces the darkness of the cave, sharp and bright. There is the crack - there where the light is coming in. I feel my muscles soften. Then they tense ready for the task ahead. I will need to draw on all the strength in every muscle I have if I am to push out the rock and create my escape.

I feel around where I can easily reach. The small stones I find I lodge into the crack, each new stone causing the rock to move outwards. Just a tiny movement, so small I do not know for sure it has happened. I keep going, hunt a small stone, push it hard, as hard as I can manage, into the crack, slowly, slowly easing the rock from its position. Wondering each time, will this be the stone to move the rock? Each time disappointment, but I keep going, one more, keep going, one more and one more, another and another.

Suddenly, a burst of sounds and sights as the rock rolls away and a shaft of sunlight swoops across the floor of the cave. Desperate as I am to leave the cave, I know I must wait. Wait and listen for more falling rocks to see if I have made the wall unstable.

I breathe in the sharp tang of the new day and bask in the shaft of sunlight while I tense and relax the aching muscles throughout my body. The wall has not collapsed. I wriggle gently through the none too big hole left by the departing stone, out into the sharp crispness of the day.

***

A very small lamb is lying here, at the entrance to the cave. The noise it makes is pitiful. It has been abandoned by its mother. I have seen this happen before. Most likely it was born as the weaker one of a pair. To be born one of two is a curse. One must be left to die. We also do this, just as the sheep do. When the weak one dies, the part of the soul resting in their body will leave to join its other half, which rests in the stronger twin. The soul will again be whole in one body.

I know I should allow the tiny body to be sacrificed to save the wholeness of the soul, but the lamb makes such a pitiful noise. The noise tells me the lamb is hungry and thirsty. I see its starving body shaking with cold and fear, a fear so like my own. I know it feels as I feel. I must name it. I know I should kill it and eat the flesh for my own survival, but I name it.

As I approach, the lamb shakes and jerks uncontrollably with an even greater fear. I don't want it to be afraid of me. I speak gently, calmly. Which words I use I don't later recall but the lamb seems to trust the sound my voice makes. It calms as I approach, quietens and stares through eyes seemingly too big for its head, straight into my own eyes. We are as one. Gently, I lift it onto the only fur they left me when they entombed me in the cave. I wrap the lamb closely in the fur, feeling bones under thin flesh. Slowly the shaking subsides as the fur warms the lamb.

I gather up this bundle of bones and fur, nuzzle close to its ear and whisper, 'Your name is Agna.' Agna turns her tired head, nuzzles into my shoulder and sleeps.

On the hillside behind the cave, sheep graze around stubbly thistles. They are not hiding, not in fear. They know the people have gone. Maybe they sense my presence but alone I am not a threat to them. One of them must be the mother of Agna. I know she won't take Agna back and nurture her but maybe she will let me take Agna to her to feed until she grows strong enough to forage and graze. Perhaps, I too can take some of the mother's nourishing milk to stave the hunger dulling my own senses.

It takes me some time to find Agna's mother, but it is not an impossible task once I recall she will have another lamb, equal in age with Agna. I carry Agna, afraid her legs are too weak to hold her. Afraid the flock will remember they have left her to die and, seeing her alive, might trample her.

We walk slowly amongst the flock, looking, looking, looking - careful not to cause alarm. We don't want them to flee before Agna at least has received sustenance. My legs become weary. I have not eaten since the rest of the people left. They left no food in the cave. What use was food if my purpose was to die? My arms become weary. I try to ignore this. The weight they carry has become precious to me.

Round the flock, through the flock, towards the setting sun, away from the setting sun, towards where the sun will return. Turning, circling, moving ever inwards, as hunters do when they have identified their next meal.

I feel Agna tighten, her head lifts, a tiny noise escapes her. I know we are near her mother. One sheep tenses. Her head lifts and she lets out a gentle, motherly bleat. Agna hears it. The other sheep, all engrossed in their foraging, do not hear it or they hear but it does not alarm them sufficiently to take them from their grazing.

Agna's mother is cautious. She knows Agna is supposed to be dying on the cliff edge by the cave. Agna wriggles. I lay her down gently and unwrap her. She nuzzles close and takes in her mother's sustaining milk until she is sated and sleepy. Then I take milk for myself before wrapping Agna once more in the fur. Already she feels heavier. We move slowly, carefully away from the flock. Agna and her mother make tiny sounds to each other.

I carry Agna back close to the cave and lay her to sleep, still wrapped in the warmth of the weak sun. We will make the cave our place of safety.

I know, from previous seasons, useful things might still be here, waiting for the next dark season when everyone will return to the protection of the caves. There will be nothing in the cave which was meant to be my tomb. It may not be opened for two seasons, just to ensure my bones have indeed been picked clean and my spirit destroyed so it cannot make a future woman barren.

But there are two other caves. One yields a fur. Dusty and older than the fur I have wrapped Agna in but still with many seasons of warmth in it. Here also there is a forgotten stash of nuts, easily opened with a sharp rock. Sufficient to ensure I am nourished for a very short while.

Before I can explore the final cave, cold and darkness descend. I carry the sleeping Agna into the open cave, this will be our home. I hold her close. We warm each other through the darkness of the night. As soon as the sun begins to appear we return to Agna's mother so both Agna and I can again take in her milk. In the days following I will bring Agna each morning and evening to be nourished by her mother's milk and by the warmth and comfort of her mother's body. Agna will grow healthy and strong but, for today, I carry her back to the cave. When I place her gently on the ground, she walks a little, testing her unsteady legs as she finds a patch of sunlight to bask in.

The second cave is narrow and deep. I have never been inside it before. It is the domain of the hunters, used to store weapons for the hunts. Women have no need to enter this cave. They do not need to hunt. Men must hunt because, beyond offering their seed, they have no role in bringing into the world those who will ensure the continuity of the people.

But me? I am a barren woman, abandoned to die. If I am to overcome this destiny I need to survive and I need to hunt.

The cave yields almost nothing, or so it seems at first. There is an axe which I can sharpen and use to split, to chop, to skin but not to hunt. Further into the cave – bones. I don't look too closely in case they are the bones of another barren woman, although they are more likely the bones of the hunters' yield.

With a weighty heart I move carefully around the dark at the very end of the cave. As I turn to leave, wondering for how long berries and fruit alone will sustain me, I stumble. There are long pieces of wood on the floor. Believing anything could be useful, I carry them to the daylight - bows and arrows.

With bows and arrows I can hunt. Not many arrows but I can make more when I need them. I do not need to die. I can hunt to feed myself. Agna will not die. I will be strong enough to care for her, to take her to her mother each sunrise and moonrise. I will find grazing for her as she grows stronger and no longer needs her mother's milk. Ahna and Agna, we are not alone.

***

I am not practised in the art of the bow. Often, I have watched the hunters honing their skills, imprinting the perfect shot in their minds. So when it mattered most, when the hunted animal was within their range and they had it in their power to prevent starvation for us all, their instinct would take over. With an arrow straight and true, success would be theirs. I have watched, also, the one who wasn't content to become a great hunter through practice and perseverance. I've seen him lose many opportunities through his unwillingness to slow down, to move quietly, to draw the bow and release the arrow with care. Rather I have seen him lumbering and bumbling, 'look at me', his quarry gone while the arrow flew who knows where, guided by nothing but a poor shot.

I know how not to shoot an arrow from a bow, now I must learn how to shoot.

Some of the bows I reject immediately. Used by hunters, strong in their youth, they are much too heavy for me to draw back, but there is a lighter bow. I think it has been used for those who had not attained their full strength, but it is still a strong bow and I trust it will serve me well.

For days Agna lies in the sun, watching me as I build what strength I can without food beyond early berries, leaves, and some milk from Agna's mother. The stash of nuts from the cave I eat sparingly, desperate to make them last until I can again eat meat.

While I try desperately not to become weaker, Agna grows stronger each day. By the time I am able to draw back the string on the bow, to produce in it the power which will send the arrow fast and true, Agna's legs have gained strength. Although we now walk to her mother for her twice daily milk, Agna never strays from me, never goes back to the flock alone. I think she knows we belong together now. Each night, as the chill of darkness arrives, Agna moves close to me, and we sleep securely.

As we settle close together one night, I know my skill with the bow has grown well. It is time to put my skill to use. My head tries to tell me I could shoot one of the sheep in the flock. They have grown used to my presence amongst them, they seem to trust me. Although they have rejected Agna, they have trusted me enough to allow Agna and me into their midst. They may no longer have a place for Agna, but I cannot willingly kill them. Besides, if I kill one, much of the meat will fester and rot before I can eat it.

Agna seems to sense my problem, my hunger, maybe also my increasing desperation. She seems to know what I need. As the light of day begins its slow fading, the first hint of pink dancing in the sky, Agna bleats. She nuzzles at me, not softly like when she wants us to sleep, but roughly, with a sense of urgency. She runs a short way from me then returns to nuzzle again. She repeats the actions several times, patiently waiting for me to understand. Dulled by tiredness and hunger, it takes me some time. Agna wants me to follow her.

Once I start to follow, she gives a quiet but unmistakably happy bleat and trots steadily ahead of me, her head turning from time to time, checking I am still there. I follow over humps in the ground, stumble over rocks, trip on the root of a tree protruding from the earth. I should have seen it. I must move more carefully. There will be no one to help me if I fall and break.

We stop. Agna bleats and settles down, eating the short, crisp green covering of the land and I think, 'she has only brought me here so she can eat?' I did not think so when we set out so urgently. I pause, still and quiet. Why has Agna brought me here?

My eyes skim the shadows created by the gathering gloom. Something moves, a quick, fleeting movement. It stops. I see nothing. Then another fleeting movement and nothing. Another and another. My eyes grow more accustomed to the low, receding light. I watch carefully where one fleeting movement ends. I see what created it. It is a rabbit, which would make a good day's eating for two. These are the rabbits the young boys growing into hunters use as their first quarry. Their first kill which they take home to share with their mother, before they play their part in hunting to feed everyone. This first kill is for a special moment of closeness with the woman who gave them life.

I watch the rabbits feeding, my heart racing, mouth dry, the taste of the meat spinning in my head. I know, for today, I have only one chance. When I release the arrow from the bow and it whistles through the air, it must find its mark or I will sleep hungry again. When I release the arrow the rabbits will sense their danger, they will skitter away and hide through the night rather than risk exposing themselves to a second arrow from my bow. I raise my arm, clutching tight to the bow. I see my arm shake. The bow is not steady. I jerk the knock of the arrow onto the string. The bow is even less steady. I feel the lurching beat of my heart which seems to move my whole body. I hold my breath tight, tense with the need to succeed. I quickly, too quickly, pull back the string and in an instant the arrow is gone. Too soon. I have not pulled enough power into the bow. The arrow falls short of the rabbits but close enough to alarm them, cause them to bound, almost as one, back to the safety of their burrows. I will not see them again this day.

The following day, just as an early pink glow from the rising sun is visible, I return to the rabbits' feeding ground. Hungry from their interrupted eating the night before, they are out early. On the first sight of the rabbits, and the thought of the meat I might have to stave off my hunger, my whole body tenses. But I am still, they must not know I am here. I take in a deep gasping breath as I nock the arrow and aim, quickly pulling back the bow, quickly releasing the arrow, hoping speed will outwit the rabbits. But the rabbits are already alerted, perhaps by the sound of my sharply indrawn breath or I have moved too quickly. The arrow lands in the ground, where just moments before, the rabbits feasted. Now I must wait all day.

When the sun begins again to leave, I am already at the rabbits' feeding ground. I wait and wait, listening to myself breathing, making myself breathe gently and evenly, poised in position, not moving. I feel certain I am as still and as calm as it is possible for a person to be. I breathe and breathe, slowly, steadily, to still the beating of my heart which threatens to spoil another hunt. I wait until all the rabbits have appeared. I wait until I see them all eating together. I know they have not yet sensed danger.

I raise my bow arm, hand lightly steadying the bow at the leather grip, arrow securely knocked on the string, bow arm still, my other arm steadily pulling back the arrow on the string, aiming at the stillest of the creatures. This time my heart does not pound. I have drawn my breath in deep as I continue to pull back the bow. I gently release the arrow, my breath exhales smoothly, breathing the arrow from the bow to its target.

Instantly the creature's soul leaves this world. It dies so I can live. Rarely have I felt such elation. At last I am able to provide for myself. Never before have I done so. Instinctively I hold Agna close for a short while, she seems to understand my happiness. I will make the meat last as long as possible for if I come here hunting frequently the rabbits will move on to a safer place. I do not need to hunt bigger prey. Their meat would fester and be wasted before I could eat it all.

In the following days Agna and I rarely experience hunger. Our visits to Agna's mother cease in time. As the sheep meander over the hillside in search of sufficient grazing for them all, it becomes further and further to walk.

Often when we reach them, Agna wants no more than to gently nuzzle her mother, who bleats softly while gently pushing Agna away, seeming to say, 'you are grown now and can graze, we must say goodbye.'

One night Agna creeps to me, nuzzling as close as it is possible for her to get. I know then our visits to her mother have ended. She has entwined herself with me. Now there are just the two of us.

Through many sunrises and sunsets rain falls almost unceasingly and so we remain in the shelter of the caves a while longer.

Agna does not go hungry. Each time the greyness of the sky clears a little and the rain breaks briefly from its falling, we venture out to find patches of good grazing to sustain her. When my meat runs out, I use these breaks in the weather to find and hunt a rabbit. My search for food is less reliable than Agna's. I go hungry when she does not through this wet time. As soon as it ceases, we will do well to move. The next dark season will soon begin its approach. My people will return and find my body gone from the cave. They will not rest until my barren soul, whether it be in or out of my body, or in the body of a child not yet born, has been destroyed.

***

The season of rain hung long over us, more unforgiving than I remembered it being or had ever imagined it could be. So damp and dull by day, Agna seemed to anticipate, as eagerly as I did, the coming of night, when we could again retreat to the dry depths of the cave, warmed by each other's bodies.

While we waited for the rains' passing, I spoke often with Agna, who nuzzled close and pretended she could understand the words, seeming to know they were important to me and I needed to share them.

Together we made plans, as I named aloud the things we would need to take when we moved on. The knife for skinning and butchering, the axe for chopping wood, the furs we have for warmth, the water carrier, my small store of nuts and dried berries – and my bow and arrows. These were the things we would need for our new life. Agna bleated gently each time I repeated the list into her softly twitching ear as we settled ourselves to sleep through the darkness of the night. After I had recited our list and sleep did not come, I moved closer still to Agna, my fingers warming entwined in her thick fleece, and told her stories from my ancestors. Agna never tired of any of these stories, but it seemed to me she most positively enjoyed the story of the bow and arrow.

***

In times long passed, Agna, our people did not hunt with the bow and arrow. We had no knowledge of such things. Instead, we followed the animals. We had to move so slowly, with stealth, but yet with desperation for this was a very unpredictable way to hunt and we were often so very hungry. When we found where the animals were feeding the hunters had to use heavy stones to try and stun an animal so they could kill it and we could all eat. The hunters had to move so carefully, so quietly the hunt was no place for infants and the very young. Their hunger made them desperate. They would call loudly if they saw an animal we might eat. Easily they frightened away the animals and we all went hungry once more. That's why the men became hunters. The women often had a baby at their breast or young ones who knew nothing of silence in the face of hunger.

One day a stranger came. We saw at once how strong and well-fed he appeared to be. He carried a strange weapon which none of us had seen before. At first, we did not trust him because he travelled alone. We thought, 'who travels alone except they mean no good?' It took time for us to trust him but he willingly joined the hunt. He showed our hunters how he could use his strange weapon to swiftly kill an animal from a distance. The animal did not even know he was near and so had a swift and peaceful end. The resulting meat was sweet and good. The stranger made bows and arrows like his for our hunters and spent many days sharing his skills and knowledge with them. In time our hunters became skilled with the bow and arrow but still the hunt needed more stealth and silence than infants and the very young could give and so it remained the role of the men to hunt. He never left our people and now his blood runs through the blood of our people. We never knew why he travelled alone but now I travel alone with you Agna and I know not all who do so are filled with ill-intent. From the time of the stranger's arrival our people rarely went hungry because he had shared his skills.

***

'And that, Agna, is the story of how our people first began to hunt with the bow and arrow. From infants we were told this was a skill for men. Now that

I have become skilled with the bow and arrow, I know this to be untrue. I too can hunt well with the bow and arrow.'

Agna and I shared this story many times through the nights, until the night when we reached the end of the story and I sensed the world was different. Something had shifted and we were no longer waiting. 'You feel it too, don't you, Agna?', I breathed as she shared my restless waiting through the dark. We both awaited the arrival at the cave entrance of the first hesitant shafts of daylight more eagerly than usual.

Agna was first out to explore the dryness and sunshine of the new day. As I followed, I saw her trotting briskly to a grassy tussock, which looked greener and more inviting than I had seen it for many days. Now the sun shone upon it. Her unfettered carefree rush to the lush grazing was shared, I noted with excitement, by the rabbits. My bow lay ready with sharp arrows. I carried them swiftly and silently towards the rabbits. Cornering my prey would be quick and easy this time for the rabbits seemed carefree and unaware of any danger.

By the time the sun had reached its highest point both Agna and I were sated and resting, knowing we would have just one more night in the cave before moving on to whatever lay before us.

***

As Agna and I leave the cave for the last time, we are alone together. Maybe we are the smallest community ever. I wonder what will become of us. I do not want to use the word 'alone.' I voice it aloud and it is such a dismal word, I don't want Agna to hear it. Instead, I call cheerfully to Agna, hiding the tremor of trepidation I feel within me, 'Come Agna, let us go onwards and find out how we might prosper and grow.' Agna bleats quietly. She skips and bounds across the hillside, as if she knows where we should go and how to get there. She looks back and bleats to me, 'trust me, follow me,' I hear spinning silently through my head and I put my trust entirely in she whose life I have saved.

The following days are kind to us. The sun rises each day high in the sky, giving us, with each passing night, warmth and light. Without the shelter of the cave and unable to keep watch over a fire through the night, the nights still find us often cold. I huddle under the fur we have carried with us. Agna fares better for her own fleece has grown thick and warm. Still there is occasional rain and wet nights are the worst of times. We seek what shelter we can, under a dense canopy of trees where the torrential rain is transposed to a steady dripping of cold droplets, or in the lee of a hill with the rain seeming to drift over us as we lie sleepless waiting for those clear nights when the sky twinkles and the moon lights the world.

I am afraid of the noises we hear through the night. I sense Agna also feels fear and senses danger as howls, screams and barks echo through the darkness. I've heard them before, of course, but with other people around me for safety. Now, alone with Agna, my security gone, I think less of the safety of numbers and more of the tales recounted of children missing in the morning, never found but for bones, or of old people, no longer able to keep up with the others, who have gone quietly to lie away from others and await a meeting with one of these animals of the night. What creatures roam the lands in darkness without so much as a glimmer of light from a rising or setting sun to guide them? 'Surely Agna,' I whisper as she slides closer to me with each new scream from the darkness, 'surely only a creature intent on harm would be about when all else are at rest and waiting for the light of the new day.'

Sometimes a dark but silent shadow swoops and swerves so close I believe they must collide with us. I believe our end is coming, but these silent creatures of the air seem not to bring fear in Agna, the way the screaming, barking, howling creatures do. I take courage from Agna.

On a brighter night, when the moon is huge in the sky and there are more stars than I had thought possible, Agna and I lie close beside each other as we watch these silent, flying creatures of the dark, awed by their ability to fly so close to trees, to rocks or to us, and yet never to collide and injure themselves. I know not what they search for, but it is not for us.

By day we travel onwards. Agna leads and I follow. I trust her. Her instincts will not lead us into danger. We stop before darkness falls. This is the best time to hunt a rabbit. I eat the meat, as well as the fresh fruits and leaves of this abundant season. They make good eating now. Agna too, eats well. She grows ever stronger.

There is quiet in the darkness, when the sun has faded and the moon is not yet fully risen. Agna breathes softly beside me in the contented sleep of the well-fed. Later the fear of the howling night animals will return to make my body tense and my mind sharp but, in the early peaceful quiet of darkness, I look for someone to thank. I find none - except Agna with her quiet persistence in moving us further and further away from the danger of the caves. Agna - with her willingness to keep believing in good pastures ahead of us. Agna - who grows strong and healthy because she takes the chances which come her way. Here a tiny patch of green - enough nourishment to give her a little strength - enough strength to reach the next patch.

Agna's faith may be simple, but it is strong. I try to follow her ways. When the wind howls or rain falls through the day and there is no hunting, I look to the leaves and berries I find to nourish me and give me strength to keep moving. In time I know I will always find meat - maybe not today, perhaps not even tomorrow but I will always find meat eventually, now my skill with the bow has grown.

After many, many days, when the moon has waxed and waned twice over, we pass close to some sheep. We hear the gentle bleats of the well-grown young as they check their flock are close by. We hear the much louder bleats of the fully grown sheep. I watch them as they settle close, one to another, for the nighttime. As still as they then are, I know I could shoot one quickly and cleanly with my bow. It would not suffer pain. I feel for my bow and bring it around my body from where it is slung across my back. I hold the bow in position and look, as if sighting my target, but I do not load an arrow. Without Agna I may not have survived thus far. I cannot kill a sheep to eat.

'Come Agna,' I whisper, 'we will move away to sleep and find rabbit to hunt when the light returns.' But Agna will not move, she has settled as if for the night. Her eyes are firmly fixed on a patch of grass, juicy and sweet from earlier rain. I know she intends to eat this grass, but it seems she has settled as for sleep to let me know we are not leaving this spot tonight. Once I have understood this and lie beside her, Agna eats.

I don't know why we cannot leave tonight. I must trust her.

As the sun rises, I wake once more from a sleep troubled by hunger. There seems an unnatural quietness. Usually I wake to the sound of Agna, searching out the first new grazing of the day, or, if she has gorged on fresh greenstuff late into the evening, I usually wake to her gentle movements near me as she waits to move on. This morning – nothing - or so it seems at first. When I pause and listen more attentively there are the calls and songs of many birds and a gentle swishing as the wind drifts through the woodland on whose edge we have sheltered through the night. I listen again but still I hear no sound of Agna.

'Agna, Agna,' I pause, listening once more, listening beyond the bird song and the wind – there is nothing. The thought passes through my mind, 'the sheep have moved on and Agna has moved with them.' I am alone with the thought. Usually, I share my daybreak thoughts with Agna. Indeed, I share my thoughts with her throughout the day and into the darkness of the night. A vision flashes through my mind, of settling for the night, alone, without the calm reassurance of Agna's warm body and gentle breathing close to me. I don't believe I can continue so completely alone. 'Agna, Agna,' I call once more, hearing the desperation in my own voice as it echoes around and around the trees and out across the grass-covered hillside. I feel my face, my whole body, tense, tight and immobilized. There are no thoughts in my head, no inner voice telling me what my actions should be, just dark cloud and fog engulfing me from the inside out.

Curled, I lie in the sheltering nest I created last night to keep Agna and I warm and safe together. I think but a moment has passed, but so many arrows of despair pass through my mind and body, I know it must be more than a moment. When next I open my eyes, it is to the encroaching darkness of a new night. In my despair I simply sleep.

'A new day once more,' I whisper as my eyes open without me asking them. I am surprised to hear myself speak. Without thinking, I wait for the answering bleat but it doesn't sound. While my mind and my body work a little more this morning, I still have the thick fog-like cloud to carry with me, burdening me, hindering thoughts and actions. I know I must eat but I have neither the strength nor the will to hunt and prepare meat. Sparingly I force my body to accept the leaves and berries which I can reach without carrying the heavy cloud far. Then I sit. I sit and close my eyes. There is nothing in my mind.

Nothing.

***

For three sunrises and three sunsets, nothing.

When there is no greater depth of despair to reach, I know I must begin the climb back. I know I cannot live on the few leaves and berries within reach. If I am to get strong again, I will need meat. If I do not hunt for meat soon, I will no longer have the strength to do so. Everything Agna and I endured together will have been for nothing.

When the sun rises for the fourth time, I gather my bow and arrows. The cloud feels less dense around me. I hope it does not spoil my shot. I move slowly, quietly, crossing the open hillside away from the sheltering forest, down into a narrow valley with a small stream of water passing along, gurgling, splashing, seemingly rejoicing in the new day. I leave a piece of my cloud in the water for the stream to carry away. Now I feel lighter and more able to focus on my shot. 'There they are,' this time I whisper to myself, just as I would to Agna. She always seemed to understand the need to keep still and quiet when she heard this whisper. The rabbits are big. They will move fast if startled. For a moment I feel Agna beside me, feel the reassurance of her stillness as she would wait for the shot. Slowly, silently, I raise the bow, nock the arrow, lift the bow, sight with the arrow point, pull the bow back taut to store its strength and energy in the arrow. Instinctively my fingers release the arrow at just the right moment, with all the bow's power in the shot. The arrow flies through the air, arcing slightly as it covers the distance, landing exactly on target. The other rabbits race to the security of a shelter only they know of. My target has died at once. Later I will have meat to eat. I will get stronger. I will move on. It seems as if some of my cloud went with the arrow. Lighter now, I will hope for a future.

For two days, I walk before realizing I am choosing my path in the same way I have witnessed Agna choose a path. I am following the grazing which looks the most bright and juicy. I don't stop, except to sleep a while through the darkness. Sleep disturbed by the echoing noises of the animals and birds which frequent the dark. They startle me more than they did when I had the reassuring presence of Agna's warm body beside me. They keep my mind and body from sleep. After the second such night I set out on my journey even before the light has fully reappeared, spurred on by a greater urgency than I have felt before.

The sky is clear, promising a bright, light day. I soon feel the chill of the dark hours creeping from me. Far ahead I can see a patch of woodland, not close enough to guess its size. 'Will I find wood for new arrows? And berries to eat?' Instinctively I speak aloud. Liking the sound in the quiet stillness of the morning I call, loudly, to the woodland, just to hear the faint echo of my voice bouncing back at me from the surrounding hills, 'Hello, do you have arrow wood?' The wood does not answer me. If I were closer, I might hear a swishing through the branches of its trees as the wind finds its way around them.

What I do hear, coming from the direction of the rising sun, is bleating. I think I have imagined it, for how many times over recent days have I heard Agna bleat just because I wanted to hear the sound of her? When there was no sound but the calls and songs of birds, or the patter of rain, to be heard?

I stop and listen. I hear it again. Shutting out all other sounds I stand so still I might be dead. But I am still on my feet and my mind is working, listening, listening. There it is again. This time I am certain. I hear not simply a bleat, but I hear, without a doubt in my mind, Agna's bleat. Then another bleat. At first, I take it for an echo of Agna's voice but doubt creeps in because it is louder and deeper in tone than anything I have ever heard from Agna. I wait and wait with a patience I did not know I had within me. I wait and I listen and I hear. Each time Agna's bleat is followed by the answering call of the louder, deeper bleat. As the sun creeps ever higher in the sky I know they are getting close to me. Agna has not abandoned me, she is coming back and she is bringing a ram with her.

My heart beats fast with joyful anticipation of being alongside Agna once more. It beats fast with the effort of moving so quickly, laden as I am with bow, arrows, fur and my store of meat and berries. But I ignore the pounding of my heart and the labour of my breathing in my eagerness to reach Agna. Her bleating stops. Looking up and about me, thinking I have lost the direction of her calls, I see her, just cresting a small hillock which had hidden her from my view. So close. Now I see her, she is moving faster than I have ever seen her move before. Is her heart also pounding and her breathing heavy as she struggles to cover the distance between us as quickly as possible?

'Agna, Agna,' I whisper as my heartbeat subsides and my breath returns to me, Agna nuzzles, bleating softly, using her head to nudge me towards where the ram is standing, waiting. When I reach out a hand to him, he comes towards me and we meet. I name him Aries.

Agna and Aries seem to know which direction we should take. I follow them back over the crest of the small hill. A valley lies beyond, abundant with good grazing for Agna and Aries - good grazing for the rabbits which I need to keep me strong. Perhaps we will stay in this valley, with its good food and clear stream running through. If Agna wishes we will stay here through the lighter warmer days. Perhaps we will stay here forever?

We don't stop moving for much of the day. We climb down into the valley and then walk along and along, beside the stream, slowly. Agna and Aries graze a while and then we move a little further and they graze again. I eat the meat I have carried with me. I know I should not disturb this slow and silent journey. Instinctively I know it has a purpose. There is somewhere we are going to.

'There are people!' I realise I have spoken, my voice loud in the surrounding stillness as the sun begins its journey beyond the horizon. I have stopped whilst Aries has increased his speed, his deep bleating alerting the people to his return. Agna stops a little ahead of me. She bleats very loudly at me. She seems anxious I should move, keep walking towards the people. She has found Aries and now she feels in danger of being separated from him. He turns and bleats encouragingly at Agna. I know I must go forward to meet these people. Are they friends or foes?

***

'Welcome.' The woman I later know to be Fearne steps towards me, her eyes searching all over and around me, searching for a threat, for weapons, poisons, danger in any of its manifestations. I too, do not meet her eyes because I also search for danger. When we are both satisfied as to the integrity of the other, she extends her hand to the other people present.

'Byrht, my twin, Astrid the oldest one, Esmond, son of Astrid, the father of my children, Luella and Felix.'

We stand, watching. It feels as if we will not be enemies.

I know I have little choice but to join this small group. I will be safer here than alone, for Agna has determined her future lies with Aries and the other sheep these people keep. I lay down my bow, my arrows, my axe and butchering knife. I place my palms upwards to the sky to show I have no weapons. I move slowly towards them, without any of the things with which I might defend myself and I am rewarded as Fearne, Byrht, Esmond and Astrid all lay down the axes and knives they carry, reach their palms upwards to the sky and, as one, walk slowly towards me. In turn I lay my palms on each of their palms, then I move towards the children, offering them my palms. Their hesitancy tells me they have not met many people and they are unfamiliar with this gesture of kinship, but they follow the lead of their kin and, in turn, lay their palms on mine. Henceforth we are one. They will have care and concern for me and I will have care and concern for them.

Returning to collect my few belongings, I find Agna guarding them. She nuzzles more strongly than ever before. Agna is happy. I understand she believes we will stay together with these people.

***

Byrht and Esmond lie, barely moving, barely breathing. What breath does come is slow, rasping, bringing to my mind images of the old ones lying out the final days of their souls and bodies being one, waiting for their soul to move on, their body no longer needed. But Byrht and Esmond are not old. They are poisoned from gorging on unknown berries when they should have been trapping meat to feed us all. For days now neither has moved, beyond the occasional moan of distress.

My bow and arrows lie, unused since my arrival, in the shelter of the trees. Byrht and Esmond have the task of finding our meat. More than once, I suggested I might hunt with them, but they guarded their responsibility closely. I have watched them from a distance. They do not hunt with bows and arrows, in fact they seem not to know the purpose of my bow and arrows and have shown no interest in them. Instead, they set traps for the rabbits, and even for bigger animals such as deer and boar.

'You lay the traps before darkness falls but don't go to take the prey until the light returns. Are the animals not sometimes left in pain and suffering for too long?' I have asked them. Each time they turned away, not wanting confrontation or change. 'But sometimes I hear the animals,' I whisper to Agna as she snuggles as close to me as the twin lambs growing inside her will allow, 'I hear their cries of pain through the dark night. With the arrows they would not suffer in this way.' Agna nuzzles and bleats loudly, I believe she hears the suffering of the trapped animals as well.

Again, the sun rises. With the promise of another meatless day, we are all becoming weaker, especially the young ones, Luella and Felix. If Agna had given birth, we would be able to let the children have some of her milk, but she is waiting for her lambs to be ready.

I whisper to Agna, 'I cannot wait for a slow dying to take us all - I will hunt.' I collect my bow and arrows, walk silently away from our shelter, scanning the horizon for bushes and grassland offering a sheltered feeding place for the rabbits.

Pausing, I am aware of footsteps reaching me and then the voice of Fearne, 'I heard you speak of hunting and came to share the task with you.' I glance at her eyes. Their eagerness masks the despair we were all feeling.

'Do you know how to hunt with a bow?' Fearne shakes her head, reaching out a hand to touch the tautness of the strung bow. 'Then I will teach you, but for today you must watch, we need meat to make us strong. Then we will make another bow for you, and I will teach you. For now, you must stay with my back to you, then I will not shoot you in error.'

Fearne is quiet. She moves slowly, silently. I know she will become a good hunter. She is a watcher. She is storing knowledge of the skills she must learn. Already she is an asset to my hunt. Once I have shot one animal, she stays guarding it and I don't have to take it, smelling of death, as I find another group of rabbits. We will need two to feed us all and to make a nourishing broth for Byrht and Esmond. They have had no nourishment but water since their sickness began.

As the sun rises high in the sky Fearne and I return triumphant to the shelter to prepare and cook the meat.

Astrid takes the meat from the bones, despite protest from Luella and Felix who had anticipated the pleasure of finishing this feast by sucking and gnawing those same bones. Astrid adds water and healing plants she has gathered to the bones. They stew together gently, all the nourishment leaching from the bones, all the healing from the leaves seeping into the broth.

'We cannot hurry this,' Astrid tells us, for we are eager to take the broth to the two ailing men. 'We cannot hurry this. We cannot heal them with lightly flavoured water. We must wait for the nourishment to be ready. By then the aroma will have reached deep into their minds, preparing their bodies for the nourishment.'

Astrid passes meat to the children.

Felix takes his meat slowly, not wanting, it seems, to appear desperate. 'And then,' he says, 'will they be well and hunt for us again, when they have eaten the healing broth?'

Astrid sighs, 'No, it will take many sunsets and sunrises before they are strong enough to hunt for us. Ahna must hunt for us a while longer.'

Fearne reaches to take the meat Astrid offers her, 'Ahna will teach me, then I will help her to hunt for us.'

Luella's eyes hold an unspoken yearning. They are fixed on me. 'Ahna, will you teach me to shoot with the bow and arrows? Will you teach me and Felix?'

***

Henceforth, when we share together in the meat I have provided, I sense I have earned my place here, I have been fully accepted, I have a purpose. As we wait for the fire to die down and the warmth of the fire to leave us, with no hunger to distract us, we hear Esmond and Byrht sleeping close by, sleeping more peacefully than we have heard for many days. Now their spirits seem content to stay longer in these bodies.

***

Luella and Felix have edged closer to the fire, closer to Astrid. They know her well and it seems to me this closeness says they are expecting something to happen, perhaps something which happens often when there is no hunger and fear. As my mind wanders gently through soft clouds of contentment, not yet willing to lose the pleasures of this day in sleep, I hear what Luella and Felix wait for. Astrid begins to share memories with us all. Memories to help us entwine together. Now I truly belong.

***

'Once I belonged to a different community.
But belonging is fragile at times, tender as the new
stem which can be broken, disconnected, without
thought or warning. I belonged to a community of
many. Very many. I believe a connection may be lost
when a group of people becomes great in number.
No longer are the names of all readily brought to
mind. No longer are the names of the mothers who
bore them readily brought to mind. No longer do we
know, without deep thought, who their fathers are.
No longer is it enough to be named at birth and to
keep only a birth name. No, when a people outgrows
its intimacy the young and, indeed the not so young,
must be henceforth known not as Esmond, but as
Esmond, son of Astrid. Not as Luella but as Luella,
daughter of Fearne, daughter of Esmond. Not as
Felix but as Felix, son of Fearne, son of Esmond.'

Astrid breathes in deep and slow. Slowly and deeply, she breathes out the sigh which has lingered long inside her.

'But no matter for it transpired I had no permanent place because, although I lay willingly with a man and we had a great fondness for each other, for many seasons I did not become with child. A woman who did not bear children was not needed.'

Luella gasps and snuggles closer to Astrid, wondering at the strange things she is hearing, although I feel sure she has heard the story many times before.

'One day, just as the sun rose red in the sky, and we prepared to move to new hunting grounds for the warmer seasons, I was taken by strong people and trapped beneath many, many heavy stones. Long before, I had seen a woman abandoned in this way. I had been young then, very young and I did not know what the meaning of this was. Things happen when we are very young which we don't even think to question. But when they abandoned me, I knew then what it meant. I was not needed, I was useless. I must stay to die alone. The heaviest stones lay on my legs, legs which to this day show the scars and strains from then. There were days of light fading, darkness arriving, darkness lifting, light arriving. Days of increasing weakness, for they left me nothing - not food nor water close by, before I was able to remove the final stones from my legs and free my body.

My people were long gone. My legs, full of the blackness of heavy bruising, were no longer strong enough to try and track them. I stayed alone. Water, herbs, the last of the season's berries and nuts were close by. In time some greater movement and strength returned to my legs and I moved on, looking for I knew not what. I became increasingly aware, as my body changed and moved inside, I would bear a child.

When a woman does not want to move along, when she wants only to make a place of her own. To warm that place with dry bracken. To have water, a stream or a river, nearby. When she rests, knowing she must keep to her body all the strength she can, not sharing it with others. When these things happen, the woman will soon give birth.

Thus, it was with me. Through the darkness of night and the breaking of the day, until the sun was as high in the sky as it would go, I stayed alone waiting for the pain to pass, which was all I could do. When the sun reached its high point and I began to feel it too hot upon me and to wish I could seek the shade and just sleep, my child entered the world. I whispered his name, Esmond, into his ear. I told him we must be strong for each other.'

***

Now I am the one to gasp at the similarities in our stories. In awe I move closer to this strong, strong mother of my new people. I had wondered why she moved always slowly, carefully.

'But Esmond?' I whisper, 'You bore Esmond as your son? Even after you had been abandoned as a barren woman?'

Then I see Astrid's face light with a deep glow I have not seen before. Esmond is her world. He, tiny as he had been at birth, was the reason for Astrid's strength and fortitude. Esmond reaches to take Astrid's hand, in a gesture so rarely seen beyond infanthood.

'Go on, Astrid, go on with the story, there is more to be told, Ahna does not yet know how the community you and Esmond created grew to who we are now.' Fearne's voice is low, soft, and warm. A smile flickers across her face and her eyes smile warmth to Astrid.

***

'Esmond looked at me, his mother. His eyes opened wide at the wonder of the world he had been born into after the time of darkness in my womb. Tired as he was from the birth, he lay awake in my arms. We waited. I knew once his spirit arrived and Esmond had breathed his spirit into the depths of his body and mind, then he would sleep. When the moment came and Esmond's eyes became heavy, his head turned towards me and the alertness of his body stilled in sleep. I knew I had to trust the spirit which had chosen him would be a good spirit. Then Esmond would grow to be strong, kind, and thoughtful of others.

After several nights of rest, Esmond and I grew a little stronger. The time had come to move on. We began our journey to this place of our own.'

Luella and Felix look with alarm at each other, was Astrid going to leave the story there? 'Astrid, you haven't told of Byrht and Fearne,' Luella whispers with desperation in her voice. 'If you don't tell of Byrht and Fearne then how will Felix and I join the story? Ahna will believe we don't belong.'

Astrid reaches out to stroke Luella's arm reassuringly.

'I have not forgotten you. I needed to make certain you recall the sequence of our story for one day the story will get longer and longer. I will be gone, and it will be for you to tell the story to those who come after us.'

Astrid breathes deeply of the night air. This time she does not breathe out the air in a deep sigh, seeming instead to retain it within herself, as if the words to the story are held within her breath and the breath will be let go slowly, one word at a time.

***

'We travelled slowly. I needed to find food along the way to give me strength for the journey and to help me make milk for Esmond. When we found food, we rested.

One day, as we rested with the sun as high in the sky as it would go before darkness began to return, we listened. We listened to the rustling of leaves in the trees. I told Esmond, 'This is the rustling of leaves in the trees.' We listened to the songs of the birds in those trees. I told Esmond the names of the birds making each of the different songs. I told Esmond of how some of the birds were good to eat but very hard to catch for, unlike us, they have also the freedom of the sky and can travel where we cannot reach them. We listened to sounds which came faint and slow from rocks nearby. Esmond stilled his body when we heard these sounds. These were sounds even he, young as he was, recognized, although he had not the words to tell me.

It mattered not. I too, recognized those sounds. Many times, I had heard the cries of hungry babies. I heard Esmond's hungry cries in the darkness of night. Esmond's eyes were wide, staring, willing me to find those hungry babies.'

'Ha,' Felix shouts aloud, almost breaking the spell of Astrid's storytelling, 'you found Fearne and Byrht.'

'Yes, yes indeed, the two hungry babies we found, lying abandoned on the rocks, were Fearne and Byrht. There were no people nearby. I knew these babies had been abandoned. Why would a people abandon their babies? They must be brother and sister, they must be from a twin birth, two babies born together, abandoned because their people believed they would share a spirit and so neither of them would be truly a whole person. They believed that in each there might be no voice of reason to quiet the voice wanting trouble and strife. There might be no voice of urgency to overrule the voice of

idleness. And, being one male and one female, they would one day become separated, one would leave to bring children into another community. Their spirit would be forever divided. These babies, it seemed, had been abandoned to die together in the belief this would bring together the two parts of the divided spirit, making the spirit whole once more.

I knew not if they carried names before that, whispered to them by their mother at birth. The girl I found with her eyes closed, nestled in the softness of the undergrowth, and so I named her Fearne. The boy lay beside her but his eyes were open and shone as bright as the stars shine in the darkness, and so I named him Byrht. These names I whispered to them as at birth. For this was a new birth, a new beginning.

We remained, just the four of us, for many, many seasons, until Esmond, Fearne and Byrht grew to maturity. Then Fearne bore her first child, a tiny child we named Luella and, some seasons later, a happy, easily contented child we named Felix. In this way we became five, and then six.'

***

'Now Ahna has joined us we have become seven.' Luella ended the story triumphantly and then, in her eagerness, she begins to predict the future, 'Ahna will bear children for Byrht. Then our numbers will grow further.'

I know she speaks the truth. If Astrid could bear Esmond after being abandoned as barren, I might, indeed bear children with Byrht. I see on

Astrid's face the look I have come to recognize as a look of knowledge and wisdom. I see Astrid has already decided this will be. These are my people. I belong.

***

When the sun begins its next ascent into the sky, I reach out to feel the warmth of Agna's wool. My hand falls, feeling the morning dampness of the earth, not the warm softness I had expected. As if in answer to my unspoken words Agna makes soft nuzzling bleats. 'Where are you, Agna? What's wrong? Are you hurt?'

Agna is calling me. She does not come to me. I rise and move through the lightening dawn towards where I hear her bleating softly. Agna is nestled behind a sheltering outcrop of rock. Two tiny newborn lambs lie close feeding contentedly from Agna's warm, giving body. Agna looks at me, seeing I am near. I whisper the promise she will keep both her twins before leaving her to nurture her young.

Today I have work to do. We must begin to make a bow for Fearne.

Luella and Felix shadow us. We had not intended to take them to find wood for the bow, but they have come of their own accord.

'It will be good for us to have a bow also,' there is determination in Felix's voice, 'we will practice many times. When you and Fearne are old, we will hunt with the bow and arrows. Then you will have meat without hearing the snared animals howling through the night.'

The days following fall into a pattern. As the sun rises, I hunt for the day's meat. Fearne, Luella and Felix follow silently. They see how the tautness of the drawn bow fills the arrow with power. They hear the swiftness of the arrow's flight through the air and the gentle thud as it reaches its target. See the animal dies without suffering, its spirit released.

Astrid takes the meat from us, always waiting to make more of the nourishing medicinal broths which are slowly bringing Esmond and Byrht back to health and strength. We, the hunters, make bows. For Fearne, a bow as long as mine but thinner, more flexible, less powerful because Fearne must build strength in her shoulders and back. For Luella and Felix, bows a little taller than they stand themselves, thin and flexible enough to match the strength of the young ones as they build their skills. They are eager learners but patient also and they persevere and listen well. They will make excellent bow hunters. I will not let them hunt rabbits, deer, or any other animal until I know they have sufficient skill to cause no suffering.

Eventually, the bows and arrows are made and finished well, to the satisfaction of us all. Fearne and the young ones spend much time each day practising this new skill, just as I did when I first clawed my way from the enclosed cave intended for my burial place. They learn quickly, especially Fearne who has more inner strength than the young ones. Fearne knows how to be still, how to be calm. She quickly becomes adept at almost breathing the arrow out of the bow, then her body finishes the shot soft and relaxed, all the strength and power flying with the arrow. Her dedication and determination mean she is soon able to hunt with me. At first her arrows are less true. Then we must go close to the prey she has shot to make a final shot with a second arrow, loosed from so close a range it cannot possibly miss its aim and so the animal does not suffer.

***

Esmond and Byrht grow stronger. Byrht more quickly than Esmond but we see now they will both recover. Astrid starts to put small pieces of meat in their broth each evening.

'The broth was good,' Byrht suddenly says one evening, startling us all after so many days of silence. We had almost forgotten how his voice sounds. 'Where has the meat come from, has Felix laid the snares?'

Astrid strokes his head gently. 'Shh Byrht, you still need much rest. Ahna and Fearne hunt for the meat using bows and arrows. We have had meat every day since they started. Don't worry about us, we are strong now. Luella and Felix have joined them. Soon they too will be able to bring meat, fresh meat, just killed.' Astrid saw Byrht was troubled. 'Quiet Byrht,' she continued her stroking, 'quiet, all is well, you must still rest.'

'No, what are they doing? No that's not possible. Do not let them do this again. We do not use the bow and arrow to find our meat, we use snares.

We have always used snares. Felix!' Felix, hearing his name, moves close to Byrht, but not too close. He finds something repulsive in sickness but knows he must listen to Byrht's words.

'Felix, tonight you must take the traps and lay them, then there will be meat when the sun returns.' Byrht falls back onto his resting place, seemingly exhausted from thinking and talking after so many days of doing nothing but regain his health and strength.

Felix does not lay the traps. On the day he kills his first rabbit, with one arrow, a clean dying, he takes his kill to where Byrht and Esmond sit. He finds them reclining tiredly against a tree, their bodies still protesting a little at being upright, but their minds more alert now their strength is returning. The dead rabbit is a symbol of the passing of the old ways. They look at it with dismay.

***

'Ahna, we cannot go back to the old ways,' Astrid holds me by the shoulders in a firm grip, surprising me with her strength. All the power in her body radiates into her grip. I realise Astrid could also become a skilled archer. But that is for the future. For now, she nurses Byrht and Esmond with a greater skill and dedication than I have ever witnessed before. We are a very small group. We need every member with us for as long as possible. We can have no place for early dying. We must grow in number.

Over the following days Byrht becomes increasingly agitated. Each time Astrid takes him water or food he grasps her arm in an increasingly strong grip. 'The bows and arrows must be abandoned,' he insists, 'and the old ways kept to.'

Astrid, skilled as she is in keeping harmony, always has the right words to placate and soothe. She tells Byrht and Esmond of how we all would have suffered starvation, deprivation, and likely death, without the meat the bows and arrows secured for us. Tells of how Esmond, the son she herself had borne, the only child she has borne, would have died, if not for the meat provided by the archers' bows. Tells of how Byrht and Fearne, the young ones, the light of our future, would have withered and died.

Reluctantly, Esmond acknowledges the broth made from meat hunted with our bows and arrows has given his body the strength and courage to escape an early dying, but he greatly mourns the passing of the old ways.

As Byrht grows stronger he often calls Felix to him, advising him the snares must be set before evening.

Felix refuses to set the snares. He knows now, as he grows to maturity and the number of our people expands, he will have skill with bow and arrow sufficient to provide for the young and the old. He sees how one day, Fearne, the mother who bore him, would rely on him. Already he has seen the strength of Byrht and Esmond almost taken from them. Already Astrid, the oldest amongst us, is less strong than his memory recalls her being.

Esmond speaks slowly. Defeat in his voice. 'If even Felix, son of Fearne who has only just learnt to set a snare, can bring meat to us.' He pauses. Drawing his breath deep into his body he begins again. 'If Felix can bring us meat with no suffering to the animal, using only a bow and arrow, perhaps there is no longer a need for the tortuous snares.'

***

One day, when Byrht is almost strong again, I hear him call Felix to him once more. 'Felix,' he murmurs quietly, 'it is not for the women to provide meat, this can only be done by men. It has always been this way. We cannot do this. We cannot change the ancient ways. Go now and set the snares in time for the animals arriving to feed. But if you have not the willpower of a man because you are not yet fully grown and you have seen the women try to take our man's role, then bring one of the lambs the sheep Ahna names as Agna has borne. I will show you how to kill it. It is small but it will make good eating until I am able to set the snares, perhaps after one or two more sunrises.'

Felix listens but does not offer any words of reassurance nor does he follow the instructions of Byrht. Felix has seen Luella, his sister, learn the skills of archery alongside him. He has seen her skills develop equally with his own. Seen her grow strong and able, just as he is growing strong and able. But still, I see he is troubled. I hear him as he seeks counsel from Astrid, the oldest and wisest person he has ever known.

'Astrid, Byrht speaks wisely when he says the lambs would make good eating and it is true to say you and Fearne, as the women, have not before provided the meat for us all. But I see how the lambs are precious to Ahna, and I see how well Ahna provides for us without killing the lambs. I see how willing she is to share her skills so we might all be able to hunt. Surely such a wealth of skill as we are building must bode well for our future?'

Astrid speaks more loudly and clearly than Felix. I do not have to strain to hear her words. Words which she surely intends to reach the ears of Byrht and Esmond. 'Felix, your words show a wisdom not usually found in one so young. The old ways are changing. Have they ever remained the same? True Esmond and Byrht have long set the snares to provide our meat, but it has not always been so. Remember the stories I have told you. I, with the infant Esmond, came upon Fearne and Byrht abandoned to await their death. For many seasons they were not old enough or strong enough to provide. Remember my legs had been crushed, I had not the strength of Ahna, but I had three infants to feed. Setting snares was the only way I could give them the meat which would make them grow strong. Now Ahna has brought us new skills we are all equal in our ability to provide for each other. Let us hope this continues. Sometimes men lack the skills of sharing.'

For some time, Felix remains silent. In the drooping of his shoulders and the cast of his eyes, he shows himself still to be troubled. Although she does not move or speak, Astrid seems to maintain her connection to Felix, waiting for his next words.

Finally, as darkness begins to fall and the colour in the sky changes, Felix speaks once more. 'But what of the lambs? The lambs which Ahna protects. Is it not the truth? They would make good eating?'

I feel rather than hear the faint mocking laugh from Byrht, sense he thinks the lambs will soon be eaten.

Once again Astrid speaks loudly enough for all to hear her words. 'Yes, Felix, it is true the lambs would make good eating but now we do not need to eat them. We have other meat. The lambs will grow and will wander on the hillside. In time we will be able to cut their fleeces from them, to provide warmth for ourselves during the cold and dark season. In time there will be many healthy sheep on the hillside to provide us with milk and fleeces. Perhaps, in time to come, those who follow us will eat the meat of the sheep but now we are very small in numbers. We have no need to eat them.'

Fearne, Byrht's twin, who has listened quietly to Astrid's words, now speaks aloud. 'There is much wisdom in your words Astrid. Truly we have no need to eat the lambs. The snares greatly distressed the animals in their dying. Many a night the animals' cries have disturbed our rest through the darkness, frightening the young ones. I recall the cries of the animals at night when I was very young, they made me fearful. I needed to stay close to you, Astrid.'

Esmond sighs deeply, his head reluctantly nodding in agreement, 'I also needed to stay close to Astrid when I was young and heard the animals' cries through the night. The cries sounded as I have felt myself during the long darkness of this sickness which befell Byrht and myself. I believe the animals felt, in their long dying, as I felt in my long sickness. With bows and arrows there is no suffering. Perhaps you are right. The days of the snares are gone. We must embrace a different future.'

For those of us listening, it seems Esmond has no longer the will to resist change. No longer the strength to fight against us.

***

Slowly Esmond and Byrht recovered from the sickness which had so nearly taken them from us before our small group had time to grow.

Byrht lost something of himself when he returned from his illness, the familiarity of his old world replaced by new skills. The sickness took from him in a way it did not take from Esmond. Byrht never truly embraced the bow and arrows, but, in time, he became skilled in the making of bows.

When Byrht spent hours watching one of us with our bow we knew it would soon be our turn for a new bow. Byrht watched until he knew each archer's body almost as well as we knew our bodies ourselves. He knew when our strength increased. He saw when it began slowly to decline as we aged. Each time the bow would be a perfect fit, in size and in strength, Byrht did indeed know us all well. As they grew Byrht made small bows for the children I bore him. Our children grew to adulthood as archers with only Byrht's stories to tell them of the old ways of hunting with snares.

Luella eagerly embraced her own new beginning as a hunter and provider. In time, Luella taught her father, Esmond, how to become as one with the bow. Then he also became a skilled archer. Quiet and gentle in his movements, he was especially adept at tracking and hunting small deer. It was always a feast day when Esmond killed a deer.

***

Many seasons passed after Astrid shared her wise words. Now I lie in the softness of bracken covered with the warmth of a sheep's fleece I am waiting for the moment when my spirit will be ready to leave and so give my body its final release. At that moment my spirit will begin its journey to the welcoming body of a newborn infant. Byrht, my companion of many seasons, waits with me. We know my body's end will soon be here.

As we wait, I feel him listening through the darkness of the night, as he has listened through the darkness of all our nights, for the calls of dying from animals trapped in snares.

This night, as always, he will be disappointed, for we have become a community of archers.

I hope the skills I have brought to my people will live on beyond the life of my body. I hope in times to come other women will use these skills to find their place in the world. I trust my spirit will carry my skills with it to the women it becomes. I know my body has not lived without purpose.

....

Marianne

1250

'Marianne, Marianne, are you there Marianne?' A rasping breath at the door alerted Marianne to her friend's closeness. Edith's voice rang out, echoing around and around the stone walls of the spiral staircase outside the door. Walls through which no sound escaped, so solid and impenetrable were they.

'Marianne, Marianne, is it true? Tell me it isn't true. Please tell me it isn't true.' This time a soft hammering from small fists on the thick wooden door accompanied the distressed cries from Edith.

Marianne rose, spindle in hand, and crossed to the door from her seat by the narrow window, where the last rays of sunlight had aided her work. 'Push,' she called. Edith pushed. Marianne pulled. After much effort between them, they managed to open the door sufficient for Edith to slip around the edge of it into the room. They collapsed rolling together and laughing onto the rug in front of the fireplace, although no fire yet burned in the grate.

Suddenly Edith caught sight of a wooden travelling box lying open to the side of the hearth. Edith stopped laughing, rose with an air of urgency, withdrawing in panic from the moment of childhood's innocent play as she recalled once more the news she had overheard Marianne's mother share with her own mother.

'Marianne, Marianne, is it true? Tell me it isn't true - go on, tell me, tell me it isn't true.' Edith clutched Marianne's arms in a grip as tight as her seven-year-old hands, and Marianne's thick woollen dress would allow.

Marianne wanted to squeal and beg her friend to let loose her arms, but she was hampered by the need to put childhood pleasures behind her now that which Edith feared was indeed coming to pass.

Marianne knew her friend's pain, for did she not also feel it for herself? Alongside their shared pain Marianne felt a bubbling of excitement. This adventure she had been told of all through her short life was becoming reality. Until this moment she had been filled only with eagerness and anticipation. Now her voice quivered a little as she realised Edith, with whom she had shared every childhood adventure, would not be with her as she embarked on this new beginning. 'Yes, Edith, your fears are indeed true.'

Marianne did not usually initiate an embrace with her friend. Even at the age of seven she was aware of their different social standing. But today she reached out with both arms extended to draw Edith close to her. She placed a kiss on each of Edith's cheeks. Holding her friend now at arm's length, their eyes locked together, Marianne continued, 'Yes, it is true. Mother says I am a very fortunate girl. She says many a girl would wish to be in my position. It is Lady

Isabella, wife to Lord Percival of Crick Manor, who has agreed to teach me all the things I need to know in preparation for the day I too marry and become lady of my lord's estate.'

'But Marianne, what will you learn there which you cannot learn right here in your own father's castle? Why must you go away? For, in truth, should you go so far from here I know we will never meet again, nevermore play together. Where will your spirit go when your body dies? Far away it will be gone. To a new life, a new body which does not belong to the kin of your father's castle, your memory will be lost to us forever.'

Marianne sighed deeply. 'The time for playing is gone, Edith. I am grown now beyond an infant and must follow the path of my destiny. At Crick Manor, in the service of Lady Isabella, I will become the lady which befits my destiny. In time I will be introduced to the Lord whom I shall marry.'

A shiver ran through Edith's small, thin body as she took in what was happening. If Marianne's carefree days had ended, so too had her own. Henceforth she would be like her mother and aunts, like her older sisters and cousins, perpetually working. In a few short years married and frequently with child.

Without warning, Marianne spun her friend around and around in a mad, giddy fit of excitement. 'I have it Edith, I have the answer. When I am married and bear my first infant you shall come to me as nursemaid. Then we shall be together all the days of our lives.'

Edith smiled, averting her gaze from Marianne's eyes, not wanting the sadness in them to mar her friend's belief in their future happiness together. Edith's heart was heavy as her head told her Marianne's vision for the future was but a dream. Once Marianne passed through the big gates of her father's castle, she would not return. This knowledge weighed heavily on Edith's heart. So heavy she felt the pain would never lift and she would be condemned to carry it forever.

***

'Marianne, Marianne, Marianne.' Edith's hair whipped loose from its braiding as the wind gusted and swirled around the battlements of the castle on which she stood. Her voice rang out as loud as she could make it. Not loud enough to reach through the wind, the stamping and snorting of the horses, the shouting, cursing and wailing noises of the everyday accompaniment to castle life. Nor yet through the churning mixture of eagerness, excitement and terror which gripped the head, heart and stomach of Marianne as she clambered up onto the ornate wagon behind the horses with what she hoped was ladylike dignity. Marianne remembered too late to turn for a last view of her childhood home and those who still inhabited her past life. Forgot to turn in time to give a final farewell to her faithful friend Edith.

***

Lord Percival had sought out his cousin's child, Marianne, to serve his wife whilst learning the manners and skills of a lady. He had hoped the close daily presence of a young girl would make Isabella inclined to those marital duties which might result in more children to continue his lineage. Lady Isabella, however, was not greatly interested in either Marianne, or in her husband.

'And so dear Edith, I am much left to make my own amusements once Lady Isabella has taught me what she deems to be the lesson for the day and after I have assisted her with dressing. Excepting, of course, I am obliged to attend my Lady at meals. Mostly we dine in the Hall with all from the manor but sometimes Lady Isabella decides we will dine alone in her own chamber. I think this happens when she is determined to avoid the advances of Lord Percival. Sometimes he has come to her private chamber, blustering and red in his face, instructing me to move to the Hall so he might dine alone with his Lady.'

Marianne's letters to Edith were written only in her own head, for Marianne had no knowledge of reading or writing, nor yet did Lady Isabella. Even had she means to record her thoughts and memories and the means to send such records back to her father's castle, Edith could not read any such missive. And yet Marianne continued to reflect on her life in such letters, which she willed towards Edith. In the early years she had little enough companionship when Lady Isabella did not require her presence. The composing of these missives served to distract her from the cold dampness of her lonely room.

'Edith, I have lived here at Crick Manor for a whole year. I cannot believe it to be true, but I arrived at the beginning of Lent and here we have Lent upon us again. Let me describe to you the manor, then you might picture me in it when you close your eyes to sleep. Lord Percival's manor house is not so large, nor yet so impressive as my father's castle and yet, at the same time it is, for it dominates the land which it surrounds - land which is littered with the tiny mud and straw homes of the peasants and their families - and which belongs to Lord Percival almost as far as the eye can see. The door is huge and heavy. When a visitor arrives at the door it opens only slowly. It is so very heavy it takes two strong men to heave it open after they have been alerted by the loud clang from an enormous bell which hangs above the door.'

'Inside is the main hall, where there is always such a multitude of people about. Even after I have lived here a full year, I do not know them, for I keep mainly the company of Lady Isabella and her ladies-in-waiting. On warmer days we are often to be found in the gardens of the manor where herbs are grown in great abundance for pottages and apothecaries. On colder days we are to be found in the anteroom off Lady Isabella's chamber. Of late it matters little where we are for I am now obliged to spend many daylight hours working on embroideries and tapestries and other fine needlework. Each night my back does ache dreadfully, and my eyes get so very

tired, especially when we work in the dim light of the anteroom. Lady Isabella is calling for me. Is this to be my life forever more?'

The gentle warmth of spring gave way once more to the heat of long summer days. On Sundays, Lord Percival required Lady Isabella to rest with him in her chamber during the hours following the second church service, prior to the evening service and the sabbath evening repast. Marianne took to walking alone at these times. Nobody sought to stop her or question her movements for those usually engaged in serving Lady Isabella took advantage of Lord Percival's amorousness to pursue interests of their own.

'Don't walk there, Mistress.' A young voice with hesitant authority reached Marianne just as she exited the churchyard by a small rear gate.

Marianne, still young enough to be immediately obedient to any authoritative voice, but old enough and experienced enough now in life to understand the increasing importance of her own position within the society of the manor, stopped in confusion. The voice, panting slightly from its owner's dash across the field towards her, but less hesitant and with a definite air of authority, spoke again. 'Mistress, it is not safe for you to walk this way. For now is the time we must all practice and improve our skills with the longbow, lest we ever be called upon to defend our land.'

As Marianne turned towards the voice, she felt confusion racing through her. The voice belonged to a youth, older and taller than she was herself. She guessed him to be around twelve years of age. He had not the ragged appearance of the local peasants. As Marianne's eyes roamed over him, she saw the hat worn by all the men and boys employed in Lord Percival's service, hastily snatched from his head as he realised he spoke with an attendant to Lady Isabella.

'Come Mistress,' the youth reached out his arm and gestured gently, indicating Marianne should follow him, 'would you care to watch the practise?'

Marianne thrilled at the thought of something new to experience in the midst of the dullness of her life at the manor. She reached without thought to the hand outstretched towards her. For the briefest of moments their palms tingled at their mutual touch.

'What is your name?' Marianne asked of the youth. If she was to go with him, she should at least know how to address him.

The youth's fingers trailed gently away from Marianne's hand. 'My name is Robin mistress. My mother named me for the bird which sat at the window to wait with her as I came into the world. The next day the robin returned but my mother had already gone to the good Lord.'

Marianne's curiosity and interest were aroused. She felt herself wanting to stay close to Robin. 'Robin,' she murmured, 'such a beautiful story. How do you know your story if you were just a new-born infant? Was it your father who told you your naming story?'

'Yes, Mistress, my father told me, and my sister Morgan also told me. Now Father is gone to his own eternal rest and so I live here at the manor and care for the Lord's horses. But today is the sabbath and so I must join the other men and boys at the butts.' Robin again held his hand towards Marianne, 'Would you like to watch?'

***

'Dear Edith

So much time has passed since I last shared my life with you. Remember the youth I told you of, the one named Robin? Well, many times now I have been to watch him with the other men and boys practising at the butts. I believe we shall be well-defended should marauders arrive, so skilful are they all with the longbow and arrows. Perhaps my father has archers also ready to defend the castle, but I did not know of them when I lived there as an infant.

But, most exciting of all, Robin says I too may learn to shoot the longbow. I am to wait next Sunday until the practising is done, at which time my Lady is most often still at her rest and does not require my presence. When all others have left the butts, it will be my time. Robin tells me his mother was skilled with the longbow and able to hunt as well as any man. He tells me also his father once instructed Lord Percival's sisters in the shooting of the longbow when they were young and not yet left their father's manor. Now I must leave you once more for I believe Lady Isabella is calling for me.'

In the days which followed, it seemed to Marianne her world had grown bigger and brighter. The hours spent attending to the whims of Lady Isabella, or engaged in perfecting her needlework skills still happened, as did the cold and damp church services each morning and three times on the sabbath. But now Marianne had a new purpose. She wanted to become skilled with the longbow. It seemed to her this was her destiny. Marianne did not admit, even to herself, the pleasure she also gained from the company of Robin. Robin who was so willing to give up the only free time he had to help Marianne.

'Edith, I cannot believe how time has passed since I began to learn how to shoot the longbow, for this is the third summer and I am becoming quite skilled. Robin says I am as skilled as he himself is, but I know this not to be true for it is a full nine years since he first pulled a longbow. But Robin is exceedingly generous in his praise of me. He says I have learnt well how to work as one with my bow. Truly Edith it is a wondrous skill to achieve. There is my longbow, full of power which it cannot release until I pull back the string, strong and slow, with the arrow firmly nocked to the string. And then, the miracle, I loose the string and all the energy stored in the bow is transferred to the released arrow. When the arrow travels straight and true it always finds its mark. If it does not find its mark, I know the fault lies within me. Edith, I am an archer.'

***

As Marianne entered her fourteenth year, a sense of urgency slowly crept into her. Without voicing the thought, even to herself, she knew instinctively her life would soon change. Within the coming few years her father would send word he had chosen a husband for her or he wished Lord Percival to make a recommendation. Marianne began to linger close to where she might expect to find Robin. Overcoming her distaste for the smell of the stables, she ventured to the edges of this unknown world, got to know the ways of the horses as she watched Robin and the other grooms at work.

Marianne asked Lady Isabella if she might ride. Lady Isabella, mistaking the intention of Marianne's question, remembered she herself, as a young girl, had often ridden with her father. She remembered they had hunted with the falcons and sparrowhawks which he had loved. 'Marianne, are you skilled in the art of riding? I believe we might ride out a way. Perhaps a ride will lift my spirits.'

Marianne jolted more upright than she already was, wiping, as discreetly as possible, the perfect bauble of blood emerging from her finger where she had stabbed it with her needle, in her wonder at what Lady Isabella was suggesting. 'Why yes, My Lady.' Marianne replied hastily, lest the opportunity be lost, although she had never yet ridden a horse.

The next day Marianne visited the stables under instruction from Lady Isabella. The grooms were to make ready two of the smaller, more docile horses on the day preceding the Sabbath. Then, Lady Isabella declared, she would ride out accompanied by

Marianne, a groom, and Lord Percival's falconer with a sparrowhawk. Lady Isabella wished to revive the pleasurable pastimes of her younger days.

Marianne, speaking with the head groom, conveyed Lady Isabella's instructions with great clarity, her words lent authority by their source. 'Of course, Mistress. I will see it is done just as her ladyship requests.' The head groom bowed, rather a deeper bow than Marianne was accustomed to receiving but the bow was intended for Lady Isabella. Marianne was no more than representative of her ladyship's voice.

Lifting her skirts from the worst of the stable dirt, her heart suddenly pounding, her breath racing, Marianne rushed through the stables. She ran out to the yard, eyes darting in all directions, until they alighted on Robin. Coming close, she grasped the thick linen cloth of his sleeve tightly. Robin turned to her, alarmed at the consequences for them both should this act of intimacy be witnessed. Marianne released his arm, struggling to catch her breath. 'Robin, you have to help me.' She reached to grasp his arm again but let her hand and her head drop instead. 'Robin, please you have to help me. Lady Isabella wishes me to ride out with her on Saturday next. I led her to understand I am a horsewoman but in truth I have never ridden. Please help me, Robin. You taught me to shoot the longbow, please, please teach me to ride a horse.'

'Oh, Edith, what great excitement I have had these past days. Robin has taught me how to ride upon a horse, leastways in so much as he has

taught me how to avoid falling from the horse, which is good for it seems such a long way to the ground from atop the horse's back. There has been little enough time to learn more, so few are the days before Lady Isabella wishes to ride out. I have even had to forgo my archery practice in order to spend some time acquiring such limited riding skills as I have. Tomorrow, I ride out with Lady Isabella and also with my Lord's falconer. Lady Isabella intends once more to set a sparrowhawk to hunt, as she did in the far-gone days before she was married to Lord Percival. Oh Edith, my greatest wish would be you might enjoy these pastimes with me but perhaps you have pleasures of your own which one day we might share.'

***

During the seven years Marianne had resided at Crick Manor she had very infrequently heard news from home. A nobleman, journeying through the country one year, reported both her mother and father to be well. From his description of her family, it seemed to Marianne she must have another sister and brother, born since her departure, for the children of whom he spoke of were too young to be the siblings she had left behind.

The following year a priest took shelter at the manor as a wild storm raged across the land. He too brought news for Marianne. Her older sister was married. Her father's castle had been attacked by marauding outlaws whose heads still graced the spikes above the castle gates.

As Marianne's first summer of riding and falconry drew to a close and summer warmth faded to the golden glow of autumn, a church painter passed through with news of Edith. Edith had entered a convent. There she would remain all the days of her life serving God, until the day her earthly body died. Marianne grieved deeply at this news for it seemed to her Edith was already lost to the world, her spirit forever trapped within the closed walls of the convent, desperately seeking salvation and a new body.

Close on the news of Edith's new life, another visitor arrived at Crick Manor. Marianne was astonished to see her brother Richard entering the Manor. Richard arrived with a small retinue of attendants, craving an audience with Lord Percival.

'Even before coming to greet me, his sister! What, Edith, could be so important he omits me the courtesy of a greeting upon his arrival? Always, with Richard there is in me a wariness, his intentions are not always good.'

As the light of day began to fade Marianne made her way to Lady Isabella's chamber, so she might accompany her to the evening meal. As she stepped daintily across the mucky, muddy stones, concentrating on avoiding the detritus littering her way, Marianne's heart pounded fiercely beneath the linen of her gown. 'Why is he here, why is he here?' she muttered, startling the blacksmith as he made his way towards his own more meagre repast. Marianne saw him not, so engulfed in her own anxiety was she.

'Come Marianne, we dine in the hall this evening. Lord Richard and his men have graced our Manor with their company, we will make them welcome.' Lady Isabella spoke impatiently, directing the flustered Marianne out of the room before she had fully entered it.

'Lord Richard, my Lady? Surely not for my father is Lord John. My brother Richard is only my father, Lord John's, second son.

'Come Marianne, did you not hear me, make haste now and let us see what manner of feast they have put together for our honoured guest, for I have a prodigious hunger following our ride out today.'

'Indeed Edith, there were good things to eat which I greatly enjoyed. The roasted venison was exceedingly fine, with the umbles seemingly greatly enjoyed by those below the salt. There was mutton, well-cooked to perfection alongside capons and quails and the small dumplings I love so much which are made from the livers of swine with soft cheese and eggs and baked in a crust. The cooks had excelled themselves with tarts containing pears and pippins as well as hot egg and cream custards such as we ate frequently on festive days in my father's castle. Although I grieve to tell you it is my father's castle no longer. Had the news my brother Richard imparted been shared with me beforehand I feel sure I would not have been able to consume but a single morsel of the wondrous feast.

Oh, Edith, Richard brings the news my father is no more, his spirit has flown free from his body, alongside the spirit of Young John my oldest brother, he who should have become my father's successor. Both dead from a sickness which took the lives of many living in my father's castle and many more of the peasants from his estates. Now Richard is become Lord and commands me to return to my father's castle from whence I must marry Lord North.

Oh Edith, what am I to do? Lord North is so very old. His youngest child was often my playmate when we were infants and I visited his estate with my beloved mother and father. In no time I shall be left a widow for his family to condemn to convent life. For certain Lord North wants nothing more than a nursemaid to care for him in his declining years. Edith, what am I to do? I needs must follow my brother's direction for what choice do I have? Lord Percival will not permit me to remain in attendance on Lady Isabella knowing I have defied the wishes of my brother. My brother reports these were also the wishes of my departed father, but I know not if he speaks the truth. We are to remain here some weeks longer, although I fear it will not be many weeks for the changing season will make our journey difficult if we linger overlong.'

***

Marianne saw little of Richard during the following days. She did not beg her brother for release from the marriage contract entered into on her behalf, knowing his mind would not be changed. Even when they had both been young children, Richard had displayed an iron will. Once set to something he could not be led astray from his target.

Marianne had always sensed in Richard something which instilled fear. As a child, she could not say what this was or why it frightened her, but she could not deny the unease felt when Richard was nearby. The same unease came upon her again now Richard was in Lord Percival's manor as Lord Percival's honoured guest. Marianne instinctively kept her contact with Richard limited, showing by her brisk movements how busy she was, always engaged in errands for Lady Isabella.

Whenever possible, Marianne escaped to the sanctuary of the stables. To the horses. To Robin, who felt her despair deep in his own heart, who feared for what she would become in the castle of Lord North, with none of her kin to lighten her days. No Robin. Feared for what she would become when, in the none-too-distant future, Lord North passed from this world and Marianne remained nothing but a burden to his family. Then they would ensure she married again - a bride of Christ, condemned to a life of prayer and silence in the cloistered world of the convent. He feared she would never again ride free to hunt with the sparrowhawk. Never again draw her longbow which he had worked to just the right draw weight for her. Never again stand close beside him so shivers tingled through his body. Robin feared for Marianne, and he feared for himself.

'There is to be a tournament, Mistress.'

'A tournament? I have not heard of this.' Marianne trailed her hand through the mane of the horse Robin had just helped her dismount from.

Robin took the reins from Marianne and began to lead the horse to its stable. He did not want to face Marianne lest his face give away his feelings. 'Yes Mistress, there is to be a tournament with jousting and displays of archery and suchlike things. Lord Percival has decreed there must be such a tournament to mark your departure from his castle.' Robin's voice came low and strained, 'It is to mark your betrothal to Lord North. The tournament will take place two days following the sabbath next. Then, when the sun rises again, you will depart.'

Marianne leaned heavily against the solid oak frame of the stable doorway, all strength seeming to leave her body. It was now. Now she must give up the life slowly carved for herself from the lonely beginnings of her years in Lord Percival's manor. Marianne remembered well how lost and alone she had felt in those early days. On her marriage, tied to a man she had not chosen, those feelings were sure to return.

***

'We will ride in the tournament. I wish to show my husband, Lord Percival, how skilful are my sparrowhawks in hunting and following prey. You must accompany me, for my display will be all the more spectacular if there are two hawks and I grant you are indeed skilled in handling the hawks, even if you could, at times, be more steady on your horse.'

Lady Isabella spoke without raising her eyes from her needlework, unaware of the churning of Marianne's stomach or the blood slowly emerging from a finger once again stabbed by Marianne's needle. Marianne swiftly withdrew the needle. 'I suppose you must take to your marriage the tapestry of hunting in a forest for it is all your own work and will serve well to show the refinement of your needlework since your arrival here. I have taught you well and you have been diligent in your learning.'

Marianne spluttered, her finger dripped blood onto the floor where it became nothing but a dark stain amidst many indeterminate stains, 'Your ladyship, will that be possible? How will Lord Percival be persuaded to agree to our riding in the tournament?'

Lady Isabella pushed away the tapestry she had been working on. 'My Lord Percival will do as I require for am I not losing your service just when you reach an age to be useful to me? And for what? For you to be married to an old man not long for this world. Everything I have devoted so many years to teaching you will be lost to a convent before many summers have passed.'

Marianne spoke without waiting to formulate her thoughts. Instinctively she knew she must speak before the moment was lost, 'Oh My Lady, may I also demonstrate my skills with the longbow, for I have worked hard at my archery also. Surely Lord Richard, my brother will want to know how dedicated and steadfast I am become in the learning of new skills.'

'Marianne, now you are leaving me you may do as you wish so long as you ride with me to show the skills of my hawks. Go now and tell Lord Percival's grooms what they will need to prepare for us. I will inform Lord Percival. We will ride together this one last time and then you will leave me for your new life, such as it might be.'

The path from Lady Isabella's chambers to Lord Percival's stables had never been longer. It seemed to Marianne she would never reach the stables, so fast was the beating of her heart and so clumsy had her feet become. Consumed in the excitement of the news she had to share with Robin, Marianne was able, for this short time, to forget the horrors she had already perceived in the life she would be compelled to lead after the tournament.

'Robin, Robin,' Marianne's words came amid ragged breaths as she sought to steady herself. Seeing Robin was not alone Marianne added a tone of authority to her voice. To allay any suspicions of an inappropriate friendship between herself and Robin. 'Ah, there you are Robin.' Marianne's chest heaved with the effort of suppressing her excitement. 'The Lady Isabella wishes us, her and me, to ride in the tournament to display the skills of my Lady's hawks. My Lady commands horses be made ready at the appropriate time and asks you convey the information also to Lord Percival's falconer.'

Marianne turned to leave the stables, there would be no chance today to speak more intimately with Robin. At the entrance archway she turned as if an afterthought had occurred to her, 'and also, Robin,

Lady Isabella has said I am to demonstrate my skills with the longbow during the archery displays at the tournament. Please ensure my longbow and sufficient arrows are prepared.'

As Marianne turned once more to leave, two hearts pounded in unison. Neither heard the other but their eyes locked in the briefest of glances such as might be exchanged between lovers.

'Oh, Edith, how I do fear for you locked away from the world in your convent, never to know true love. For now, I am sure it is true love I feel when I speak with Robin, when he stands close as I practice my skills with the longbow, when he steadies me as I mount and dismount my horse. And yet, Edith, perchance I envy you, for locked away in your convent you will never know true love and so will never know the pain of loss. I am to take part in the tournament, not the jousting, which is for the knights and other of the men of Lord Percival and my brother Lord Richard. I am to ride with Lady Isabella to display the hunting powers of the hawks and I am to join the display of archery, right at the end when the very skilful archers have shown of their best. I am eagerly anticipating the joys of the tournament and the feast to follow but beyond that all is despair. For, Edith, I am to be married, married to Lord North, taken far away from this place, never more to see Robin, except, perhaps, when my spirit flies free from my body.'

***

'Come Marianne,' Lady Isabella declared, 'let us sit a while in the shade of the pavilion, the knights for the jousting will parade shortly. You must decide which of these gallant knights to grace with your favour as they go into battle. Of course, it is not a real battle for no one will be killed here today. But still, there will be winners and losers. Let us hope we have chosen wisely, and the winners are carrying our favours.'

Marianne tried not to clutch the delicate lace handkerchief too tightly, lest it be crumpled when she handed it to the knight of her choice. Desperately she wished she could grace Robin with the favour of her handkerchief, but Robin was a groom not a knight. He would not be jousting.

As the knights began their parade a slight breeze carried the crackling of the fire over which the ox for the feast to follow was roasting, the aroma intensifying as the tournament progressed. The peasants, who had eaten no meat for many weeks, but for the occasional rabbit poached from Lord Percival's lands, were torn between a desire to witness the wonders of the tournament and a desire for the tournament to end so the feasting might begin.

'Make ready Marianne, the knights ride by once more. It is time to give your favour. I will give mine to your brother Lord Richard. He is a fine bold figure upon a horse and I feel certain he will outwit my Lord Percival's knights.' Lady Isabella inclined her body forward, meeting the eyes of Lord Richard who slowed his horse to take Lady Isabella's favour. He tucked it securely into his tunic before moving on so the other ladies might choose their knights.

Marianne determined she would not present her favour to any of her brother's knights, here to escort her to an unwelcome and likely unhappy, marriage. Instead, she chose the youngest of Lord Percival's knights, imagining in her mind this was Robin.

The young knight took the favour from Marianne with evident pleasure, he had not expected any of the ladies to choose him.

Lady Isabella laughed, 'Why Marianne, I believe you are giving your favour for desire and not for hope of victory. You are indeed ready for the marriage your brother has arranged, you are become a woman.'

Marianne smiled, she was giving her favour for desire, Lady Isabella need not know where her true desire lay.

'Truly Edith, the jousting thrilled us all. The knights so brave and daring - only imagine them in battle! I feel none of them could lose, so skilful were they all. Their horses so strong and steadfast, and fearless too it seemed, as they charged towards each other, hooves pounding the ground. The very manor seemed to shake on its foundations. The great crowd watching, cheering, stamping their feet. Their enthusiasm fueled no doubt by the barrels of ale Lord Percival had provided so everyone might quench their thirst through the heat of the day and the dust churned up by the horses. A truly wonderful

display although my young knight did not win, taken as he was from the ground where he had fallen to have his arm set in a splint.'

Marianne tried to rejoice in her brother being declared victorious, but she could not truly find it in her heart to do so.

Robin stood nearby. 'Marianne, who is this youth standing by us?' Lady Isabella inclined her head so Marianne might know to whom she referred.

'My Lady, he is one of Lord Percival's grooms. The one who rides out with us. I see they are setting up for the archery display so perhaps he has come to tell me I need to prepare.'

'Go then Marianne - but see they have made ready the horses and the hawks for we will ride with the hawks when the archery is done.'

Marianne felt a wave of pleasure pass through her as Robin reached to help her step down from the pavilion but quickly let go his hand lest any should be watching. Marianne's hand shook as she took her quiver from Robin. She expected her brother would feel some dismay when he saw his sister taking part in the tournament in this way, but Marianne knew it would be nothing to the dismay she had felt when the purpose of his visit had been imparted to her. Dismay which had not left her in the intervening days.

As Robin handed Marianne her longbow, she felt a calmness seep into her mind and body. With the bow in her hand, her mind had pushed aside these troubles, focusing instead on what was to come.

Marianne was experienced enough as an archer now to know she would not shoot true arrows if she allowed dismay and despair for the future to inhabit her mind. More experienced archers with heavier bows than Marianne were first to the butts to show their skills.

'Although Mistress,' Robin said softly, 'they are little more skilled than you yourself. They are stronger and so can pull more weight but some practice only as they must and have little skill. See how this man nearest to us does not pull back the string. With a lighter bow he could pull back the string fully and achieve the same end as he does now but he does not want the other men to witness him pulling a weaker bow and so he shoots a bow which is beyond the weight he can truly manage.'

Safe from the eyes of others Robin's hand rested lightly on Marianne's shoulder, just as it so often did when they went together to the butts to practice. A reassuring touch leaving Marianne inwardly prepared to shoot well.

Today, alongside Marianne would shoot several youths not yet strong enough for a heavy bow and also Robin, who had willingly forgone the opportunity to shoot with the men so he might shoot alongside Marianne. Together they approached the designated shooting line, as Lord Percival's trumpeter sounded the start of their display.

'Marianne, Marianne,' Lord Richard's strident voice could be heard loud and clear, 'Lord Percival what is my sister doing at the butts? Marianne, Marianne.'

Many of the people watching the tournament neither knew nor cared who Marianne was but they heard the call from Lord Richard and, fueled as they were on ale, took up the call. As Marianne reached for her first arrow the wind carried her name from many directions as if all were willing her to victory. Marianne nocked her first arrow, focusing, thinking only of the shot to come. She raised her bow arm, hand lightly steadying the bow at the leather grip, arrow securely on the string, bow arm still. Marianne steadily pulled back the arrow on the string, back to its full draw, all the draw weight of the bow ready for the arrow to receive, aiming at the stillness of the target in front of her. As she lifted the bow Marianne drew her breath in deep, her heart stopped pounding, she pulled back the string. Gently she released her breath, smoothly and gently loosing the arrow from her bow, breathing the arrow from bow to target. The arrow found its mark. The crowd cheered. Lord Richard unwittingly continued to fuel the cries for Marianne so great was his dismay at what he was witnessing. In despair he prayed fervently for news of this not to reach Lord North until Marianne was securely given in matrimony.

Marianne knew that once each arrow had left her bow it became beyond her command. She kept her thoughts firmly focused on achieving the best possible shot with each of the arrows. The crowd continued to cheer each shot as it reached its mark. As the final arrow left Marianne's bow, a good arrow, a strong release, all the power of the bow called for and responding, two boys began a race. One, a youth of eleven years, son of Lord Percival's chief carpenter, ran from east to west, crossing behind the butts, safe from all but the most wayward arrows. The second boy was a simple lad of twelve years, named Thomas after the father he had never known. Sensing no danger in the invincibility of his youth, Thomas ran from west to east crossing in front of the butts. Fast, but not fast enough.

Marianne, her sight focused on the centre of the target, did not see Thomas until her well-aimed arrow passed through his side and pierced his heart – and the crowd slowly fell silent.

Nothing moved. It seemed even the birds in the air ceased their calls. No wind ruffled the leaves of the trees. No horse whinnied or snorted. In the midst of silence, a single cry of despair still rose from Lord Richard, 'Marianne, Marianne!'

The crowd, as one, drew in its breath and it seemed to Marianne there was no air left for her. She gasped, spluttered, and struggled to draw even the smallest of breaths. A crowd of men and women surged around the fallen boy. Marianne prayed he lived, although her instinct told her otherwise.

When those nearest the boy saw his staring eyes and lifeless body the crowd turned, almost as one. They surged towards Marianne raising a tremendous hue and cry. A boy had been killed. Each wished to be the one to fulfil their responsibility for maintaining law and order on behalf of their king by apprehending the killer, delivering her to the sheriff.

The blacksmith, first to reach Marianne, grabbed her by the shoulder with the full strength of his muscled hands and arms. 'I have her, stand back, I have her,' he called, his call taken up by those near, 'He has her, stand back he has her.' The forward surge of the crowd abated. Those intent on immediate justice and retribution largely being held back by the more god-fearing in the crowd who wished to see justice done on behalf of God and their king, perhaps with a public hanging for all to witness.

Mistress Martha broke through the crowd with such fierce determination none was able to stop her, from the back of the surging crowd where she had cradled her dead son one last time, to the front where the blacksmith still held Marianne in a tight grip.

Marianne's head span out of control, only the grasp of the blacksmith kept her upright. The hue and cry raised by the crowd rang through her head and her heart pounded as her fear of the crowd grew. Faintly she heard cries of 'Marianne,' sounding first as Robin's tender voice, then as her brother's despairing voice. She knew not from whence they came. They could not save her.

Mistress Martha, a tiny woman worn thin by the years of her disgrace following the birth of Thomas, screamed the agonizing scream of the violently bereaved. She had no wish for God or the King's justice, she would exact her son's vengeance at once. She leapt at Marianne, ripping at Marianne's face with dirty jagged nails, burying her teeth into the soft flesh rising from the neckline of Marianne's gown, clinging tightly to Marianne, the better to use her feet to kick and kick at Marianne's legs. Marianne's knees buckled.

The blacksmith held her tight with one hand, pulling Martha away with his other hand. 'Take her, take her,' the blacksmith called to those around him. 'She is driven mad with grief. We do not want another killing. This one I will deliver to the sheriff.'

Willing hands reached out none too gently to drag Martha away from Marianne, for she was not a well-liked woman being somewhat given to causing discord in a number of marriages.

The dark, damp cellar which served to house miscreants awaiting the attention of the sheriff was cleared of the two men from a neighbouring town held on charges of drunkenness. The blacksmith pushed Marianne into the cell. Using his wide girth to block access he called his apprentice to bring tools with which to chain Marianne to the wall, before securing fast the door so none might enter to do harm to the prisoner.

As daylight began to fade the crowd gradually quietened and dispersed, most pausing to peer, jeer, or spit at the prisoner through the grille on the door as they departed. A few offered up a short prayer for her eternal salvation.

As night fell and the manor and its environs slept, a hand quietly pushed bread and water through the door.

***

The following morning Marianne woke from a fitful sleep filled with nightmares and plagued with pain from the deep scratches and bites inflicted by Mistress Martha. Her body was sore and bruised in many places from Martha's kicks, from the over-firm grip of the blacksmith, from the stones of the ground on which she lay, from the rough iron which held her chained to the ring in the wall by both hands. She shivered uncontrollably, feeling her gown filled with the dampness pervading the cell, wishing for a dry gown, a fire to warm her. She called, faintly at first, her voice hoarse with the terror she felt, then louder, shouting for someone, anyone to come and save her.

And come they did, but not to save her. There was little enough entertainment in their lives, such an opportunity for amusement could not be passed by. They came to stand, peering through the iron grille, lifting the youngest children so they too might glimpse the prisoner. To taunt and mock her with talk of the noose which was surely coming her way. To offer her fresh bread, withdrawing it swiftly when her grimy blood-stained hands reached for it, leaving her only the stale bread and dirty water passed through by her goaler each morning and evening.

'Oh, Edith what is to become of me? I am so wretched here, so very cold. It seems my bones shake with the coldness and damp engulfing me in this darkness. I dare not move my hands and arms more than is needed to reach for the scraps of food they pass me. Poor as these are I eat, for without this meagre repast each day I will surely die.

Sometimes I believe death would be a salvation. In the end I will die on the hangman's noose. Would that I could die before such a time arrives, while my spirit can fly free through the grille in the door. I have tried not to eat the bread in the hopes I might die but my hunger overcomes me. Deep inside me I believe there is a will to survive for as long as possible. It is dark now. The hours of darkness relieve me of the torment inflicted by those who pass by. They are less in number now than in those first few days. Perhaps their curiosity has abated. The mother of the boy comes each day, demented in her grief, to vent her anger. I feel greatly for her pain, but I did not aim to kill her boy. Now it seems all have forsaken me.'

***

'Marianne, Marianne,' a whisper from the grille, 'Marianne, Marianne, are you awake?' the whisper more urgent this time. Marianne, startled, momentarily confused. Never before could she recall having heard Robin's voice calling her name, always he called her 'Mistress'. Now Robin's voice called once more, 'Marianne, Marianne.'

Marianne stirred and stood in the darkness. Her gown heavy in its dampness. Faintly she made out the grille and staggered unsteadily, on legs weakened by her imprisonment, towards it, as far as her chains permitted.

'Robin is it you?' she whispered startled by the sound of her own voice, a sound she had not heard for so many days.

'Yes, Marianne, it is indeed. I am come to bring you fresh bread and meat. Take it quickly for I must go at once should anyone pass by.'

Marianne took the bread and meat, wrapped in a cloth. She could feel the warmth of the cooked meat take some of the chill from her fingers. Tantalizing aromas reached out to her. 'Thank you, Robin. Oh Robin, what is to become of me? They will hang me for murder Robin, for sure they will hang me for murder?' Marianne's voice became louder.

'Shush Marianne, none must know I am here, or I will not be able to come again. Each night I will bring you bread and meat to help you get strong. I must go now before I am missed and needed. Have the cloth ready for me to take tomorrow or it will be missed, everyone is very anxious now. I will come tomorrow.'

Marianne, her spirit lifted by Robin's visit, slept less fitfully through the night. The meat had been good, she hoped Robin would be able to fulfil his promise and return with more.

After darkness fell, but before the light of the rising moon appeared each night, Robin came, always calling her name softly, 'Marianne,' and she answering just as softly, 'Robin, I am here.' Both welcomed the brief moment when their hands touched as they exchanged an empty cloth for one filled with warmth and nourishment.

After many days, a night came when Robin did not appear at his usual hour. Marianne kept watch by the grille, seemingly for hours before retiring to a despairing, disturbed sleep, to be awakened as the very first hint of dawn appeared by the familiar whisper, 'Marianne, Marianne'.

As Marianne stumbled to the grille Robin pushed food through, whispering urgently, 'Quick, Marianne, I must go and prepare the horses. Lord Percival rides out at first light to meet the Assizes judge who is due in the city. Today or on the morrow you are to be taken to the city to be tried at the assizes. Keep heart Marianne, the judge is known to be a fair man. I must go. Farewell I will return this evening.'

'Edith, I feel so far from you. I wish you could hear my despair and offer prayers to God for my salvation. I am certain I am pitiful to behold, filthy as I must now be. At least the fresh bread and meat Robin brings has nourished me a little. Robin tells me not to despair but what else am I to do? Alone as I am here in the cold and the dark, knowing my arrow killed the boy. That cannot be changed. For certain it was my arrow which took his life. Even a judge known to be a fair man will be bound by the facts. I will surely hang, although I fear I will no longer have weight on me for an easy hanging. Edith, I do not know if my spirit will fly free from such a dying.'

***

Few witnessed Marianne's departure from the dank holding cell, not for lack of interest but rather from the need to go about their daily tasks. Following Robin's final visit to Marianne a large crowd had gathered, expecting the entertainment of a look at the now filthy and bedraggled prisoner. Marianne, hearing them long after darkness had fallen, shook with more than the damp coldness of her prison throughout the night, not daring to close her eyes for fear of the crowd. Many of the crowd remained through the night, warmed and rowdy with the ale willingly supplied from the village inn. Calling for Marianne, they took turns to peer through the grille, but Marianne was hidden to them by the darkness.

As dawn showed its first rays over the roofs of the cottages, the crowd dispersed, disappointed at being robbed of their entertainment. Once it became clear Marianne would not be moved at dawn most were compelled to go about their daily business.

As quietness returned Marianne unwound herself from the stiffness of her tightly folded efforts to keep warm and unseen through the night. Eyes and body heavy with exhaustion from her own silent vigil, she slept intermittently in short bursts, each time startled awake by some clanging or banging from the outside world. At noon Marianne was once more awakened, this time the banging was indeed a herald to her departure for the assizes court. The sheriff himself had arrived to oversee the delivery of this prisoner accused of wanton murder, to the judge who would surely see her hang.

The blacksmith strode behind the sheriff, pausing from time to time so the sheriff might stay in the lead, the sheriff being a considerably smaller man than the blacksmith with a markedly shorter gait.

A loud rasping sound told Marianne the key was turning in the lock.

'Break the chains, Blacksmith, let us have done with this sorry business.' The sheriff, his nose assailed by the rank odour of the cell and of Marianne, held a grubby handkerchief to his nose, regretting the infrequency with which his wife permitted him a clean handkerchief.

'Come man, hurry and do your work, the cart is waiting. We must have her to the city by dusk or the gates will be closed. I have no wish to spend the night in the cart with such as this.' He waved his grey handkerchief towards Marianne as he exited the cell to make way for the blacksmith.

Believing Marianne's conviction all but confirmed and her death imminent, the blacksmith, took none too much care as he went about his task of freeing her from the chains. Marianne staggered out of the cell, her arm gripped tightly by the blacksmith. She lacked the strength to climb onto the cart. The blacksmith lifted her and dropped her onto the floor of the cart, before climbing after her to bind her hands with rope and to tie more rope around her waist to secure her inside the cart.

Marianne was thankful for this. As a child she had seen prisoners taken from just such a cell, tied at the waist to a horse or cart, their hands bound, to walk the miles to the nearest city. The sides of the cart kept her largely hidden from view. The blacksmith, accompanying the sheriff lest the prisoner attempt an escape along the way, sat in the back of the cart, aiming the occasional kick at Marianne to ensure she was as far away as possible.

'Edith, oh Edith, I fear my end is near. I have barely the strength to send my thoughts to you. Even though you are secluded in your convent I believe you will enjoy a longer life than I. Tomorrow I go before the judge. There is no doubt it was my arrow killed the boy, Thomas. I have taken a life and now I have no hope remaining within me. I do not think I will sleep tonight, so much do my heart and head churn within me.'

***

Sighing heavily, the Judge peered through the gloom of the courtroom as Marianne was led in, dishevelled in her dust-covered dress. Blood, the legacy of the bites and deep scratches inflicted by Mistress Martha, dried hard and crisp in the intervening weeks, showed now only as dark patches on the filthy gown. Marianne's hair, long fallen loose from its ribbons, hung matted with dust and grime of dubious origin, all head covering torn from it by the drunken crowd in the first moments following the death of Thomas, moments when Marianne had feared for her life every bit as much as she feared for it now.

Marianne stumbled across the uneven floor. Terror raced through her. Her eyes refused to adjust to the dimness. She felt, rather than saw, the mass of people come to view her, the murderer. Come to see her condemned to death. She heard, rather than saw the rustling and jostling as all struggled for a view of the prisoner. Heard the stamping of feet and the rising and falling of the murmur of many voices. Marianne felt her hands shaking, her arms, her legs, her whole body. She grasped tightly the wooden barrier before her, her head spinning inside, wanting only for this to be over.

The Judge was long accustomed to the sorry state in which many prisoners were brought before him. It passed through his mind to wonder if prisoners could not be cleaned up somewhat before being brought into the courtroom, his courtroom. This one put him considerably in mind of the half dozen witches he had condemned to hang just the week previous. Filthy, wild and bedraggled looking all of them - all skin and bone and rags. They had been twelve months in a cell awaiting trial. Their appearance suggesting they had been fed little in all their time of imprisonment. But they were witches. They were going to hang anyway. What matter if they had been fed well or not? No doubt the God-fearing children of their jailors had grown plump on the extra rations.

However, the Judge considered himself a fair man. He sighed deeply once more as he tried to empty from his mind all thoughts of witches and witchcraft. Both put great fear into him. The prisoner before him might resemble a witch in appearance but the charge was not witchcraft.

'Marianne.' A single cry rose from the crowd in the courtroom. Marianne, startled, followed the cry through the gloom. She found herself looking straight into the eyes of Robin, silent now, keeping his peace so he might witness proceedings.

The cry brought also the stern eyes of the Judge, his displeasure was abundantly evident. There being no further disturbance beyond the underlying, subdued heckling of the crowd, the Judge ignored Robin's cry. He proceeded straight to the evidence for the prosecution.

The case for the prosecution began slow and lugubrious as one witness after another was brought forwards to give almost identical testimony. Lord Percival had organised a grand tournament to celebrate the visit of Lord Richard and the subsequent departure from Lady Isabella's service of Lord Richard's sister, Marianne. Two of the witnesses seemed hazy as to the cause for celebration but had agreed to stand witness on the promise of liquid sustenance to follow. Having nothing new to add to the testimony of others, being somewhat offensive in appearance and demeanour and clearly desperate for their promised reward, these were quickly dismissed by the Judge.

Hours passed. The courtroom grew increasingly hot, stuffy, loud, and lively. Such entertainment was not often to be had. The crowd clapped and cheered as each witness began and ended their testimony. The Judge grew tired of calling for order. He was anxious to draw this case to a conclusion with adequate time in which to readjust his sensibilities sufficiently so he might do justice to the fine roast beef dinner being prepared for him in his Judges' lodging house. However, the Judge was also conscious of the need not to deprive the crowd of peasants of their anticipation, their entertainment and so each witness came forth in turn until finally it was the turn of Lord Percival's chief archer.

The Judge listened. His stomach rumbled. The crowd continued its murmuring and jostling, more used to enduring hunger than was the Judge.

Finally, the Judge's stomach won through. He would tolerate no more. He raised his hand and coughed loudly to still the sound of the witness's voice.

'From your testimony and the testimony of the many others we have heard it seems I am to understand the prisoner was practising archery at the butts at the time of the alleged offence. Would you agree my presumption is correct?'

The witness, who had been revelling in his testimony, was somewhat startled at the Judge's interruption of his long, slow recounting of his evidence. He stopped in mid-flow.

'Why, yes Your Honour, at the butts for the archery display at Lord Percival's tournament.' It passed through his mind to wonder if the Judge had been fully awake through the previous testimonies.

The Judge looked directly at the witness, then cast his gaze slowly around the courtroom, taking in the myriad of previous witnesses, now standing open-mouthed in astonishment at the interrupting of the head archer's account. He brought his gaze back to rest sternly on the witness once more.

'Pray tell me, what is the purpose of practising at the butts?'

'Well, Your Honour, 'tis to be ready to defend King and country against threat.'

The Judge folded his arms over his stomach with an air of satisfaction. 'Miss Marianne, therefore, was practising archery in order she might defend King and country against threat should the need arise, do you agree?'

'Well, well .... No, your Honour, I find I cannot agree. She,' the chief archer pointed with a sharp jabbing motion towards Marianne, 'she cannot defend King and country for she is a woman.'

'My good man,' the Judge spoke loudly over the sound of his stomach and wishing his voice to reach the far corners of the courtroom for all to hear, 'I have read nothing in the laws of this land to say a woman may not defend King and country.'

Astonished gasps spread through the courtroom. Silence descended. The mouth of Lord Percival's chief archer opened and closed rapidly several times. No sound came out. The Judge waved him from the witness stand, 'You may step down my good man, I have no need of further testimony from you.'

The Judge turned his gaze from the gasping, drooping mouth of the witness towards Marianne.

'Miss Marianne, I pronounce you are not to be convicted nor punished for the death of Thomas, son of Mistress Martha and – ah I recall we know not the boy's father.' The crowded courtroom let out a communal snort of derision directed at Martha, some recalling her downfall when she bore Thomas out of wedlock. 'For it was declared in the time of King Henry the first, an archer who kills someone during archery practice at the butts, that is, when perfecting of skills needed to defend their Lord, their King and their country, shall be absolved of said person's murder.'

Martha Todd let out a wail of despair, declaring loudly for all to hear. 'But she is a woman, she will not defend our Lord, nor our King. She is a woman,'

The Judge held up his hand for silence in the court. When the level of outpouring from the crowd subsided sufficiently for his voice to be heard once more, he continued, speaking quickly, wanting to get this sorry business over with. He doubted Miss Marianne would be allowed to live the night if she did not make haste to leave the district and the remaining daylight hours in which to do so were short.

'Miss Marianne is indeed a woman. However, I find nothing to tell me a woman cannot practice the art of archery in order to be able to defend her Lord, her King, her country. I, therefore, declare Miss Marianne to be free from guilt and hence free from punishment.' He turned towards Marianne, 'You are free to leave the courtroom and make your way to the house of your family. I doubt your presence in Lord Percival's Manor will be very much welcomed.'

The Judge cast his eyes around the courtroom, his ears deafened by the noise of the crowd. Obliged to remain unnaturally silent during court proceedings, the crowd had released all their anger, fear, delight, each to their own and between them created an almighty clamour, putting the Judge in mind of the tower of Babel. He knew he would not get order back in his court until Marianne had departed. His eyes finally alighted on Marianne's brother Lord Richard. 'Lord Richard, please remove Mistress Marianne before some harm befalls her.'

Lord Richard and the Judge looked to where the grimy, bedraggled Marianne had stood just moments before. She was gone.

***

'I am Morgan, sister to Robin. I have lived here in these Forest caves since the day Lord Percival first cast his eyes to me when I was aged but fourteen years and a servant to Lady Isabella. To run away to the Forest caves was Robin's idea. Although he was but a young boy then he no more wanted such a life for me than I did for myself. As children, before our father's spirit flew and he left us for eternity, Robin and I played in these caves. None will look for us here for almost none know of the caves.'

Marianne became aware she was resting against Robin, warm and secure. The noise of the courtroom fading from her ears, slowly freeing her senses to the new world around her. The flight from the courtroom she could barely recall, beyond a jumbled blur of sights, sounds and feelings. Robin had been at her side the very moment the Judge set her free, tugging at her hands, urging her to go with him hastily, lifting her, with a strength even he did not know he had, onto the strong back of one of Lord Percival's horses. Climbing up behind her as he urged the horse to swift movement, they were outside the city walls before any sought to pursue them. Riding, riding, almost for an eternity, or so it had seemed to Marianne, weary and famished as she was.

Marianne knew now Robin had taken her back almost to Lord Percival's castle, certainly to Lord Percival's lands, to hide her there in plain sight.

Morgan stood. She walked softly towards Marianne, stooping to hold her and offer support for her to rise. 'Robin is certain you must remain here with me. If you go to your brother's, you will be obliged to spend the rest of your days doing penance on your knees in a convent. However, if you wish to return Robin will take you with him. He must leave now to be back long before daybreak.'

Marianne, leaning on Morgan's strong arm, gasped loudly, 'Does Robin not remain here with us?' Set adrift from all things familiar to her Marianne could not picture a world without even the comforting presence of her friend.

Gently, Robin held Marianne's hand, 'Marianne, now, at last, may I call you Marianne?' He did not wait for the affirmative reply of which he was confident, 'Now Marianne, I must return to Crick Manor, at least for a time, I must return the horse. The horse is one of Lord Percival's best, it is swift and strong and will certainly be missed by his Lordship if I do not return it before daybreak. Morgan will care for you while you grow strong again.' Gently, hesitantly Robin kissed Marianne on each cheek. He kissed his sister in the same manner and then began to lead Lord Percival's horse quietly from them.

Marianne shivered, she started a little towards Robin, 'Robin,' she called softly, 'Robin, will you bring me my bow and arrows?'

Robin turned back towards Marianne, he was surprised to hear her ask for the bow and arrows which had led to her imprisonment. For a moment he hesitated but he could not deprive her of something which gave her so much pleasure. 'Yes, yes I will bring them.' Robin looked into his sister's eyes and laughed as he switched his gaze to Marianne, 'When you have them you and Morgan will be able to hunt together for food.'

Morgan laughed gently, 'Robin has told me you are also skilled in the art of archery, we will practice together. For today, however, Robin must leave us.'

Again, Robin made to leave, but once more he turned to speak with Marianne, unwilling to leave her but knowing he must, 'Morgan has a pony here, it is safe to ride out to the north. I will bring you a sparrowhawk to train. The land to the north is barren but a sparrowhawk will find some prey. Farewell, I will return often until I am able to leave the employ of Lord Percival without arousing suspicion. Then I will return to be with you always.'

Marianne felt a shiver run through her. Her whole body thrill to the thought. Surely Robin meant he was hers.

Morgan, mistaking the shiver for cold and discomfort, remembered how dirty and dishevelled Marianne had become during the long days of her confinement and how thin and hungry she appeared. She took Marianne by the hand, leading her gently so her gaze could no longer fix on the spot where Robin had stood and kissed her. 'Marianne, there is a stream close by where you might bathe and then be comfortable in my spare gown. I will turn the rabbit I hunted this morning into a fine supper for us to share.'

'Edith, I cannot think of you for long, I am so very weary, my eyes are heavy and need to close in sleep. Edith, I am safe, I am free from my prison. I will never be married to old Lord North, nor confined to a convent. Robin has brought me to this forest cave to be safe. Oh Edith, seldom have I been so happy with my lot in life for Robin will be mine, I am certain. Soon we will be always together, and I am sure God will bless our union even if we do not visit a church. I will live here with Robin all the days of my life until my earthly body is weary and seeks its rest and my spirit flies free and happy to its next life. Edith, I will think of you every day. I so wish you could be here with me.

Marianne'

....

Hannah

1642

When Hannah turned seventeen, her mother requested to speak to her in the sitting room. This, it being January and the fire not yet lit in the sitting room, caused Hannah to know at once the serious nature of the conversation to come. Hence, she followed her mother to the appointed chamber with more than a little trepidation. Her mind spun quickly through her recent misdemeanours which she knew were, in her mother's eyes, many, searching for what might be the cause of this meeting.

'Close up the door, Hannah, we do not wish to be disturbed before your father joins us, do we?'

Hannah agreed with her mother, this being the accepted thing to do, but she had no inkling as to why any of her brothers must be excluded. And as to why her father would join them later, Hannah could recall no misdemeanor serious enough to warrant the presence of the father who terrified not only Hannah but her mother as well.

Thus, Hannah's mother succeeded in reducing Hannah to a quivering wreck capable only of quickly acquiescing to any request made of her before the arrival of her father's fearful might.

Later, at the evening meal, Hannah ate little. She was searching for a quiet space inside her head to make sense of what had come to pass.

'Hannah, fetch the bread.' 'Hannah, serve your brothers some pie.' 'Hannah, sit to the table now.' 'Hannah, bring the butter.' Hannah's mother, exasperated by her slowness and forgetfulness, issued a stream of instructions until all at the table were weary of hearing her voice. But none dared to speak, for their father forbade idle talk during meals.

Without warning Father's fist thumped heavily onto the table, causing much shaking about of the crockery. Joseph caught the hot pie dish on its slide to the floor. His yelp of pain caused Father to once more bring his fist down upon the table, sending the dish of cabbage to the floor. The resounding crash delivered silence for father's words.

'Hannah, I do not wish to hear your mother say one more word to you. You are of an age to know how to serve a meal, so it is a time of peace and tranquility in which I might enjoy my food. Once you are married this nonsense will not be able to continue. Think, my girl and behave as your mother has taught you all these years or your married life will be less pleasant a life than you now enjoy.'

Later, seated in the darkest corner of the room so others should not see her tears fall, Hannah leaned on Joseph's strong shoulder.

'Hannah,' Joseph whispered, 'why did you agree so readily to marry the merchant Collet, or Mister Collet as I suppose we must now call him? He is almost of an age with father and is already twice widowed with many grown children.'

'Oh Joseph, of course I agreed to marry. I feared father might come to the room and find me in disagreement with mother. You yourself know what consequences any such disagreement would surely have, both for myself and for mother. You also have seen and heard his wrath when he is crossed. I have sacrificed my hopes of a happy marriage made for love so I might save mother from his fists just once.'

'Let us hope Mister Collet is not so free with his fists as father. I know almost nothing of him beyond knowing his business lies in Gloucester city. No doubt you will be obliged to reside there,' said Joseph, turning and grasping Hannah's ice-cold hands. 'I will visit as often as I am able.'

Hannah clutched her favourite brother close, lowering her whisper further, 'Joseph, thank you. I know you will do what you can.' She glanced towards her parents anxiously, assuring herself they were engaged in their own reveries as the flames of the fire licked and crackled around the dry logs. 'I have heard Gloucester is for the Parliamentarians and against the King. I have heard this is the way of things in the whole city of Gloucester.'

Joseph looked towards the father who had done this to Hannah. In a moment he determined to seek his own fortune in Gloucester rather than leave his sister isolated amongst Cromwell's supporters.

***

Father, prepared though he was to sacrifice his only daughter to a needy old friend, had no wish to bring any who might possibly support the Parliamentarians, to the Forest. Hannah and Mister Collet, shipping merchant of Gloucester, were married in the city on a fine spring day.

In the months following her wedding, Hannah saw nothing of her father, mother or the brothers remaining in the village. Her own journey to Gloucester for her wedding had been hazardous and filled for the two days with trepidation at the thought of encountering Parliamentarian troops or desperate deserters. Even the possibility of encountering the King's troops caused nervousness among the small travelling party. In those times of strife, the desperate would not ask, 'friend or foe?' before taking what they needed. They would have no regard for the lives of the travellers.

Father, reminding everyone of his responsibilities to protect his wife, home and family, refused to leave the Forest to see his unwanted daughter wed. Father forbade Hannah's mother to travel to Gloucester. Father was still strong despite his advancing age. When he forbade something only the foolish went against him. However, realizing he could not send his daughter to her future entirely alone, he instructed Joseph to escort her, accompanied by the stable boy and an orphaned village girl.

'You may keep her Hannah. You will be able to train her. In time she will make a serviceable maid and it will give a purpose to your life when your husband is engaged on his own business - until next year when you will, doubtless, have an infant to care for.' Mother declared with much more conviction in her voice than in her heart.

Hannah had felt her heart lift at the thought of this little band of Foresters gathered around her in the strange new life awaiting her. At her mother's next words her heart sank deep.

'You may keep the girl, but Joseph and the stable boy must return just as soon as you are wed and in the care of your husband.'

***

The small party had arrived in Gloucester just as the city gates were to be closed for the night. The gateman, reluctant to admit the unknown party to the city, caused much delay whilst the merchant Collet was fetched to claim his bride. The stable boy and the orphaned girl, however, freed from the tyranny of Hannah's father, however, had made their own plans for their future lives. In the bustle and confusion of arrival, they did not wait to be shown to their dark, cold lodging places. Silently they put their faith and trust firmly in each other as they turned from the city gates unseen, to seek their fortunes elsewhere.

Joseph, also relishing freedom from his father, fulfilled the promise he had made to his sister and failed to return home.

The marriage between Hannah and Merchant Collett was not an event of any note in the city. Joseph attended as witness, as did, after much bribery and coercion, one of Merchant Collett's adult children, who later reported to any of his siblings as cared to listen that she was, 'but an overgrown child, speaking in the incomprehensible dialect of the Forest but she will serve well-enough to meet father's needs, I suppose.'

Although she had spoken his name as Matthew in the awe of her marriage service, Hannah long continued to address her new husband as Mister Collett.

'Will you bide a while in my house, Joseph?' Matthew Collett clasped Joseph's extended hand between his own hands, surprising Joseph both by the offer and by the strength extending through his fingers.

Joseph had not anticipated such a welcome or such an offer. Tempting as the offer was, he knew if he were to stay in Gloucester against his father's wishes he would do well to bide somewhere he could not easily be found. I have, he thought, no wish to bring my father's wrath upon my sister's new household. All except Hannah must believe me returned to the Forest. 'Alas, Mister Collett,' Joseph declared, returning the hand pressure as he looked down into Matthew Collet's eyes and keeping as close to the truth as possible, 'my father requests my prompt return. I must hasten forth and make preparations.'

Joseph left, taking employment and lodgings where he found them, desperately seeking ways to maintain communications with Hannah.

***

Lying awake each night beside the snoring of her husband, Hannah re-lived the more carefree times in her growing up - times she had mostly shared with Joseph who had been born just ten months after her own arrival in the world. Joseph was unwanted by his mother, who was all but worn away by the demands of her husband and the needs of the children she already had. Hannah, however, was unwanted by her father. ‘A girl, what do I want with a girl, I thought you might do better,’ had been his first words to his exhausted wife, who had tried in vain to have him look at the infant Hannah following her birth.

Joseph and Hannah, when not required for chores or learning, meals, or evenings by the fireside, had made their own amusements roaming free in the Forest surrounding their village.

When Joseph was called upon to learn how to shoot the longbow, ready to defend the realm for the King should the need arise, he stole the bow away between each sabbath day, so he might teach Hannah how to shoot it and they might have their own tournaments of skill and precision, just between the two of them, hidden deep in the Forest. They had proved evenly matched in skill. As Joseph grew to manhood his strength outstripped that of Hannah and of the bow. Provided by the bowyer with a stronger bow Joseph permanently stole away his first bow for his sister. Then they would shoot side by side, vying to outdo each other in the distance their arrows travelled or the precision of their shot.

Hannah drifted to sleep each night, secure in the knowledge Joseph had brought both their bows and a good stock of arrows to Gloucester. One day, she was certain, they would again shoot side by side.

***

Joseph walked slowly through the streets of Gloucester. He was unfamiliar with the city, unfamiliar, indeed, with any city, having lived all his life in a small village nestled on the edge of the Forest of Dean. He had never before had cause to travel the miles to Gloucester. The city was a fascinating mystery to him, at once new, exciting, full of possibilities and opportunities and at the same time crowded with dark buildings, roads, and pathways muddy from the rain and people. More people than he usually encountered in a year passed him as he walked at the end of each day, trying to plan his future. Trying to overcome the image of Hannah, small and lost, beginning her married life.

Through the long winter, it seemed, everywhere Joseph walked, Cromwell's Parliamentarian troops were to be seen. Should he be concerned? Joseph did not know. Did they know some Foresters professed to be for the King? Could they tell he was a Forester just by looking at him? Even if they did not hear him speak? He took work and lodgings where he could, speaking little - trying, when he must speak, to mimic the speech of those around him, anxious not to draw undue attention to his origins.

***

As the evenings lightened with the turning season Hannah took to strolling through the garden before the maid brought the supper tray to the parlour.

At this hour Matthew had put aside the cares of the day's business proceedings and rested a while by the fire. Dozing, he allowed only the brighter parts of his life to intrude upon his solitude, sometimes sleeping lightly, sometimes verging between sleep and wakefulness as gentle thoughts swirled softly through his mind. Today perhaps, after they had taken supper, he would ask Hannah to play for him on the spinet, an instrument which had belonged to his mother. His mother had played each evening as he listened from the depths of his slowly warming, childhood bed, drifting to sleep on its gentle sounds. Neither of his previous wives, now deceased, had cared for the effort of playing in the evening and he had not yet asked Hannah.

'But she plays,' he murmured to himself, 'I have heard her playing as I have returned home at the end of the day.' He sighed, heaving himself more upright in his chair. 'It's then that she busies herself. She cannot know I would like to hear her play.'

On a warm spring evening, while these thoughts were drifting through Mathew's mind, Hannah, walking in the garden, stopped alongside the wall marking the boundary between the property and the street outside. Seeming to admire the emerging spring flowers she took a pointed stone from a nook in the wall. Shielding any view of the wall from the house with her body she tapped, as loudly as she dared, on the wall. From the other side of the wall an answering tap told her Joseph was there.

'Joseph, are you well?'

'Hannah, I am well. I have new lodgings with the merchant who employs me.'

'Are you comfortable there, Joseph?'

'Yes, Hannah, it is more comfortable than the inn, which was often visited by the troops garrisoned nearby.'

'Joseph, listen carefully I have only a short while before I need to go and attend to my household.'

Hannah paused for the silence which told her Joseph was listening.

'If you follow this wall around its corner, Joseph, what is there?'

'Hannah, which direction would you have me travel? One direction leads to a busy thoroughfare whilst the other leads to open land, which one should I take?'

Hannah did not know. 'I will take the stone and tap the wall as I walk, listen and follow.'

Hannah moved around the edge of the garden, tapping the wall so Joseph could follow on the other side. She stopped and called, 'Joseph, just here, what land lies there beyond the wall?'

'I am on the open land, no one is here.'

'Listen well Joseph for I need to leave you now. Standing here, I am hidden from all view of the house. None but I venture here. Next time you come put my bow and arrows over the wall and I will be able to send out messages to you on arrows. I must go Joseph, farewell.'

Joseph softly called a farewell, knowing Hannah was already beyond its range.

Swiftly Hannah shook the burrs and tangles from the hem of her dress, hung her shawl on a hook just inside the door and proceeded to the parlour only a little ahead of the maid carrying the heavy supper tray.

'Good evening, Mister Collett,' she stood, warming herself beside the fire, facing her husband's chair, 'I trust all has been well with your business today?'

Matthew smiled gently at her and reached to take her hand. His previous wives had rarely expressed interest in the day-to-day affairs of the business which provided them with the comforts they enjoyed. Hannah asked after his affairs each day.

'Your hand is cold, Hannah. Have you been walking in the garden? You must take care not to catch a chill. Did you have your shawl about you?'

'Yes, Mister Collett, I made sure to wear my shawl but even though the light is returning there is still a cold dampness in the evening air.' Hannah did not withdraw her hand. Unexpectedly it felt warm, comfortable, and secure in Matthew's hand, perfectly complementing the warmth seeping into her from the fire. She looked up to find the softness of Matthew's hand reflected in the softness of his eyes. Hannah did not think she had ever looked into Matthew's eyes before. The thought passed through her mind that his evenings here by the fire must have been lonely in the years since his previous wife had died.

'You should drink some wine, Hannah. It will warm you.' Gently Matthew released her hand so she could pour wine for them both.

A brief moment of loss passed through Hannah as her hand was returned to her. She buried the thought as she poured wine, relishing the easy domesticity of the moment.

Once the meal was finished, Hannah tidied everything onto the tray, ready for the maid to collect. A slight shiver of anticipation passed through her. She sensed Matthew had something further to say, whereas most evenings they sat on opposite sides of the fire, each lost in their own thoughts.

'Hannah,' Matthew spoke quietly, more quietly than he had intended, so anxious was he not to alarm his wife.

Hannah sensed, rather than heard him speak. 'Yes, Mister Collett, did you need something? Is there something I can fetch for you?

Matthew reached out his hand towards her. 'Come sit closer.'

Without thought of refusing, Hannah moved to sit closer to Matthew so he might take her hand again as he spoke to her. Once more Hannah felt the glow of warmth and comfort which spread through her from Matthew's hand. Unthinking, her fingers closed around his hand with a very gentle pressure.

'Hannah, I have two things to ask of you.'

Hannah looked hesitantly but enquiringly into the soft warmth of his eyes.

'Firstly Hannah, you have been here some months now and I have hopes you might see your way to addressing me as Matthew. I know I am much older than you are yourself but at the same time you are my wife. Hannah, there is really no cause to continue to address me as Mister Collett as if we were strangers. Would you do this for me?'

Hannah nodded slowly, 'Why yes Mister…' she hesitated, 'I mean to say, yes Matthew, I will do so, although I fear it will be strange at first.'

'I trust it will soon become less strange, I hope it will be a sign you are tolerably happy and comfortable here with me.'

Their eyes held each other for moments before Matthew took his gaze to the hand he still held. With his other hand he stroked her fingers gently. 'There is one more thing I seek to ask of you, Hannah.'

'What is it you desire,' again a slight pause, 'Matthew.'

'It would very much lighten my evenings if sometimes you might play upon the spinet. Until your arrival in the house, it had remained silent since my mother played when I was a child. I would very much like to hear its music again.'

***

Hannah strolled in the garden early in the evening almost every day, knowing, trusting, believing her bow would arrive just as soon as Joseph could deliver it without arousing suspicion.

Joseph did not walk close to Mister Collet's house every day, anxious as he was to blend unnoticed into the life of the city and avoid undue interest from Parliamentarian supporters. It was a full two weeks before he returned with Hannah's bow and a bundle of arrows. He chose an evening just following the waning of the crescent moon, the darkest night of the month. Joseph knew the darkness would be too great for Hannah to be still walking in the garden but was thankful it was dark enough for him to pile stones into a high mound beside the boundary wall unobserved. Thus, he was able to slide the bow and arrows over the wall without noise or damage. Despite his caution he still heard faint clattering as the precious load slid down into the garden, the sounds seeming to resound loudly in the quiet of the drawing night.

Joseph dismantled the mound of stones, removing the evidence of his visit. He trusted Hannah would be the first to find the bow and arrows. Silently he withdrew across the open land towards the city centre. He kept close to the shadows, changing his route to narrow alleyways to avoid Parliamentarian soldiers rolling from the taverns. If they saw him and spoke, he would have to reply. To not reply would likely arouse their latent desire for a fight. If he became a target for the soldiers there would be no reasoning with them, no escape. He had witnessed such beatings and enforced recruitment to the Parliamentarian cause more than once during his time in Gloucester. Best to keep to the shadows, be just a fleeting glimpse to the drunken soldiers, so they might believe they had seen no more than the ghost of their own mothers berating them for their drinking.

Joseph returned to his lodgings – a dusty but mercifully dry corner of the Merchant Mitchell's warehouse. A hunk of bread, cheese and an onion had been left for him on a wooden board, carefully covered with a bowl to keep the mice from it. A small tankard of Mistress Mitchell's home brewed ale rested beside it. Joseph realised afresh, as he did on his return each evening he had walked out late, how fortunate he had been to be taken into the employ of Mister Mitchell.

Both Mister Mitchell and his wife spoke little about his evening excursions beyond Mistress Mitchell warning him to have a care around the taverns - to stay clear of Cromwell's soldiers. Mistress Mitchell lay alert each evening waiting for the sounds of his return, followed by the sounds of her husband quietly barring the door before climbing the stairs in darkness. She breathed deeply, trusting to their safety for another night, as she waited for her husband to join her.

***

The day following Joseph's delivery of Hannah's bow and arrows the sun lingered long in the sky, delaying Hannah's evening stroll. The mild warmth of spring would soon give way to the heat of summer. Already the middens, slaughter yards, the alleyways, and the gulleys lining the main thoroughfares, were assailing the nostrils of all whose business or pleasure took them around the city. Hannah guessed the stench would only increase as summer progressed, guessed soon the mere opening of a casement to bring air into the house would suffice to allow the aroma of the city's waste to enter also.

Childhood memories of practising archery with Joseph filled her mind as she walked slowly, seemingly without purpose, to the quiet side of the house. How she longed for the lost freshness of forest and fields.

As on so many previous evenings Hannah slowed as she left the sight of the house. She moved slowly, eyes piercing into the bushes and undergrowth, searching, searching, long patience today rewarded. There was her bow, resting upright against stones. The bundle of arrows proved harder to locate, tangled as they had become in a mass of bramble and nettles. Nettles, which despite her best efforts to avoid them, stung her hands, leaving them red and swollen.

Leaning against the blank wall of the house, Hannah rested briefly. Swelling fingers gently stroking her bow, she waited for rustling footsteps which might indicate Joseph was close by. She tapped the wall with a stone and was rewarded with an answering tap from the other side. Praying Joseph would know she had found the bow, would anticipate the arrow and so would stay close to the wall she drew from the pocket tied around her waist a small piece of paper on which she had written, 'Thank you.'

Hands shaking, Hannah pierced the paper with the arrow. She pushed the paper along the shaft. Experimentally drawing up the bow she realised the paper would need to be close to the point of the arrow to avoid it being ripped away as the arrow curved through the bow.

'I must take care not to draw to the point,' she muttered, as if she were discussing the shot with Joseph during their practice. In her mind she heard Joseph agree.

As she nocked the arrow to the string Hannah felt a familiar joy surge through her. To be holding her bow once more, to be ready to shoot an arrow once more, she felt there to be no greater pleasure in life. She listened. There were no further sounds of movement, of others passing by. She stepped backwards a short way, judging the distance to the wall, the height of the wall, the angle of her shot. A steep arc would be needed to clear the wall and ensure a close descent on the other side. A different shot to their regular practice when they had vied to reach the furthest distance or to accurately hit a far target. Hannah drew back the bow a little, adjusted the line of the arrow by raising her bow arm higher in the air, drew a little more, raised a little more. Too high and the arrow would not clear the wall before descending, too low and it would travel far into the darkness.

Hannah eased the tension from the bow. She had identified her aiming point at the apex of the wall, had estimated the angle needed and the draw needed to keep the paper on the arrow, had assessed the possible impact from the slight breeze. Now she must put them all together in a smooth shot.

Joseph heard the soft sound as the arrow released from the bow. He watched it descend in a smooth, steep arc to the ground a short distance from the wall. He tapped on the wall, retrieved the arrow and faded almost soundlessly into the night.

***

'Would it please you to hear some music this evening, Matthew?' Hannah asked as the maid removed the supper tray.

Matthew Collett allowed his head to rest in the wing of the fireside settle, he smiled gently. A quiet pleasure seeped through him. This was the first time Hannah had herself suggested playing for him. 'Thank you, Hannah it would greatly please me. When I hear your beautiful music the cares of the day leave me, my soul is lifted.'

As she played the spinet, Matthew noticed the redness, the swelling of her hands. Later, he held them and stroked each in turn gently, concern in his eyes, enquiry kept close - not escaping from his lips.

***

As spring blossomed into summer Hannah found pleasures in this life she had not chosen, knowing Joseph was close by. Deciding she could not be confined solely to the house and its large garden, she took to accompanying the maid to the market, choosing for herself the produce for her small household. Passing the church of St Nicholas, Hannah would oblige the maid to stand and wait while she walked around, studying the beauty of its exterior. She sensed the maid fretting at this wasted time, which would leave her rushing the cooking to have the dinner prepared on time and working late into the evening to complete her tasks, instead of resting by the dying fire, dreaming of the young man whom she had yet to meet.

Returning towards the house Hannah would again oblige the maid to stop while she admired Greyfriars, the Franciscan Priory. These pauses were much shorter. The maid did not wait quietly, instead whispering frantically to Hannah, 'Come Mistress we best not linger here where the soldiers are garrisoned.' Shivering, even in the warmth of summer and keeping close to one another, they would hurry away from the unknown danger, the maid to her work and Hannah to write a reply to Joseph's latest message.

Joseph, do you continue well? I walked in the city today. Are the soldiers truly garrisoned at Greyfriars?

Indeed, they are, Hannah. You will do well to avoid them. It worries me to hear of you walking in the city. Much love, J.

I do not walk alone, Joseph, I go with the maid to the market and sometimes we pause to admire the fine buildings. They are bigger and grander than any I have seen.

Joseph, where else are the soldiers to be found? Today two soldiers tried to halt our passing. Then they were distracted by their fellow soldiers who were assaulting some men accused of being for the King. We left at once and quickly. The maid was very frightened and I was obliged to warm a little ale for her to calm her on our return or we should have had no dinner today. Is it safe to visit St Nicholas' church and walk to the city walls?

Hannah, you must be always cautious and not linger where there might be danger. Do not speak with strangers. They will know you to be foreign to the city and so possibly a supporter of the King. Stay close to the house. The maid will fare better alone for no doubt she knows the safe places and the people who will help her. Much love, J

Joseph, before I received your reply, we again encountered soldiers. Once more we have returned safely but I fear you are right. Henceforth, I will send the maid to the market alone. I may be obliged to confine my walks to quieter places, accompanied by my husband no doubt.

Joseph, you did not reply to my previous message, are you well?

Hannah do not include my name on your messages. I fear your message has been intercepted. Send messages only when you have heard me tap on the wall. Much love J.

Where are you living? How will I find you if I need you?

Hannah, I bide with the Merchant Mitchell and Mistress Mitchell. They are good people and I do not want for food or shelter. Much love J.

J, now autumn is upon us and the nights are drawing in I fear I may have few opportunities to send messages. I will come each day at twilight and tap the wall but if I hear not your response, I will not shoot a message.

***

As the seasons changed the exchange of messages between brother and sister slowed. The chilly winds of autumn gave way to frosts, rain, and snow. Hoarfrosts turned the bare trees white. They glistened in the winter sun in seeming defiance of Parliament's wish to restrict the celebration of Christmastide to a single day of fasting and religious observance. The feasting and fun of the twelve days of Christmas were no more. Many of the people of Gloucester found themselves quietly perturbed. Parliament had sat on 25th December, continuing the business of government whilst the populace went without their festivities.

Hannah kept her thoughts to herself, anxious not to give voice to support for the King and the old ways of celebrating which had done much to lighten the darkest days of winter in years gone by. She dared not even mention Christmas festivities in her messages to Joseph, excepting to offer him, 'compliments of the season' in a message hastily dispatched on the morning of 25th December, just prior to leaving the house for the first church service of the day. On her return she did not find a reply.

Like Hannah, Matthew did not express any thoughts of loss for the festivities of the past. Sighing, almost inaudibly, he said to Hannah, 'You had best ask Cook to prepare only a modest repast. We will save the meat for another day. A day on which we can freely enjoy it.'

In the evening Matthew sat quietly by the fire. He did not ask Hannah to play for him. She had not expected him to, given the new solemnity of the day.

In the weeks following, Matthew continued about his business during the days but, it seemed to Hannah, he sank into a somewhat despairing gloom each evening as they sat by the fire. Even as February brought light to the end of the day and he was sometimes able to take a turn around the garden before darkness fell, his spirit seemed not to lift. Hannah, worried he might be sickening, felt him fade from her somewhat. Sadly, she realised she missed the feeling of her hand in his, missed sitting close to him beside the fire. She missed playing the music which had brought him so much pleasure and contentment. the music which had brought them together.

On an evening when Matthew seemed a little less sunk in gloom Hannah ventured to ask, 'Matthew, would you like me to play the spinet for you this evening?'

Matthew nodded slowly, letting out a deep sigh, 'Yes Hannah, please play. Perhaps some music will lighten the evening.'

Slowly the weary winter dragged on into the wet and stormy spring of 1643. Matthew's mood continued low most evenings. Even his solitary walks around the garden seemed not to lift his sadness, indeed Hannah was almost certain he became quieter and more withdrawn from her on those days when the weather had permitted such a stroll.

Hannah too began to sadden and despair. The promise of a happy gentle life with Matthew was fading and she rarely found a message from Joseph. She knew Joseph should be more easily able to send messages during this time. Believing none but Hannah ventured to the side of the house they had agreed he would send messages when he could. Hannahs must wait to send a reply until she knew Joseph was on the other side of the wall. They could not risk another message going astray.

Hannah despaired, even when dry weather persisted for several consecutive days and she was able to walk in the garden looking for messages, she found none, whilst the days of wet and stormy weather also hampered her own efforts to communicate with Joseph.

Hannah's despair deepened. There were few messages from Joseph and Matthew only listened to her music when she guessed his mood to be receptive. Then she offered to play for him. He no longer asked her to play, seeming content to sit staring into the fire, lost in his own thoughts.

When the ceaseless rain began to ease, Hannah was again able to walk more frequently in the garden near sunset, trying to prolong the day, shorten the evening. Each dry day Hannah searched but rarely found a message. Each day she tapped but no reply came for many days until very late one evening, just as the wind began to pick up, she heard Joseph's familiar tap.

Quickly Hannah prepared the bow, her heart beating fast at the prospect of once more communicating with her beloved brother. She pulled back the bow, allowing the arrow to take flight in a steep arc which saw it drop smoothly, close to the other side of the wall.

'J, Not hearing from you for so long has caused me great anxiety. Have you been unwell? Is there any help I can offer you?'

Hannah dared not linger. Turning towards the house she had the briefest glimpse of a shadow fading round the corner. Guessing it to be no more than the waving of the branches of the big, old apple tree, Hannah hurried on so she might be in the parlour when the maid brought in the supper.

Unbeknown to Hannah, Joseph had lingered to send an immediate reply, concerned because Hannah had not received his recent messages.

'Hannah, I am well and thinking of you each day. One day we will again be together. Much love J.'

Hannah walked along the passageway, only just ahead of the maid with the supper. She was surprised to find Matthew not yet arrived but, happy to have made contact with Joseph again, she busied herself pouring wine and setting out the music which she determined to offer to play to Matthew later.

Matthew was not long delayed, soon entering the room with the scent of the garden still around him and the coolness of the wind sending its chill from him. He spoke little beyond polite necessities when Hannah offered him wine. Hannah was distressed to see the sadness in Mathew's eyes during the evening as he sat gazing more intently than ever at the fire in the hearth. When Hannah hesitatingly asked if he would like her to play for him Matthew replied, 'No Hannah, not this evening. I do not believe I would enjoy the lightness of music this evening.'

***

All through the spring and into the blossoming of summer Parliamentarian troops remained garrisoned at Greyfriars. News of turmoil and battles around the country arrived sporadically, borne by those still willing to travel.

Matthew continued quiet through the evenings. Hannah sensed his sadness. He seldom responded positively to her offers to play for him. Hannah's heart was heavy. Silently, she longed to once more look into the softness of his eyes, to feel the tenderness of his hands. As the evenings grew long in their light and warmth, Matthew walked late in the garden.

One day, with no word spoken between them, Hannah walked with him. Matthew made no comment, uttered no word of encouragement, raised no objection and so Hannah ventured to walk with him each evening. Each evening, they paused, seemingly as one at the corner of the house beyond which lay the tangle of bramble from where Hannah sent her messages to Joseph. Joseph's messages arrived there also, although now very few and far between, thought Hannah, shivering in concern.

Matthew spoke and Hannah was startled, so seldom did he direct any but the most mundane of comments to her these days, 'Are you chilled, Hannah? Or perhaps something different ails you?' Matthew's gaze cast itself over the bramble.

Hannah, seeing the end of an arrow showing slightly above the bramble, was anxious to draw Matthew away, 'Thank you Matthew, yes, I feel a little chilled, it seemed so warm I did not wear my shawl. Shall we return to the house? I could play a little music for you?'

'Yes, let us return, you should not catch a chill. There is no need to play, so little of the evening remains. Perhaps some other evening.'

Matthew sat thoughtfully by the empty hearth for the rest of the evening.

The following morning Matthew left early to attend to his business in the city. Household duties kept Hannah in the house for much of the morning but, as soon as she was able, she walked quickly around the garden to the overgrown corner. She was eager to gather in the news and good wishes undoubtedly contained in the message she had spotted the previous evening.

It was gone.

Hannah's heart beat rapidly. What had happened to the message? Someone must have found it, there had been no wind to blow it away. Besides the arrow was also missing but surely no one else came clambering around these brambles. No one else would be expecting a message. Hannah's thoughts spun wildly.

Suddenly she understood why Joseph had seemed to send so few messages in reply to her many. She understood why Matthew had paused at this corner of the house, looking carefully over the brambles instead of the fine cultivated plants on the other side of the garden. She understood why Matthew sometimes, as he had done this day, left early for his walk to his business. But the messages were only from Joseph, from her brother whom Matthew had been so cordial to when they had first arrived in Gloucester. A picture played through her mind, an image of all the messages from Matthew addressed, 'Dearest Hannah,' and signed, 'Much love, J,' their content expressing desire to meet soon, to be together again.

Slowly Hannah leant against the wall. She knew without doubt Matthew had found all the messages she had missed. She guessed he had mistaken them for messages from a lover, believed she had forsaken him for another. She understood why he had withdrawn from her. Deep in her heart she knew she wished to make it right once more, for him, but also for herself. She wanted once more to see gentle love in his eyes and feel the tenderness as he held her hands, held her close.

Later that day Matthew returned home tired and troubled.

'Hannah, I have distressing news. The city gates are closed, none may enter or leave.'

Hannah studied Matthew's face, somewhat puzzled, 'I understood the city gates to be closed always as night falls. They are opened once more each morning to allow people to go about their business and to permit travellers entry to the city.'

Matthew moved to the settle, a deep sigh escaped from him as he sat, 'No Hannah,' he said not looking at her, shaking his head, 'it is more than closing the gates for the night. Cromwell's soldiers have closed the gates. Soldiers for the King are amassing outside the city walls wanting to take back the city for the King. There is rumour of cannon being sent down the river from Worcester. Gloucester is under attack - we are besieged. You must not leave the house and we must trust to the loyalty of the servants, for if word gets about you are for the king there will be plenty here who would betray you – us – to Cromwell's troops, in the hope of reward.'

Hannah's heart missed a beat, 'But what of Joseph, my brother Joseph?'

'I do not believe we need have too great a concern for Joseph. He is safe back in the Forest.'

'No, Matthew, no. Joseph did not return to the Forest. He remained here in Gloucester where he might be free from our father's violence and where he might offer me protection should it have transpired that I was in need of such.' Hannah leaned heavily against the fireplace struggling to prevent the tears escaping from her eyes. 'I must send Joseph a message, make sure he is safe.'

Rising from the settle to stand beside his wife, Matthew asked where Joseph was to be found.

'He has work and lodging with the Merchant Mitchell and his wife Mistress Mitchell. They are good to him, he is happy and settled but others must know him to be for the king.' Hannah reached as if to grasp Matthew's arm, but memories of their recent coldness led her instinctively to withdraw her hand and grasp her own arm instead, pulling and kneading at the cloth of her gown in her distress.

Matthew spoke slowly, 'Many know Merchant Mitchell to be against the Parliamentarian cause. I fear your brother will not fare well there for much longer. I will send a message to Mitchell requesting Joseph's presence here, although I fear there will be a danger of the message being intercepted.'

'No Matthew,' Hannah spoke rapidly, thinking even faster. 'I will send a message. I have often sent messages to Joseph. If I send it in my usual way, he will know it to be from myself. Come let me show you.'

***

Hannah's eagerness to carry out the task of alerting Joseph to the impending danger of his situation swept Matthew along in its wake. He watched and waited as Hannah took from the bureau a small scrap of thick paper on which she wrote, *J, you must come to the house and rest here with my husband and I. You will not long be safe at Mister Mitchell's.*

Matthew followed Hannah as she walked swiftly to a little-used back door. He was astonished to see her take a longbow and an arrow from a deep alcove beside the door, hidden by all manner of unused household utensils.

'Come, Matthew, we must send the message before darkness falls. If we are fortunate in our timing Joseph may even be nearby, waiting.'

The distance between them of the last weeks disappeared from Hannah's mind. Her only purpose now was to send the message, to try and secure for Joseph the greater safety of the house she now called home. This time, as they approached the corner of the house beyond which lay the bramble strewn path and the garden wall, Hannah wasted no time in looking to see if she had been observed. She was trusting Matthew with her deepest secret.

Hannah stooped for her tapping stone and tapped the wall, waiting and listening before tapping again. A faint but clear reply came from the other side of the wall. Joseph was there. Carefully Hannah eased herself and her cumbersome skirts along the narrow path deeply edged with bramble. She secured the message to the arrow and nocked the arrow to the string. Carefully she raised the bow, adjusted the angle to take account of the breeze, a final adjustment to ensure the arrow cleared the wall. She pulled the bow to full draw, followed by a smooth and swift release. The arc of the arrow's flight peaked as the arrow passed the top of the wall. It fell steeply.

'Come, we must step back around the corner, Joseph may reply at once.' Hannah indicated the direction they should take. Matthew, astounded by what he had just witnessed, obeyed. Silently they waited, each listening to the muffled sound of the other's breathing, waiting for another sound, jerking visibly as they heard the swish of an arrow and the gentle thud of its landing.

'Wait Hannah, I will retrieve the arrow.' A moment later Matthew returned, his badly scratched hand holding tightly to the same paper Hannah had sent over the wall. On the reverse Joseph had written, *Dearest Hannah, I fear you are correct. I will come tomorrow with news, much love J.*

Hannah listened as Matthew read the message. 'Come Hannah,' he said, reaching for her hand. She felt the old familiar warmth and tenderness in his touch, 'let us return to the parlour. I have intercepted Joseph's previous messages. Believing Joseph to be returned to the Forest I did not know who '*J*' was. I believed I was losing the love which had been growing between us. I have misjudged you, Hannah. I wish to make amends and offer my sincerest apologies.'

***

The following day, with Matthew gone to the city to attend to his business, a restless Hannah tried to still the anxiety and joy which were causing her heart to beat so loud and fast. She and Matthew were reconciled. Matthew was offering shelter to Joseph. Joseph would arrive at the house, surely just as soon as he was able. Not wanting to alert the maid unduly, Hannah prepared a bed for Joseph herself, although she found the task wearied her quickly.

Just as the clock struck noon, the maid announced the arrival of two visitors. Hannah and Joseph each threw themselves into the outstretched arms of the other so great was their pleasure at being together once more.

Hannah withdrew slightly, still clasping Joseph's hands. 'Let me look and see for myself you are still my brother Joseph.' She sighed with satisfaction. 'It seems they have treated you well. Now what news do you bring?'

Joseph turned, taking Hannah's attention to the heavily pregnant woman who had entered the house with him. 'Hannah, here is Mistress Mitchell, come to seek shelter and safety. Mister Mitchell, the merchant who has given me employment and shelter is with us no longer, we buried him yesterday.'

Hannah dropped Joseph's hands as she reached for those of Mistress Mitchell. Mistress Mitchel grasped Hannah's hand tightly as a wail of despair and grief escaped from deep inside her.

Hannah guided the widow to a seat, offering what condolences she could to the newly bereaved woman. She looked enquiringly to Joseph, praying silently disease had not been the cause of death. Surely Joseph would not risk bringing disease to her household. 'Joseph, pray tell me what has befallen Merchant Mitchell's household? I can wait no longer for news.'

Joseph sank wearily onto a chair, clasping the arms tightly in his hands. 'Hannah, the news is not good, the city is besieged by the King's forces. Cromwell's soldiers are becoming desperate. If the King's forces gain entry to the city, Cromwell's men will be killed or taken prisoner. They are desperate. They are a danger to others. Four days ago, hearing there were Royalist sympathisers, they came to Merchant Mitchell's business, where his home lies also. Taking Mitchell by surprise they killed him. Whether by intent I know not, but Mitchell is dead. Seeing him lifeless and, perhaps fearing the consequences for themselves, they fled, thus sparing Mistress Mitchell, Jane, the maid, and myself.'

Hannah sank beside Mistress Mitchell on the settle, clasping a cold hand within her own warm hands. 'You must rest here with us. I trust my husband will agree. It was his thought to bring Joseph here and I am sure he would not wish you to remain alone and unprotected.'

'Joseph,' Hannah looked towards her brother, 'what has become of the maid, surely she does not remain alone, is she returned to her family?'

'She is here, she has no family. Your maid has directed her to the kitchen where no doubt your cook will find work to take her mind from what has happened.' Joseph sighed as he rose from his seat to once more take his sister in his embrace, 'I fear, Hannah, we may none of us be safe for long.'

From the doorway Matthew spoke, taking them all by surprise for none had heard his arrival, 'Joseph, welcome to my home. Mistress Mitchell welcome to what little protection my home may offer you.' He turned to Hannah, 'I too fear we may not be safe for long, desperate soldiers and citizens are very unpredictable. News has got through. The cannons from Worcester have arrived, although one was lost overboard to the river. There is grave danger for all who remain in the city, but it seems there is no way out.'

***

Over the following days Matthew went seldom to his business. Without access to the river's trade route there was little business to attend to. When he returned, he offered what reports he could as to the damage wreaked by the incoming cannon fire. Westgate street, he reported, had fared badly. Many houses had been damaged and the church of St Nicholas had lost its spire. The cross at Tosley was all but destroyed. Greyfriars, where the

Parliamentarian troops were garrisoned, had sustained serious damage.

Somehow news still crept into the city and, as Mistress Mitchell observed one evening after the cannons were silenced for the night, 'no doubt it creeps out also.'

'But, yes, this must be so,' declared Joseph, excitement in his voice. Surely if news is getting out it might be possible for us too, to leave the city.'

Silence fell on the room as they each absorbed Joseph's words. Any attempt to leave would be difficult, treacherous, but to remain could also mean death or injury.

That night, as the household slept fitfully in their beds, Joseph silently slipped from the house determined to discover how news was entering and leaving the city.

***

Midsummer had passed and the month of August was progressing towards autumn. Nights were dark. The new moon, appearing late in the evening, gave just sufficient light to guide Joseph on his return to the house.

For several nights Joseph slipped silently from the house as everyone slept. Although few were abroad in the darkness of those night walks, Joseph moved cautiously around Gloucester, careful to avoid the attentions of any who might seek to question him or do him harm. He wished not to be too much observed.

At first, the dark, the quiet and the stillness disturbed him, made him fear for what he might encounter with every step he took. Then, as he met no one and no danger befell him, Joseph became less guarded. Some nights he found himself enjoying the quiet aloneness of the city after the sounds of battle which had raged through the day. He knew it would not be long before he was called upon to take a place in defending the city. Joseph shuddered. He had no wish to support the Parliamentarian cause. Such thoughts brought swiftly back to mind the true purpose of these nighttime wanderings. Joseph realised he had wasted several evenings enjoying the solitude of the darkness. He had not ventured beyond the parts he knew well, not reached the city walls or gates, the very places where he might find the information he sought. Once more Joseph set out, determined to trace the path of the city walls each night until he discovered how information passed in and out.

Each day Hannah watched as Joseph's face became more and more pale and drawn. He slipped into sleep whenever he sat without purpose. She knew him well, knew his determination and she guessed from whence his tiredness and growing despair came. She guessed the duty of protection he felt to the household now weighed heavy on him, knew he would find what he sought if it were there to find. Each night she lay in her bed, fighting to stay awake, until she heard the reassuring creak of the stairs as a weary Joseph climbed to what little rest was left for him before daybreak.

***

On the tenth night, Hannah woke sharply. She had drifted into a deep sleep but immediately on waking she realised the sound she heard was different. Careful not to disturb Matthew, slumbering by her side, she raised herself on one elbow, leaning towards the bedroom door and the stairs beyond. The noise came again. A heavy footfall, a deep rasping breath, the creak of the banister as it bore the weight of Joseph pulling himself painfully up the stairs. Another heavy footfall, a pause, a deep breath, the slap of a hand grasping the banister, the creak as the banister again took Joseph's weight. Hannah slipped from her bed, waiting, listening, until she judged Joseph to have ascended the stairs, not wishing to startle him and cause him to falter in his painful climb. With the slightest click she lifted the latch of the door. Matthew's snores reassured her that he slept on.

'Joseph,' Hannah whispered, 'Joseph, is it you?'

'Tis I Hannah, go back to your rest - all is well.'

'No Joseph, I will not go back to my rest, clearly all is not well for you climb the stairs like a cripple or an aged man. You have sustained injury.'

Joseph, despite his pain, laughed quietly. Hannah knew him so well and shared his determination. He knew she would not rest until she had ascertained the extent of his injury. He reached out an arm, resting it heavily on her shoulder, 'Come sister, guide your poor brother to his chamber, the moon will be coming through the casement now. You will be able to satisfy yourself I am not bleeding excessively, and no bones are broken. I fear, however, I have many bruises and will be stiff and sore on the morrow.'

'But Joseph, what happened, whom, or what, did you encounter?'

Joseph sat heavily on the bed, 'Hannah, I need to rest now. I will give you a full account when the sun rises, and I have counted my bruises. I'm sure there will be no more than following a beating from Father. Perhaps 'tis lucky I am familiar with bruises. They will run their course and I will be none the worse for them. The ruffians who set upon me have a few bruises of their own.'

***

The morning dawned warm, the sun shining brightly above the cannon fire which started early and continued relentless through the day. Jane, Mistress Mitchell's maid, approached Hannah, clearly wishing to speak with her. Jane was generally a quiet girl who Hannah could not recall having heard speak in the short time since she had arrived in the household.

'Good morning, Jane, did you wish to speak with me?' Hannah asked gently, hoping to put the maid at ease, for she generally liked to see everyone comfortable.

'Yes, Miss ... Madam, I helped Joseph, your brother. Forgive me - I have always called him Joseph when we worked together for Merchant Mitchell. I helped him in the kitchen last night when he returned, beaten by the soldiers.'

At once Hannah recognized the tones of a fellow Forester. Slowly, she took Jane's work rough hand, seeking to encourage her to keep talking.

'Miss… I'm sorry Madam, I know why Joseph roamed the city last night. I know what he looked for, whom he sought. He was injured so I could not tell him then, but I know where and how they send the messages, and where the King's troops from the Forest are tunnelling from the outside. I have brothers amongst them and have sent my own messages to them.'

The creaking of a door behind her, and the look of caution spreading on Jane's face alerted Hannah to the fact they were no longer alone. Indicating to Jane she should say no more, she turned to leave the room, to go about her morning's business with such an air of normality as she could muster.

Matthew stood before her in the doorway.

'Hannah, let the girl continue speaking. I have encountered Joseph already this morning. He is in a sorry way. I believe we may none of us be safe here for long if news of our sympathies is spread abroad, especially amongst the soldiers and those who seek only their own protection.'

Matthew turned to address Jane directly, 'Jane, if the King's troops from the Forest are tunnelling under the walls might it be we could leave the city by their tunnels?'

'Indeed, Sir, such an escape may be possible. I was minded to attempt it for Mistress Mitchell and myself. Mistress Mitchell must soon be confined for the birth of the infant. I had hoped to be able to escape Gloucester and take her to my own mother in the Forest for her confinement. Mother has much experience in these matters following her own fifteen confinements.'

Hannah sought to speak, questions poured through her mind. There was so much to know, maybe plans to make so they might leave the bombardment of the city, return to the Forest. Memories of her father's violence crept around the edges of her thinking but no, she had no cause to worry for she was married now, Matthew would be her protector. She knew even her father would not assault another man's wife.

Before Hannah could gather her thoughts into words Jane spoke once more, looking at Hannah, 'You might accompany me this evening, Madam. There may be a message waiting with news of the tunnel's progress and we can send out messages requesting passage.'

Hannah nodded her assent, 'Go about your work now Jane, I will go with you this evening.'

Matthew raised his hand to halt them, wanting to express his concern for their safety, to say he would accompany them, but Jane did not see his gesture. She had already turned to the kitchen door, pausing only to say, 'Bring your bow, Madam, two arrows are better than one, we shall not be able to linger long.'

'Matthew, how does Jane know about my bow? She cannot have seen me use it - she has been here but a short time and I am always so very careful to avoid observation.'

Despite the severity of their situation, Matthew laughed as he reached to enclose Hannah in the warmth of his arms. 'I believe her skills of quiet observation come from her Forest roots. Perhaps also Joseph has spoken with her about his fearless sister. But, recall, I too discovered your secret.' Gently he pulled Hannah closer to him. 'I will accompany you this evening.'

***

When darkness was fully upon Gloucester, Jane, Hannah and Matthew set forth. Jane and Hannah carried bows. They walked swiftly to the west walls of the city.

'My brothers and their fellow soldiers will be close by the walls. We must shoot the arrows well clear but not so far they cannot be found easily,' Jane whispered to Hannah. 'I have two messages. They both ask for news of the tunnel's readiness. We will send both, lest one might go astray.'

Jane turned to where Matthew was faintly outlined in the darkness, 'Mistress Collet and I will climb these steps to give us a better chance of clearing the wall with our arrows. The steps are steep, it would be best, Sir, if you remain here. We will be gone but a short while.'

Jane's hands shook, she was unused to giving orders to her social superiors. She did not wait for a reply.

At the top of the steps, Hannah and Jane silently braced their bows, attached the messages to their arrow points, stood alongside each other, drew up their bows and, almost as one, released their arrows over the city wall and into the night. 'There will be news in the morning,' Jane said confidently as she led them back through the stillness of the night.

***

None but Jane left the house the following morning and she returned as swiftly as she was able. The cannon's bombardment was relentless from the first light of day. Hannah, attempting to distract herself from the battle outside, played on the spinet but her hands jumped as the music vanished from her mind with each firing of the cannon.

'Come, Hannah.' Matthew gently placed his hand on her shoulder. Hannah rose to stand beside him. Matthew's next words remained unspoken. Cannon fire crashed in the street, destroying the house next door. In the moment it took them to recover their wits they felt their own house shudder. The splintering of wood and the crashing of crumbled masonry drowned any words. They staggered backwards, colliding heavily with the tallboy behind them.

Silently they waited. Not yet aware of their own bruises. They waited for the movement of their house to cease. They heard the next cannon ball, fired from beyond the city walls, drop, knowing from the sound it had landed some distance away.

In what remained of the kitchen they found the crushed and lifeless body of Cook. The agonised shrieking of their maid alerted them to her presence in the pantry, legs trapped under a fallen beam.

Joseph and Jane arrived at the pantry just behind them. Together they were able to lift the beam sufficiently to ease the maid from under it, her blood-curdling shrieks continuing until the pain overtook her and she succumbed to unconsciousness.

All wished to speak but it seemed none could find the words they needed. Jane was the first to recover composure sufficiently for thoughts to form into words.

'I believe we must leave this very evening. The Forest troops have a narrow tunnel ready, there are others leaving this evening. The Foresters plan to desert tonight. It would help us greatly to have what protection they can offer on our journey back to the Forest. Now I must be with Mistress Mitchell, I pray the shock does not bring the infant before we are gone from the city.'

'I fear this house, such as it now is, may not stand long. Its structure is weakened,' Matthew sighed heavily. 'I had hoped to have news others had successfully left the city before we made our attempt. But Jane is right. We must attempt to leave this evening. Joseph, the maid's family are to be found at the far end of Eastgate Street, they must send bearers with a litter to carry her home where they can care for her. I fear she may lose her leg if not her life. Seek out also Cook's family. They must take her body for burial. I will make up a purse for each family to help them with the expenses they will incur.'

***

Late at night, carrying little but the bows and arrows belonging to Hannah and Jane and moving almost silently, the party set forth through the moonless streets of Gloucester. Jane, being most familiar with the city, led them, Joseph close behind. Mistress Mitchell breathed as deeply and quietly as she could to quell the palpitations of her heart and to quiet the infant lying within her. She walked behind Hannah, who made certain they did not lose sight of Joseph. Matthew brought up the rear, glancing anxiously behind him with every other step.

Jane moved swiftly, always seeking the darkest paths. An occasional swish from the unbraced bow she carried alerted those behind her to the rats, stray dogs and other vermin which had ventured from their hiding places to scavenge in the sleeping city.

Hannah and Matthew paused to enable Mistress Mitchell to catch her breath. Hannah prayed silently but fervently for the infant's arrival to be yet some days hence. For herself, she felt a quiet exhaustion, brought on, she believed, by the worries of the past few days - the constant bombardment of cannon fire, the death of Cook, the maiming of her own maid. Hannah sensed Mistress Mitchell wanted nothing more than for the nightmare to be over. As they rested together Hannah felt the same for herself, but she knew they could not linger long. The merest hint of a shadow ahead and the very faintest whisper, such as they had used in childhood games, reassured Hannah Joseph was waiting for them.

'Come,' Hannah's voice, close to Mistress Mitchell's ear, was almost silent, 'we must continue.'

Mistress Mitchell grasped Hannah's arm tightly. She let out the very faintest squeal as a rat, fooled by their previous stillness, scuttled back to the building it had emerged from.

Ahead Joseph felt Jane's shiver of exasperation. Her mistress's indiscretion might yet lead to disaster for them all.

Fleeting shadows, whispers floating on the gentle breeze, the skittering of stones, told them others were about their own secret, silent, missions in the darkness. No doubt all were as anxious as they to reach their destinations unobserved. They encountered no soldiers but for glimpses of shadows atop the city walls, watching for enemy incursions under cover of darkness.

They made slow progress. Joseph glanced frequently skywards to the east, expecting with each glance to find the first glimmer of daylight ready to overtake them. But the darkness held.

Once more the total stillness behind them alerted Joseph to the need for another pause. This time he heard Jane's sharp intake of breath as she fought to keep her frustrations quiet within her.

Standing close beside her Joseph felt the stiff tension in her body. He wanted to offer reassurances but did not dare to voice them. Instinctively he reached out in the dark, finding her arm, clasping it with gentle pressure. He kept contact as they again resumed their walking.

Suddenly, Jane reached out her free hand, seeking Joseph's arm in the darkness. 'We are here,' she murmured, her voice just slightly above a whisper. 'We are here,' she repeated as the others joined them, 'wait while I seek information.'

Hannah became aware of an almost silent, rustling, bustling, hubbub around her, alerting her to the presence of others but she knew not how many nor their identities. All of them cautiously trusting there were no enemies amongst them to betray their purpose to the Parliamentarian soldiers.

Keeping close to each other Hannah, Joseph, Mistress Mitchell and Matthew felt the thoughts and fears of those strangers drifting around them - felt their own fear - wished for nothing more than this to be over - to be safe outside the city walls.

Joseph felt again the touch of Jane's hand on his.

'Come,' she beckoned, although none could see the gesture, 'there is a tunnel ready to leave by,' she murmured, hoping her voice did not travel far.

Mistress Mitchell, who knew no life but the city, reached despairingly for Jane's arm. Unable to find it in the darkness, her hand grasped Hannah's arm instead.

'No, Jane, surely there is no need for such haste,' she whispered. 'One more day will do no harm, besides,' she patted gently her heavily pregnant body, 'I do not believe I am able to pass through a tunnel.'

'No,' Jane whispered, understanding the time for protecting her Mistress from the reality of their situation had passed, 'we must go this evening, there is no possibility of delay. Those who have dug the tunnel, the King's troops from the Forest, will not remain risking their lives in a battle for a city which means nothing to them. Tonight, those from the Forest who wish to escape are able to use the tunnel. When all have left, the Forest troops will block the tunnel once more and none remaining in Gloucester will know of it. We must go now or not at all.'

***

'Come with me,' a voice whom none but Jane recognized, spoke firmly beside them. 'There is no time for delay - others are waiting.' The voice became fainter as its owner began at once to move away. They must follow or remain inside Gloucester's walls, for they knew not how long, to face whatever dangers remaining might bring them.

They followed.

Faint lights from rush torches glowed around the tunnel entrance as it sank beneath the city wall. All around them the fears of others drifted in the night air. They must move quickly. If they hesitated, others would take their place. The voice on the night air which had summoned them to the tunnel now chivvied them to make haste, reassuring them, 'The tunnel is not long, one by one, keep moving, don't stop in the tunnel, keep moving.'

Joseph went first, commanding Mistress Mitchell to follow and keep close to his heels. As the tunnel narrowed, he could hear the sharpness of her breath, feel her fear that the infant within her would wedge her in the tunnel. Matthew felt the dank earth above and around him - knew there would be space enough. He heard the muffled voice of Jane urging her Mistress forward just as he felt the first drifts of fresh night air.

'Come, Mistress,' Joseph urged, this time more loudly, 'we are almost through, keep close, we are almost at the end.'

Suddenly Joseph was free from the dankness of the tunnel, was able to stand, could hear the call of an owl and feel the dry chill of the night. A voice urged him to make haste away from the city, but Joseph turned, reaching for Mistress Mitchell's hand, urging her to open her eyes, to feel the freedom of the night, to know she had escaped Gloucester.

Jane very quickly followed her Mistress, cursing quietly. Jane and Matthew assisted Mistress Mitchell to her feet. Hannah and Matthew emerged from the tunnel. Swiftly, damp and cold, they melted into the night, away from danger.

'Come,' Hannah urged, 'we must continue our journey before the sun rises. It is a good day's walk to the Forest, but I fear we may be longer. Mistress Mitchell will have need of rest upon the way. Let us pray the infant can wait a while longer.'

***

As they began their long walk it was evident Mistress Mitchell was not the only one slowing progress. Matthew, somewhat more elderly than the rest of the party, was unaccustomed to walking great distances. Even Hannah soon found the walking exhausting. It was an arduous journey which found them at the edge of the Forest only after two days and nights.

Hannah and Jane, with the aid of their longbows and some quietly grazing rabbits, were able to provide food to sustain them.

Joseph laughed. 'Remember Hannah, rabbits were our prey when we spent the days of our youth hiding from Father's wrath in the caves. Mother was pleased with the rabbits.'

Hannah grasped Joseph's arm. 'The caves, of course Joseph, the caves. I have been deeply worried thinking how this journey might end. If we go straight to the house Father will certainly have cause to be angry with you, for were you not expected to return from Gloucester once you had delivered me?'

Hannah stopped. She looked at Joseph, concern showing deep in her eyes, 'Father will not, I fear, welcome us with any great alacrity. Joseph, we will go first to the caves.'

On the third day, lighter in spirits, they travelled through the Forest towards the childhood play place of Hannah and Joseph.

The caves were cool, dry and sheltering. Jane gathered bracken in great armfuls to make a comfortable place for her Mistress to rest and recover from the journey. Both waited anxiously for signs of an imminent birth.

Once Matthew had rested a while, Hannah took his hand gently and led him to a second cave. She stopped, facing the wall. Slowly she raised her fingers to trace the outline of drawings scratched into the stone. 'See, Matthew, this is my drawing, and this,' she pointed further along the wall, 'is Joseph's.' Hannah laughed as she traced the drawings. 'We drew ourselves. I had the easier task there, my gown being more straightforward than Joseph's attire. Then we drew our braced bows. Those were not so hard, the lines and curves are smooth to create, even with a stone. We tried also to draw the rabbits we shot in those early days.' Hannah traced the rounded shapes with their pointed ears. 'They don't look much like rabbits, 'she laughed. 'It's difficult to draw rabbits on a stone wall with nothing but a small stone to do it with. But look here.'

Hannah led Matthew further along the wall, 'Others have done this before us. This one has drawn herself I think. There is her gown. She holds a bow ready to release an arrow. There's a funny shape drawn in front of her. At first when I was very young, I did not think of it being any kind of a creature but later when I tried to draw my rabbit and found how hard it was to keep the shape true, I thought maybe this person too had tried to draw a rabbit.'

Once more Hannah's hand reached out to trace another picture. 'This picture I think is very old. She seems wrapped in a sheep's fleece rather than wearing a gown, but she too has her bow drawn ready to shoot an arrow and there, see, she too has tried to draw a creature. The ears give it the appearance of a rabbit.'

Matthew reached out his own hand to trace the features of Hannah's face, 'thank you, Hannah. You have provided well for us on this journey, but I see weariness in your face. You must sleep now. When the sun rises, and we are all rested, I believe it would be best if I visited your father to discover how he might receive us. He and I have been long acquainted. Your father will pose no danger to myself as he might to you or Joseph.'

***

For much of the following day, Joseph and Matthew found themselves banished from the cave as Mistress Mitchell's infant made a long, slow arrival into the world, aided by the knowledge Jane had acquired through her own mother's many confinements.

Joseph accompanied Matthew to his childhood home. Matthew doubted the wisdom of this, but Joseph reasoned, 'Father will surely not resort to violence against me whilst he has you, Matthew, as guest in his house. As for the future, I will judge when I have met with Father.'

Later, as the heat of the day began to sink into the trees, Hannah stood at the entrance of the cave, her shawl wrapped around the soft newness of Mistress Mitchell's infant. Hannah's gaze moved from the infant to the forest path along which she saw Matthew and Joseph returning, accompanied by her mother. She felt the first flutterings of movement from the infant growing within her.

Hannah's mother reached to take Mistress Mitchell's infant, examine him and return him to his own mother, not quite trusting her daughter with the care of anything so precious.

Hannah smiled at her mother, 'Do not worry, Mother, his arrival was not left to myself, but mostly to the very great care and skill of Jane, Mistress Mitchell's maid.'

Hannah almost spoke again, but much as she wanted her mother to know her own news, she wanted Matthew to be the first to hear it.

'Hannah, I have news of your Father. Joseph was to tell you but when I heard of Mistress Mitchell's confinement I came swiftly, and so I will share the news with you myself.'

'What news do you have, Mother?' Hannah sensed a lightness about her mother which was unfamiliar.

'Your Father is gone, Hannah. We shall see him no more, he will torment us no more.'

'Gone, Mother? What can you mean, he is gone? Wherever has he gone to, surely, he would not leave without cause? What has caused him to leave? '

Hannah's mother lowered her voice and glanced all around her before continuing. 'The neighbours believe him gone to Gloucester. No doubt they will be none too surprised to hear of his demise there when news of the battle Joseph has described reaches them. They will believe him buried without ceremony in Gloucester during the heat of the battle.'

'Mother, has Father truly gone to Gloucester? If so, there is surely every possibility he will return here to resume his old ways.' Hannah moved close to her mother, she too glanced around and kept her voice lowered. She did not fully understand what her mother was telling her.

'Hannah, you must repeat this to no one, your brothers and I do not even speak of it amongst ourselves. I will tell you once and then you must know him dead in Gloucester. After much torment for us all your oldest brother, Peter, stood up to your father. Their fight was fierce. If Peter had not taken your father's life, then he would surely have lost his own. We none of us mourn the loss of your father but we would have deeply mourned the loss of Peter.'

Hannah gasped, hands covering her face in horror, her heart beating fast but soothed - her Father dead - her unborn child never to be exposed to his brutality. ‘But Mother,’ she gasped, ‘the body - where have you buried him, so none are aware of his death?’

‘I believe your brothers have fed him to the swine.’

Autumn gave way to winter, then winter began to loosen its icy grip as the first shoots of spring appeared before Matthew was able to stand beside Hannah’s bed cradling their newborn daughter. ‘Hannah,’ he commanded, with tenderness in his voice, ‘when she is grown a little, you must teach our daughter the art of the bow. She too must be able to defend and provide should the need arise. She will be strong, as her mother is strong.’

……………………………

Annabelle

1860

With creaking wheels and suspension ill-fitted to modern-day travel, the ancient carriage lurched slowly along the rutted lanes, towards the only slightly less rutted highway, which would see Annabelle delivered to Gloucester soon after nightfall. Annabelle felt a farmer's wagon would have provided transport of at least equitable comfort with the advantage of a farmer to converse with along the way. However, Mrs Lily Collett, Annabelle's mother deemed it more fitting for a rector's daughter, albeit a rector now deceased, to travel within the lonely confines of a carriage, especially as she travelled alone. Mrs Collett had, therefore, hired the carriage and driver at no little cost, despite her newly straightened circumstances.

'No Mother,' Annabelle had declared upon hearing her mother's plans for the future of her daughter, 'I have no wish to go as governess. I, too, have considered the necessity of employment to ease your burden now Father is gone, but I do not wish to become a governess. Rather I shall go as a nurse to Miss Nightingale's training school at St Thomas' Hospital.'

'Indeed, you will not!' Annabelle stepped backwards from her mother in alarm and fear. Rarely had she seen such anger in her mother's face. 'You are not yet turned eighteen, you will do as I say. Just because Father is no longer here does not mean you may go against my will. Father dedicated many hours to teaching you Latin, Greek and French, as well as instructing you in the scriptures. I, myself have devoted much of my limited energy into transforming your clumsy fingers into those of a skilled needlewoman and pianist - all training which will serve you well as a governess until such time as you might marry and raise your own family. You will not waste all of your training in becoming a nurse, exposed daily to all manner of diseases, infections and indecencies.'

Annabelle wept, pleaded, made every manner of promise until, having exhausted all entreaty and with no independent means of her own, she found herself obliged to take up the employment Mrs Collett had secured for her in the household of the Reverend Thornton of Gloucester. The ancient carriage now conveyed her to her new life through the heat of the late August day and into its declining warmth as the evening progressed and Gloucester approached.

The driver not being inclined to lift Annabelle's trunk down for her and seeing no entrance but the imposing front door of the house outside of which they had come to a halt, Annabelle was obliged to immediately go to this door. She pulled the tasselled bell cord to announce her arrival and seek help with her trunk.

The door opened to give sight of an imposing butler. Taking in the decrepitude of the carriage and Annabelle's mourning cloak and gown with a somewhat disrespectful air which left Annabelle in a state of some discomfiture, he enquired, 'You are perhaps the new governess for the young ladies?'

Annabelle, still struggling with the stiffness in her limbs induced by the hours of jolting in the carriage, made to mount the steps to enter the house. 'Indeed I am. I require assistance with my trunk.'

The butler pointed towards a smaller side door before giving the merest nod of his head and closing the front door.

Annabelle's discomfort grew. She could not pull the bell cord for the main door again. She had been dismissed from there. She must perforce go to the lesser door and knock there instead.

After some considerable time, the second door was opened by a maid. She stared at Annabelle, 'You the new governess for the young ladies? Supper time's a funny time to arrive,' And, without waiting for a reply, 'ain't you got no luggage? Follow me,' and, after some further delay, 'Please Miss.'

'No, I mean yes, but wait, please wait.' Annabelle appealed to the disappearing maid who was clearly anxious to return to her interrupted supper.

The maid turned with an audible sigh, 'Yes, Miss, what is it?'

'My trunk is on the carriage. Someone must lift it down for the driver is not inclined to do so.'

'Well, is that right Miss? Someone must lift it down, must they? Wait there - I'll get one of the men.

I'm going back to my supper. Nanny will be here directly to show you to your quarters.'

Annabelle felt tears of frustration and aloneness tingling behind her eyes as she entered the narrow hallway, squeezing uncomfortably past a perambulator. Turning to close the door to the street she saw the butler carrying her trunk on his shoulder as he disappeared through the area entrance to the servants' domain.

It is small comfort to me, but at least I know whilst I remain in this house, Mother will not seek out and read this, my diary. I am almost at the top of the house, and it is indeed a tall house, only the rooms the servants sleep in are above me. My chamber is small and dark with one tiny window. However, it is my own. I had feared I must spend even my sleeping hours with the young ladies and so am thankful for this sanctuary.

I have yet to meet the two young ladies who are to be in my charge, Nanny has cared for them since their previous governess left. Nanny alluded to some scandal attached to her departure but as she did not elaborate I did not believe it my place to ask further.

I fear I cannot write much this evening for I am overcome with hunger. I had only the bread and cheese mother packed for my journey and now I have arrived Nanny tells me supper is finished and I must wait until the morning.

***

The following morning Annabelle stood, somewhat awkwardly, beside the empty hearth in the schoolroom. Reverend Thornton had himself climbed the stairs to welcome her to his household, to inform her of her duties, and she was unsure of the social niceties required from her as governess. Perhaps, she decided, it would be best to behave as she had done in her father's presence and only sit if requested to do so.

Reverend Thornton did not instruct her to sit and so she remained standing for the hour it took him to inform her she was to have sole charge of the Misses Beryl and Florence. She was to attend morning and evening family prayers in the drawing room with the young ladies. She was to attend church services with them morning and evening on Sundays. She was, he informed her, responsible for turning them into marriageable young ladies by teaching them enough to ensure they were able to engage in light conversation and were equipped with the skills to entertain. Singing and drawing masters visited on Wednesday afternoons and she might consider these hours to be hers to enjoy as she wished.

Having confirmed with a nod of his own head Annabelle understood his instructions, he took the long route around the big table, on which books and a globe lay ready, thus passing unnecessarily close to her as he departed to his breakfast.

I fear once more I must keep my writing brief.
The day has been long, with so much which is new

and unfamiliar. After supper, with the young ladies abed, I had hoped for a short time of peace but Nanny came from the nursery, anxious I suspect for respite from her own charges.

The Reverend Thornton, it seems, has many children. His oldest son, Master Theodore, is Rector to a neighbouring parish. His oldest daughter, who is named Josephine, is married and gone with her husband as missionaries to China. Master Miles is of an age with myself. He studies at the university in Oxford. Miss Beryl and Miss Florence are in my charge. They are turned sixteen and fourteen years, respectively. These are the children of Reverend Thornton's first wife who died some years past.

Nanny tells me Mrs Thornton will not concern herself with my charges. She has her own brood of five infants in the care of Nanny and wishes only to have the Misses Beryl and Florence grown sufficiently to be married and no longer a concern of her husband.

How glad I am to have walked to the caves before my departure from home in order to say goodbye to the gallery of ladies etched on the wall of the main cave. Those ladies with their bows and arrows who were so much a part of the stories of my imaginings when I had the freedom of youth. I know not when I might see them again. Already my heart is heavy for my childhood games and walks during which my thoughts were free to wander.

***

Meals were reluctantly delivered to the schoolroom by Tessa, the belligerent under-parlour maid who had first admitted Annabelle to the house. Three times each day she huffed her ample body, arms bearing the loaded tray, up three flights of stairs, stopping after two flights to rest her legs and arms and to sample the tray's most enticing foods. Annabelle quickly came to ignore a missing lamb chop, a shortage of roast potatoes or a finger hole gouged in the butter, fearing comment would lead to greater loss. Three times each day Tessa climbed the stairs again and huffed the empty tray down to the kitchen, stopping on the way to look under the cloth for any tasty leftovers.

Rarely did Tessa engage in conversation beyond, 'Here's the dinner.' Seldom did she waste her time and energy on the niceties of spreading the cloth and setting places at the table. As this was clearly a task beneath the dignity of the young ladies, Anabelle was generally obliged to perform it herself.

When Annabelle had been a few weeks in the household Reverend Thornton once more visited the schoolroom, 'To be informed on such progress as the Misses Beryl and Florence are making in their studies.' Although they all attended twice daily prayers with all of the household, Reverend Thornton did not feel it fitting to use those occasions to communicate with his daughters or their governess. He sat sprawling by the window whilst Annabelle reported. Annabelle held tight to the folds of her dress so Reverend Thornton might not see any quivering of her hands for he was a large and imposing man whose questions boomed with demand for answers. In truth, he cared little about his daughters' studies and, in the silence of his thoughts, occasionally cursed his first wife for dying before they were off his hands and the responsibility of some other man.

Tessa, hearing his heavy tread on the uncovered stairs, had quickly loaded her tray for its return journey to the kitchen and exited hastily, casting over her shoulder to Annabelle, 'Master's coming, no doubt you'll be a favourite.'

January 1861

How glad I am to see the turning of the year now the festivities of the Christmas season are behind us. Miss Beryl and Miss Florence were permitted to dine with Reverend and Mrs Thornton and the visiting family on Christmas Day itself and so I took my own dinner in the nursery with Nanny and the babies. We had a restful time by the fire as the children slept, once Nanny had administered a few drops from what she terms her, 'magic bottle', into their milk.

The weather continues bitter. So much so, on some days the young ladies and I do not take our usual morning constitutional. In addition, we rarely walk in the gardens later in the day now the darkness draws in so early. How desperate I am for trees, flowers, birds, summer breezes - sometimes I even wish to be walking in rain or wind. But my time is not my own, excepting for the short hours when the drawing and singing masters visit each week. Even then if I am to leave the house unimpeded, I must slip silently down the stairs before Nanny suggests tea by the nursery fire. I fear Nanny is anxious for company beyond that which the babies can give for she has been trapped in the nursery for nigh on twenty-five years.

Here is Rose come with coals for the schoolroom fire. How would we manage without Rose, always so bright and helpful despite the quantity of work she must undertake each day.

'I've come to do the fire, Miss.' Rose heaved the coal bucket across the room, lowering it carefully to the hearth. 'I'll be quick Miss. I overheard the Master say he was coming to enquire as to the young ladies' progress. I've no wish to be still here when he arrives. I keeps out of his way.'

Just as Rose finished with the fire Annabelle heard the Reverend Thornton's heavy tread on the uncovered stairs. Rose glanced anxiously towards the door as if judging the time still available for her escape.

'Take care with the Master.' Rose whispered as she disappeared with her brushes and coal scuttle, silently along the corridor to the nursery rooms, where Nanny would keep her chatting too long.

Annabelle allowed her glance to sweep over the clock as Reverend Thornton entered the room, closing the door behind him.

With the smallest of curtsied greetings, Annabelle felt her heart pounding and her hands begin to quiver. 'I beg your pardon Sir, but I fear we must leave the door open a while. Rose has only now added fresh coals to the fire. I fear they were somewhat damp, for the fire smokes unpleasantly, and it is much too cold to open the window to release the smoke, besides evening is drawing in and the night air is not good for the young ladies' health.'

With a show of good humour, belied by the thunderous expression on his face, Reverend Thornton opened the schoolroom door before moving to warm himself by the fire. Annabelle positioned herself close to the door in its cold draught. For the following hour they made pretence of discussing the academic virtues of the Misses Beryl and Florence until, with a relief which caused her shoulders, her whole body, to sink into itself, Annabelle heard the dainty steps of the young ladies ascending the stairs.

Commanding his daughters to be on time for evening prayers the Reverend took his leave, finding himself having to squeeze past Tessa carrying a laden tea tray.

I know not why but I am somewhat fearful to be alone with Reverend Thornton. I am certain a man in such a respected position has no ill-will in his heart, but he does seem somewhat over familiar at times. I wonder he does not visit the schoolroom when he is sure of his daughters being here, then he could speak directly with them. Rose seems afraid of him, but she is several years younger than I and this is her first time in service. At first, I thought perhaps she is afraid of everyone but she is comfortable with Nanny and myself. I do not make any demands of her but just leave her to carry out her duties.

1861

'Tessa says Master Miles is home from Oxford where he has been studying.' Nanny settled into her chair by the fireside ready for a long chat with Annabelle, although no fire was lit there due to the warmth of the spring day. 'I don't expect you met him when he was last here for Christmas. Of course, he came to see me, for wasn't I his Nanny too when he was but an infant? Such a fine young man he is now. By all accounts in trouble with his father but it don't stop him being a fine young man, does it?'

'Indeed not, Nanny. You will be happy to see him again, no doubt.'

'I will, he was always my favourite of all the Reverend's children, took the death of his mother very hard. He's gentle like his mother and Miss Josephine. Of course, she's not Miss Josephine since her hasty marriage which has taken her to China with her six-month-born child. Master Theodore and your young ladies take more for their father.' Nanny sighed wearily, 'You'll have heard Mrs Thornton has been delivered of another infant this morning. Tessa is airing the room next door for the wet nurse. We will have another squalling child keeping us all awake through the night - at least until such time as the wet nurse can be dispensed with and we can rely on my magic bottle to soothe it into sleep.'

I find myself saddened by the bitterness I feel lies deep in Nanny's soul. She has seen so many of the years of her life slip away, confined to the needs of infants. Is this what will become of me also? For Nanny must have been but a young woman when she first took up her post in this household, as I am now. Already she begins to suffer the afflictions of the elderly. This must not happen to me. I must not allow it. I must find a way to regain what I have lost, lest I too become trapped, as Nanny is trapped.

Although they both attended the twice daily family prayers, it was some time before Annabelle made the acquaintance of Master Miles. News from the rest of the household was slow to make its way to the upper reaches of the house. For several days nothing more was heard of Master Miles. Nanny, fretting lest he had, after all, forgotten her, sought news from Rose.

Rose, weary from climbing the stairs with coal, welcomed the opportunity to pause for a minute or two, but she had no news.

Tessa declared it to be none of her business. Nanny worried.

Ten days after his arrival home, Nanny's lack of patience was finally rewarded. Master Miles climbed the stairs at a respectful distance behind his father. While the Reverend entered the schoolroom, Master Miles slipped along the corridor to visit his beloved Nanny.

Beryl and Florence, dismissed from the schoolroom by their father, found Miles sitting beside Nanny on the settle, resting his head on her shoulder as he had done when his head was weary since the day of his birth. Entertainment of the infants was left to their half-sisters whilst Nanny reacquainted herself with her favourite.

Taken by surprise, Annabelle made to rise from her seat at the table, where she had been instructing the young ladies in the finer points of Latin. 'Please remain seated Miss Collett,' the Reverend declared.

Annabelle's hands rested on the book she had been reading from. Reverend Thornton seated himself alongside her in the place vacated by Miss Florence. Annabelle did not know how to withdraw her hand from the table. She flushed with discomfort.

'Now, Miss Collett, my son Miles is woefully ill-prepared for his future as a priest. His knowledge of both Latin and Greek are pitiful. I fear he has not dedicated his mind fully to his studies. You are to have him here with,' he paused, seeking for the names of his daughters, 'Florence and Beryl during those hours dedicated to such study.'

Annabelle nodded, 'Yes, Sir.' She spoke more quietly than she had intended before once more attempting to rise.

Reverend Thornton placed his hand heavily on her arm, pinning it to the table. With his other hand he reached to stroke her fingers. She saw his fingers move upwards as though to touch her face and jerked her whole body painfully backwards to avoid the contact.

Reverend Thornton laughed and rose from the table, keeping for a moment a tight, painful grip on Annabelle's arm. 'There's no need for such behaviour Miss Collett, just remember who pays your salary and keeps you from the workhouse now your dear Papa is dead. You and I are going to be friends. But first you will teach my son Latin. I must go now and see where the wretched maid Rose is got to.'

My thoughts are in turmoil, I know not what to do. Reverend Thornton declares we are to be friends and yet he has bruised my arm shockingly and has put fear into me. I cannot leave - where would I go? Mother lives now with her sister and her sister's family. There would be no place for me there. I cannot go elsewhere as governess unless Reverend Thornton furnishes me with a reference of my good character and hard work. If he does not want me to leave, then I am certain he would not provide such a reference. I fear he is correct in surmising only his benevolence keeps me from the workhouse. And what of Rose? Why was he gone to seek out Rose, she is but a very young under-housemaid. He would not concern himself with her work surely.

I am lost and bewildered, reprieved I think from whatever is to come whilst I teach Master Miles Latin and Greek. Then what? Perhaps I must write to Miss Nightingale after all and see if I might become a nurse in her hospital, although I fear she too would require a reference of my good character from Reverend Thornton.

After Reverend Thornton departed from the schoolroom I sought my young ladies in the nursery, anxious, despite the pounding of my own heart, to resume their lessons. There I encountered also Master Miles, sharing happy memories of his childhood with Nanny. He seems a personable young man without any of the intimidating ways of his father. He even carried the coal scuttle from the nursery to the schoolroom for Rose who had been hiding afeared of I know not what, until Thornton was gone.

Master Miles appeared happy to share lessons with his sisters for an hour or two each day. He seemed to care not he was almost two years older than Annabelle and had been educated at both school and university. He was, Annabelle soon discovered, fond of Florence and Beryl and sought ways to bring more pleasure into their restricted lives. He gained his father's permission to escort all three young ladies, for Annabelle was but a young lady herself, to the communal gardens for the houses in the square. He brought to the schoolroom a selection of books and pamphlets on subjects with which they were unfamiliar. Annabelle eagerly devoured the content of these in the quiet of the evenings, while Miss Beryl and Miss Florence painstakingly struggled to perfect their needlework skills amidst many pricked fingers and blood-stained samplers.

On evenings which found the Reverend Thornton engaged with his own acquaintances and a large bottle of port, Master Miles returned to the schoolroom to teach his sisters, their governess and his old Nanny the game of chess, a game at which both Annabelle and Nanny proved especially adept. On those evenings Nanny was often to be found in the schoolroom, the infants, aided by her magic bottle, all sleeping soundly under the drooping eyelids of the nursery maid.

Late in the evening, when all eyelids were drooping and all were ready for their repose, he escorted Nanny along the corridor to the nursery before creeping to his own chamber, hoping a creaking floorboard or stair would not betray him.

***

As spring passed and summer sun began to warm the city, all those who regularly inhabited the nursery floor of the house found a greater pleasure in their lives than they had experienced before the return of Master Miles - all excepting for Rose. Despite her youth Rose seemed to find the carrying of coals and water up four flights of stairs equally as exhausting as the older, stouter Tessa found the carrying of laden trays. Like Tessa, Rose too, now frequently needed to pause on the climb to gather her remaining strength for the final flight.

Early in the month of July Reverend Thornton once more found it imperative he should climb to the schoolroom whilst his daughters were with the drawing master in the back parlour. He found Annabelle tidying books from the morning lessons preparatory to taking a short stroll in the garden.

'Ah, Miss Collett, I am pleased to find you here. You are alone? Why yes, of course, it is Wednesday. Florence and ... and yes Beryl must be with the drawing master. How fortunate. By which, of course, I mean how fortunate they are to have the skills of such a talented drawing master at their disposal.' Reverend Thornton sat heavily on the chair beside Annabelle.

Annabelle slid as far to the edge of her chair as possible. She did not look at Reverend Thornton but kept her eyes firmly on the pile of books in front of her.

'Now Miss Collett...' Reverend Thornton rested both of his hands over Annabelle's arm, despite having to reach across the table to do so. As he spoke Annabelle became uncomfortably aware of the increasing pressure of his hands. Gently she tried to move her arm. The pressure increased still further.

'Now Miss Collett, you have been in my house for some months, I believe it is time for us to be on ... more friendly terms. Perhaps I shall come regularly to visit on Wednesday afternoons. We might speak together of less weighty matters than my daughters' education and so become more as friends.'

As one they heard the latch of the door lifted somewhat noisily, as if the opener had been outside the door for some moments before deciding to make their presence known. Reverend Collett turned quickly in his seat. 'Miles my boy, what brings you to the schoolroom at this hour of the day? Should you not be engaged upon your private studies?'

As they waited for Miles to reply Annabelle gathered her released arm to her, feeling where the bruise would appear in the morning.

'Excuse me Sir, I am come to enquire of Miss Collett if I have left here the Latin text which she wishes me to translate for tomorrow's lesson. I see it there on the table, my thanks to you Miss Collett. Father, may I escort you down the stairs? An invitation has been issued which I would very much appreciate the opportunity to discuss together.'

I am greatly afeared of Reverend Thornton's intentions towards me. Once more he has declared we are to be friends and yet he wishes to pursue this friendship when my young charges are engaged elsewhere. I cannot think but his intentions are less honourable than they should be. What am I to do? From whom might I seek advice?

And Rose is gone! I know not why but her leaving was sudden. Nanny has it from Tessa that Rose returned to her family home late last night. She has not been given a character to take forward to another employer and so I wonder what is to become of her.

The following morning Miles appeared at the schoolroom door in high good humour. He pushed open the door, which had been left ajar, with not even an attempt at a knock to alert the inhabitants of the room.

'Ladies, I have news for you,' he declared loudly. Glancing over his shoulder to be sure none beyond the room had overheard his exuberance he repeated in more moderate tones, 'Ladies, I have news for you, exciting news.'

When no more words came from him Annabelle indicated his place at the table. 'Come Master Miles, sit ready for the lesson and then you might share your good news with your sisters, for I fear they will think of nothing else until you have done so.'

'We are all to go away from the city for the heat of the summer.'

Beryl could restrain herself no longer, 'Miles, what can you mean? Go away from the city? Where shall we go, there are so many of us with all the infants. Has Father taken a house for us?'

'But what of our lessons?' the more practical Florence interjected, 'if we go away and have no lessons for the whole summer we will never be done with learning and ready to move out into the world.'

Annabelle remained silent, waiting for the excitement in the room to subside a little, waiting for Miles to tell them more, wondering, with a heavy heart what plans Reverend Thornton might have for her in his daughters' absence.

For long moments Miles ignored the pleading of his sisters to tell them more, enjoying having the secret to himself. Finally, he could hold on to his secret no longer.

'We are to travel to Ashworth Manor, the home of my school friend Rupert Ashworth. It is but twelve months since the death of Rupert's mother. Rupert has two sisters of an age with yourselves dear sisters and their father worries they are still sunk in melancholy. Their spirits need lifting and so their father has welcomed the opportunity for them to have other young ladies with whom they might enjoy entertainments to lighten the burden of their loss. Sisters, we shall picnic, ride, row on the river and engage in all manner of entertainments. You might paint and draw and play music for each other if you so wish.'

His sisters could not resist the temptation to abandon the airs of young ladies, to become once more the excitable children of their earlier days. They leapt on their brother with hugs, kisses and questions, but Annabelle remained seated, her heart seeming to turn upside down inside her. With his daughters away from home Reverend Thornton would doubtless find many opportunities to become more friendly.

When their excitement subsided sufficiently, they regained their seats and remembered their status as young ladies. Fanning their flushed faces they glanced guiltily towards Annabelle.

Miles, too looked towards Annabelle, a frown evident on his face, 'Miss Collett, it seems you do not share my sister's excitement for the pleasures the summer will hold?'

'I trust,' said Annabelle with the faintest of smiles, 'you are all able to take pleasure in your visit and the amusements it promises for the summer days.'

'But, Miles, what of our lessons?' there was concern in Florence's voice.

Miles let out a dramatically deep sigh, 'Ladies, I fear none listened sufficiently well to heed exactly what news I brought, for I said we are all to visit at Ashworth Manor. All,' he turned eagerly towards Annabelle, 'includes you, Miss Collett. Father was reluctant at first, but I have persuaded him my sisters must continue with some of their lessons less they become imbeciles over the summer. In addition, the Misses Ashworth, being now motherless, and their governess having given notice, Miss Collett will be able to act as chaperone for both yourselves, and the Misses Ashworth whilst you engage in outdoor country pursuits. Is this not splendid news Miss Collett?'

Annabelle struggled to hide her relief. She was not to be left alone to the mercies of Reverend Thornton. She had been given time in which she might consider her options and plan her escape from him.

'Imagine sisters,' Miles continued, 'Father declared, 'tis but a few short weeks and I will have all my young ladies home once more so I might enjoy their company.' Just as if he had ever bothered himself with you or your welfare since the arrival of his second brood of infants.'

I felt a shiver pass through me at the Reverend Thornton's words uttered by Master Miles, 'Tis but a few short weeks and I will have all my young ladies home once more to enjoy their company.' Perhaps I should be feared for the safety of Miss Florence and Miss Beryl as well as for myself.

But we are, indeed, all to remove to Ashworth Manor in just four days' time. We now find ourselves in a flurry of preparations. Nanny is not happy to find Master Miles, with whom she is so recently reacquainted, is to be again taken from her. The young ladies are in such a state of high excitement they are not at all able to concentrate on their lessons and so we spend our time in preparations instead.

August 1861

Released from the confines of the house in Gloucester, with its limited opportunities for entertainment suitable for young ladies outside its walls, the Misses Beryl and Florence flourished over the summer weeks. Quickly they established firm friendships with Beatrice and Helena Ashworth. The weather treated them exceptionally well with plenty of warm sunny days and just sufficient evening rain to prevent the heat building up uncomfortably.

Mr Ashworth, it seemed, had always so much enjoyed the company of his son and his two daughters he had long since closed up the wing of the house where nurseries and schoolroom were situated. This presented something of a conundrum to his housekeeper as she allocated accommodation for the visitors. Miss Beryl and Miss Florence would occupy guest rooms near to Miss Beatrice and Miss Helena, as would Miles be accommodated in the room besides Rupert. But what of Annabelle? The housekeeper felt Annabelle to be somewhat above the servants' rooms in the eaves of the house whilst she herself had taken over the room previously occupied by the recently departed governess, having persuaded Mr Ashworth she had best be near the young ladies. Thus, Annabelle found herself escorted to a chamber referred to by the housekeeper as the pink bedroom.

'It's little used Miss.' the housekeeper declared, 'being on the corner of the house it does suffer dreadful in the winter months from the weather pounding the windows and the wind howling round it. But 'tis summertime now and likely the weather won't be too much of a bother. I've had the maids give it a good airing seen as it's not been used for many a year.'

Annabelle found herself delighted with the room. Somewhat removed from the other occupied chambers, it provided a quiet retreat each evening when she had finished taking her dinner with the housekeeper. The young people all spending the remainder of the evenings with Mr Ashworth, they had no need for Annabelle as a chaperone.

How very calm I feel now we are settled into this household for the coming weeks. During the day we spend much time out of doors as I accompany the young ladies and their brothers to their pursuits. I do believe all of the young ladies are safe enough, for are they not accompanied by their brothers? But Master Miles insists I must not only accompany them but must have also the opportunity to take part in whatever the chosen activity for the day is. I have a delightful, gentle-natured pony for our rides around the estate and the surrounding lands. I have not ridden for a number of years and yet I find I have come back to it with as much ease and enjoyment as in those days past.

Miss Florence and Miss Beryl delight in the company of the other young ladies and are much taken with Master Rupert who they behave towards as if he were their own brother. The young men delight in showing off their skills of horsemanship. After their displays they frequently declare themselves exhausted and command one of their sisters to fetch lemonade to quench their thirst. To begin with I made to carry out the errand myself, but it seems electing a sister to do the task is all part of the enjoyment and the young ladies take equal pleasure in the game.

The gardener has rolled a croquet lawn. I have not played croquet before now, but it is a very fitting sport for young ladies, especially on those days when one might not be feeling up to the rigours of cricket. Master Miles is an especially adept teacher for the game of croquet, which I confess at first, I struggled to master. He was so patient with me, keeping close to me to check my movements, perhaps for longer than was absolutely necessary. He is very gentle in his manner, and I found myself learning swiftly from his tutelage. He seemed somewhat unwilling to relinquish his role until Miss Florence called him to please assist her also.

Tomorrow we are to try our skills at archery. I had my doubts as to the suitability of such an activity for the young ladies, going so far as to raise my doubts with Mr Ashworth. However, he assures me archery is considered good exercise for young ladies. He says he and his late wife practised it for some time before she began to sicken and it is he, himself who will come to the parkland with us to teach the necessary skills.

Their first archery lesson proved successful. Mr Ashworth was a resourceful teacher, quickly finding ways to overcome the hesitancies and self-doubts of his pupils. After the first lesson all were eager for the following day. Miss Beatrice and Miss Helena pleaded with their father to be allowed to continue beyond the hour he had allocated to them, but Mr Ashworth insisted it would do no good to continue further until the following day. They must, he said, build their strength a little each day or they would soon exhaust their abilities and tire of the sport.

'For today, you have done well. We shall continue tomorrow but now look,' he pointed towards the direction of the house where a groom appeared leading a pony and trap, 'I have had the housekeeper organise a picnic. I thought you may like to go to the river and so have also had the oars for the rowing boats placed in the pony trap.' He laughed lightly, 'Rowing will build strength in your arms for archery.'

Delighted with the prospect of rowing on the river, Miss Beryl and Miss Florence quickly forgot they were no longer small children and positively squealed their excitement. Miles and Annabelle found themselves exchanging amused glances before Annabelle felt once more the demands of her position. She remonstrated with the young ladies, although none present took her words with any great seriousness, so great was the general feeling of enjoyment in their circumstances.

'Come Miss Collett,' Miles called cheerfully from his position at the oars of the bigger boat, 'sit alongside and help me to row these lazy girls, for I doubt they will even consider taking a turn with the oars but will, instead recline under their parasols, exhausted from their morning of archery.'

Annabel's hand tingled as she placed it in the hand Miles proffered to aid her boarding of the boat. Miles kept hold of her hand rather longer than was necessary.

‘Release Miss Collet’s hand, Miles.’ commanded Miss Florence with a shower of laughter, ‘Helena and I wish to be rowed along the river whilst we recline here and make as if we were indeed fully-grown, sophisticated ladies. Look, Rupert has already departed with Beryl and Beatrice. They are cool on the river whilst we continue to suffer from the heat here at the bank. Please row us at once.’

Master Miles made light of his holding of my hand, but I felt a pressure from his hand as he released mine to pick up the oars and row along the river. Later, when the picnic was eaten, and the young ladies all gone exploring with Master Rupert, he sought my company as I rested against the supporting trunk of an old chestnut tree. We conversed lightly and easily. I complimented him on the natural ability he had shown at archery. He insisted I was just as competent and has decreed we will all of us have a tournament together when we have learnt and practiced a little more. He sat perhaps more closely to me than propriety allowed but, as there were none to observe and I felt no discomfort, I raised no objection. When we heard the others returning, he quickly regained his feet and ran to meet them to raise the young ladies’ excitement further with news of the tournament he proposed.

***

The weather at Ashworth Manor continued calm and warm throughout the month of August. Days were filled with outdoor pursuits of riding, croquet, picnics, rowing on the river and archery practice. Annabelle abandoned all hope of the young ladies spending their morning hours on lessons and permitted them to spend as much of their time as they wished outdoors. Miles, however, professed to be concerned about his father's anger should he not progress in Latin and Greek over the summer.

'Miss Collett,' he declared, 'my sisters may care only for the pleasures in life and so wish to be uneducated, but I must keep Father content with my own progress. You must instruct me each morning for an hour or two in the twin torments of Latin and Greek. We shall set up school in the summer house overlooking the croquet lawn. This way you will be able to have sight of my sisters and there will be no impropriety to sully your good name.'

Unable to refuse the request, Annabelle set about preparing a sequence of lessons which she then tried in vain to instil in Miles.

Miles bored easily with the lessons, instead telling Annabelle tales of growing up alongside his sisters and tales of his life at school and at Oxford. When he tired of talking about himself, he requested Annabelle tell him tales of her own early years and of the circumstances which had led her to become governess to his sisters. He sat alongside her, rather than in the place opposite which she had allocated him, 'We must both be able to observe my sisters. After all,' he laughed, 'perhaps Rupert has plans to snare one of them into marrying him, or worse.'

'Master Miles, I'm sure you do Master Rupert a disservice, I am certain he has no dishonourable intentions towards either of your sisters, but perhaps it is best we both are able to content ourselves it is so.'

The month of August has passed so quickly. It is about to give way to September and I find I have given almost no consideration to what might await on our return to Gloucester. I had thought to find a different situation, so I might not have to make such a return, but now I find a difficulty even beyond the lack of a reference.

I do not wish to have to return to a household over which Reverend Thornton holds power and yet if I do not, I fear I will see Master Miles no more. There now, I have admitted it openly if only to myself - I wish to stay close to Master Miles. I believe he perhaps shares my feelings for he does not miss an opportunity to be close, to sit beside me, to row with me, to be partners at croquet. He takes my hand always when I board the rowing boat, or we encounter a stile on our walks, and he releases it so reluctantly. He cares not his sisters tease him over this, even the Misses Ashworth have begun to join the teasing. He makes light of their jest and pretends he is my beau, taking my hand again and pretending to kiss it for their entertainment. My heart is heavy at the thought of losing this.

Tomorrow is the final day of August. It is the day of our archery tournament and then I know not how many days we have left before our return to Gloucester. It cannot be many.

***

The morning of the archery tournament dawned bright with sunshine and with the eager anticipation of all the participants. The summer weeks had done much to ease the grief of the Ashworth family. The archery lessons he had given had brought Mr Ashworth even closer to his son and daughters.

Consequently, Mr Ashworth had planned the tournament in great detail. He had given instruction to his gardeners on the positioning of archery targets to ensure the young archers were not facing directly into the sun. He had ensured a plentiful supply of straight, well-honed arrows and had instructed Cook to provide a picnic so the young people might enjoy relaxing on the river once the tournament was completed and a winner declared.

Annabelle had presumed she would not take part in the tournament herself. She had thought Miles and Rupert would compete against each other. Beryl and Beatrice, as the elder sisters in each family, she thought would compete together, as would Florence and Helena as the younger sisters.

Mr Ashworth, however, had made his own plans. The young ladies, he declared, would all compete together, 'for you are all much of a muchness in age and strength. You too, Miss Collett, you must also compete. It will be a fine tournament indeed to have five ladies and three gentlemen competing. First the ladies against each other, followed by the gentlemen and then…' he paused smiling in turn at each of the eager young faces turned towards him, waiting in unrestrained anticipation for his next words, 'and then the winner of the ladies' tournament will compete against the winner of the gentlemen's tournament. Then we will see who is to be crowned Victor Ludorum.'

Florence and Helena joined hands, swinging each other around in a wild dance, each declaring she would be the winner until, feet tangled in their gowns, they tumbled to the ground in a laughing heap.

'Three gentlemen, Father?' asked Rupert. 'Are you to compete also with Miles and myself?'

'Indeed I am my boy. I fear you boys are too lazy to try hard unless you have serious competition. Besides, I should very much like to compete once more. Your mother and I often competed together.'

Rupert and Miles groaned loudly in mock despair. Mr Ashworth ignored them, 'Come ladies, you are first to compete. Let us brace the bows. Gather up your quivers and arrows. Are your arm guards firmly tied? We want no bruises on arms, do we? Do you each have your finger tab? Good, good, now follow me.' He pointed to a line marked on the ground, 'See I have had a shooting line marked out for us and see, I have had the targets set at fifty yards, which is the longest distance we have shot so far. Come ladies, we will shoot four dozen arrows. This will mean shooting eight ends of six arrows each, as you are accustomed to do. Rupert and Miles will do service as your scorers, in order to keep them occupied and out of trouble and so you will not have to worry yourselves with recording your own scores. Remember, call your scores from the centre out and call a miss for a fallen arrow. Everyone ready? Rupert, Miles you may rest idle for the first end of arrows. We will have an end of sighting arrows.'

On Mr Ashworth's command each of the five young ladies nocked an arrow to their bowstring, looked towards their target and pulled their bowstrings to full draw. Five arrows swished strongly through the still air, landing with gentle thuds on the straw targets. And then again and again. When each archer had shot six arrows, they put down their bows and Mr Ashworth gave the command to collect the arrows.

Miles and Rupert were not left idle for long. Once scoring commenced with the next arrows, they were required to walk with the ladies to the targets in order to record the scores as each young lady called them. Being taller than the ladies they were needed also to remove those arrows which had landed high in the target and they must, of course, help look for any arrows which had missed the target.

After four dozen arrows, the young ladies quenched their thirst with lemonade which had been keeping cool in the shade of an oak tree. Mr Ashworth himself added up the ladies' scores, not quite trusting the basic mathematical abilities of the two young men.

'We have a winner for the ladies,' he declared. 'In second place by just three points is Miss Collett and the winner is Miss Beryl Thornton.'

'Now gentlemen, are we all three prepared? We will shoot the same round as the ladies have shot and then we will know who is to compete against Miss Beryl for the overall first place. Miss Collett, will you record the scores for us, whist the young ladies rest awhile?'

The gentlemen's tournament proved an altogether rowdier affair than the ladies' tournament. Even Mr Ashworth became volubly excited when it was clear an end of his arrows had scored more highly than those of his competitors. The younger men were in no way restrained by the presence of the ladies – so great was their eagerness to declare their scores and to announce loudly how well they had achieved, or how badly their competitors had fared each time they went to the target to score their arrows. Once they had rested a while, the young ladies could no longer resist joining the excitement and so all went to check on the scoring of arrows and to pass judgement on the scoring of line cutting arrows.

When the required four dozen arrows had been shot Annabelle sat on a fallen tree to add the scores, Miles to one side of her, Rupert to the other, both eager to be first to know the winner. When she had added the scores, Annabelle gently tugged her skirts from under Miles, who had seated himself rather more closely than necessary. She rose to give the score sheet to Mr Ashworth, leaving the younger men with their anticipation for a moment longer.

'Ladies and gentlemen,' Mr Ashworth declared with great formality, 'We have a winner for the gentlemen. In first place we have Mr Rupert Ashworth.'

The young ladies applauded loudly.

Mr Ashworth held up his hand, requesting quiet, 'Rupert', he declared, 'Congratulations, you must now compete against Miss Beryl Thornton. To make things more even, given Miss Beryl is both younger than yourself and of the fairer sex, you will shoot at sixty yards and Miss Beryl will continue to shoot at fifty yards.'

A loud groan escaped from Rupert, causing much amusement amongst the ladies. 'And are we to shoot another four dozen arrows Father, for I declare I am exhausted already now the day is warming so considerably?'

'You are a weakling, Rupert,' said Helena, 'I am sure Beryl is happy to shoot another four dozen arrows, aren't you Beryl?'

Beryl responded with an animated nod, although in truth she too felt the increasing heat of the day.

'Perhaps,' said Mr Ashworth, 'The same number of arrows again would be too much. No, I think we will decide the overall winner on just one more dozen arrows. Come Miss Beryl, come Rupert, approach the shooting line. I see the gardener's boy making his way towards us with your picnic and oars in the pony cart. We will discover who is our Victor

Ludorum and then you may go to picnic by the river. You might, perhaps row a while if you still have strength to pull the oars.'

Beryl and Rupert found new energy, both determined to win. Annebelle scored for Rupert on the sixty-yard target whilst Mr Ashworth scored for Beryl on the. As they approached the line to shoot their final end of six arrows none knew who was in the lead. Beryl put all of her thoughts into her arrows. Rupert shot each arrow only after observing where Beryl's arrows had landed, so eager was he to take the lead.

When the scores for all arrows had been recorded, Mr Ashworth gave Beryl's score sheet to Annabelle, saying, 'Miss Collett, please compare the scores. I will make the announcement and you will add the name of the winner.'

Mr Ashworth stood before the young people, Annabelle at his side, 'Ready Miss Collett?'

Annabelle nodded.

'I declare the Victor Ludorum for the Ashworth Manor 1861 grand archery tournament is...' he paused.

Annebelle filled the gap, 'Miss Beryl Thornton.'

Rupert feigned despair before reaching out to take Beryl's hand and be the first to offer his congratulations.

***

Once more my mind is in tumult, such a glorious day we have had. Mr Ashworth organised the most splendid of tournaments which we all enjoyed. After Miss Beryl had been declared Victor Ludorum, Mr Ashworth said we are all to keep our bows and arrows. He has gifted them to us. He says he hopes we will all return next summer for another tournament. At this, of course I became saddened, although I trust I hid it well. I became saddened because I do not wish to be still in the employ of Reverend Thornton next summer. I also became saddened because I have permitted the whole month of August to pass without seeking out alternative employment. Reverend Thornton has sent word we are to return to Gloucester within the week. I find I am in despair at this news, but the fault is my own. I should have dedicated my time to making plans for my future and not in following the pursuits of the more wealthy and fortunate young ladies. I am now, however, almost determined the only course open to me is to go against Mother's wishes and train as a nurse in Miss Nightingale's hospital. When we return to Gloucester I will compose a letter of enquiry. I trust I am able to avoid the attentions of Reverend Thornton until my departure.

But also, my mind is in tumult because I find I have no wish to so distance myself from M Miles. After we had rested with the refreshments Cook had sent in our picnic M Miles declared he would row along the river to enjoy the coolness. None rose to accompany him, Master Rupert and the young ladies each professing they had no energy for rowing and no inclination to enjoy the delights of the river. M Miles reached as if to take my hand, 'Come Miss Annabelle Collett, you must permit me to row you along the river a short way as no other will accompany me.'

Indeed, the river was cool and pleasant and M Miles almost the perfect gentleman. I say almost because, when he took my hand to assist me from the boat so we might explore the small island a little, he called me by my given name and then did not release my hand for quite some considerable moments. I found both the sound of his voice uttering my name and the feel of his hand warm in mine to be most pleasurable.

September 1861

Following the return to Gloucester lessons commenced in earnest once more. Even Master Miles seemed anxious to make up the learning they had missed lest his father think they had been too much engaged in amusements during their absence.

On Wednesday, the drawing master arrived and took Miss Beryl and Miss Florence into the garden to refine their skills in the sunshine. He carefully positioned them outside the window of Reverend Thornton's study, thinking to avoid the need for a chaperone.

Annabelle fetched her bonnet and prepared to take a turn around the garden whilst the drawing lesson progressed. She missed the fresh air from Ashworth Manor greatly. Turning to the door she was startled to find Master Miles standing there, also appearing ready for outdoors.

'Ah, Miss Annabelle Collett, I see you are preparing to take a constitutional, as indeed am I, myself. Would you care to accompany me? We can walk a little in the Square's gardens where all will see us, surely there will be no impropriety in such a stroll?'

Annabelle tried to avoid making contact with the laughing eyes of Miles. She hesitated in her response so long Miles spoke again.

'Come, Miss Annabelle Collett, you are in need of fresh air and sunshine after a morning of trying to instil knowledge into my sisters and myself. We will walk but a short way and you will feel the benefit of the exercise and thus be better prepared for my sisters' return to your care.'

This afternoon I walked with M Miles in the gardens of the Square. They are indeed beautiful, even at this late stage of the season. M Miles insisted I take his arm lest, he said, I stumble on the uneven paths. My hand and arm did tingle so holding his. From time to time, he reached with his free hand and made to gently pat my hand as it rested on his arm. I am certain his hand sometimes lingered to make it almost a caress. Or perhaps it is just my imagining. Surely, he intended nothing by such actions. But he no longer addresses me as Miss Collett, always as Miss Annabelle Collet, which greatly amuses his sisters. On occasion, indeed, he has dispensed with Miss and simply addressed me as Annabelle Collett. Perhaps I should correct him, but I find I very much like the sound of my name carried on his gentle voice.

***

Annabelle's reprieve from the interest of Reverend Thornton was short-lived once she returned from Ashworth Manor. Reverend Thornton soon decided he had waited long enough and it was time, once more, to monitor Annabelle's work. After two flights of stairs, he paused in order to regain his breath, before continuing to the schoolroom. Finding the door closed he dispensed with the ceremony of knocking to announce his presence. The sudden opening of the door startled all three of the young ladies within, whose heads had been bent over the globe studying the location of the continents.

'Well daughters, I trust you enjoyed your sojourn at Ashworth Manor. Perhaps the young Misses Ashworth might enjoy a return visit in the spring. It would greatly please me to welcome them and to have so many charming young ladies in my house at one time.' A smirk, seemingly of anticipation, passed over his face. 'Daughters, you look pale, go now and take a stroll around the garden to restore the colour to your cheeks whilst I ... discuss your progress with Miss Collett.'

Beryl and Florence, delighted to be released from both their lessons and their father, departed hastily. Annabelle could find no words of objection, so swiftly had the instruction been given. She edged closer to the door, which Reverend Collett closed behind his departing daughters.

'Annabelle, may I call you Annabelle?' Reverend Thornton took Annabelle's hand in his. She pulled gently, trying to exert just sufficient pressure to free her hand without a fight. Reverend Thornton tightened his grip.

'It would seem more fitting sir, if you did not.'

'But Annabelle how are we to be friends if I am to forever call you Miss Collett? 'Tis so very formal and I do not think our friendship will be so formal from this day forth, do you? Annabelle?'

'Reverend Thornton, although it is not my position to contradict you, I find I must, on this occasion, disagree.' Annabelle again attempted to ease her hand from his grasp, 'Please, release my hand, we are not friends - you are my employer. As such I must request you do, indeed, maintain the formalities I might expect from such a relationship.' Annabelle's heart beat so fast and heavy she began to feel as if her breath was being taken from her. From the gaze of Reverend Thornton's eyes, she thought he too must see how heavily her heart pounded.

Reverend Thornton stepped towards Annabelle, closing completely the space between them. 'You wish me to release your hand, Miss teasing Annabelle? Then I will do so, and I thank you for the invitation.' With a sudden sweeping motion Reverend Thornton released his tight grasp of Annabelle's hand and swung his arm behind her, around her waist, drawing her closer still into his coarse embrace. 'Now Annabelle,' he muttered, his face so close to hers she could no longer focus her gaze, 'Now you, yourself, have invited me so close let us talk about being friends.'

Annabelle grasped Reverend Thornton's hand at her waist in both of her own, much smaller, hands. Desperately she tried to prise his fingers from her. She wanted to call out, scream for help, but none would be nearby, even Nanny and the younger children were out walking in the gardens.

Reverend Thornton laughed, 'Well, Annebelle, I see you like to play teasing games! Perhaps you are more experienced than I had supposed. No matter, you are still a fine young woman who will satisfy my needs admirably. I have always found a little experience to be only a good thing in these matters.' He promptly succumbed to the pressure of Annabelle's fingers and released his left arm from around her waist whilst swinging his right arm into the same position as he took another step to force her backwards, away from the door, close to the wall.

A scream escaped from Annebelle, she felt herself falling, felt herself obliged to grasp tightly to Reverend Thornton's waistcoat to prevent the fall. Her pounding heart leapt and turned. She struggled to find each new breath. She put all her strength into trying to push him away from her. She had no breath left for words beyond a gasped, 'Reverend Thornton, please leave.'

Reverend Thornton laughed heartily as he looked down at Annabelle, trapped against the wall by the height and weight of his own body. He kept his right-hand firm around her waist whilst his left hand began a none-too-gentle exploration. 'Well, Annabelle, as you seem reluctant to engage in idle talk about being friends, I must presume you wish to dispense with the niceties of such formalities and move straight to actions. You are eager indeed for my attentions, young lady, I am not accustomed to such willingness. Mostly I meet with at least a degree of opposition before the young woman fully realises the benefits of bestowing her favours generously upon me. You are a dark horse Annabelle, let us hope your experience in these matters does not outstrip my own or I may soon tire of you.'

Annabelle felt tears of frustration and desperation sliding down her face.

'Mmmm, happy tears of anticipation,' Reverend Thornton wiped them roughly away with his hand, drying his hand inside the bodice of her gown, 'we really are going to enjoy our time together are we not Teasing Annabelle? Already I feel your whole body shaking in anticipation of the delights I am about to bring to it.'

Desperately Annabelle struggled to free her arms and push Reverend Thornton from her, 'Please, please,' she called as loudly as her thumping heart allowed, 'release me. We are not to be friends. Release me at once.'

Reverend Thornton was deaf to all sounds, intent only on his urgent desire for pleasure. He did not hear Annebelle's desperate entreaties. His head buried deep into her bosom he could not hear the sharp click of the latch, could not hear the crash as the door swung open, nor the roar of fury escaping from his son's throat. Taken by surprise, he heard only his own scream of pain as Miles pulled him from Annabelle and his head hit the jamb of the open door.

An emptiness fell over the room, gradually filling with breathing. Annabelle found herself able to calm her breath as the leaping and pounding of her heart subsided. Miles let out ragged breaths. Thoughts of the consequences to come spun through his head. Reverend Thornton's breath came accompanied by squeaks as he tried to suppress any show of pain in front of his son.

The stumbling steps of small children and the puffing of Nanny climbing the stairs echoed around them.

'You, boy, come with me,' roared Reverend Thornton. He pushed down the stairs past his younger children, who gazed in awe at the blood spreading slowly down their father's face.

Miles glanced back into the room, seeking Annabelle's eyes. He found her gaze for the briefest moment before prudence led him to follow his father's wishes. He eased himself gently past the children.

What am I to do now? I fear I must flee straight to Miss Nightingale's hospital and beg the good lady to train me as a nurse. Where else can I go? I have no means to support myself. I need the presence of other ladies which perhaps the hospital will offer me. I am sure there are others with the same evil intent as Reverend Thornton, amongst whom I would be no safer than I am here. How I regret so enjoying the time at Ashworth Manor I allowed my fears to drift away and I did not then make provision for my future.

I waited in great trepidation for the return of my young ladies from their drawing class, lest Reverend Thornton should come once more to our rooms in their absence. So gleefully did I welcome them back, I was sure they thought me bereft of my senses until I heard Miss Beryl whisper to her sister, 'I believe Father has paid a visit whilst we have been at our drawing lesson.' Then my heart began once more to pound so heavily I could hear it. Are visits such as this the way in which they expect their father to behave? Were visits such as this responsible for the swift departure of their previous governess? And what of Rose, who left us so suddenly?

Did M Miles follow his father knowing I was in danger? Did he come to protect me? I cannot know but he was so brave in his actions, for his father is a formidable man. I fear I may never more see M Miles. He will surely no longer be permitted to join his sisters to learn Latin.

My thoughts are in such turmoil I know only one thing, I must leave this house as soon and as safely as possible.

Master Miles did not appear at the schoolroom door the following morning. All three of the young ladies within the room cast their glance towards the door several times until Annabelle finally declared, 'We must proceed without Master Miles.'

It was a dismal morning of lessons. Annabelle's thoughts so frequently drifted elsewhere Miss Beryl was easily able to continue the reading of a novel secretly borrowed from her stepmother's meagre library of such books.

At the end of the morning, Tessa struggled up the stairs with a heavy tray, stopping on the second landing to fortify herself with a large piece of haddock. 'Master's not happy today. Someone's upset him. They'll be trouble coming.' Tessa announced wearily as she lowered the tray to the table.

Annabelle's fear rose once more, she tried to find appropriate words with which to question Tessa, but Tessa turned and left the room before the words could be uttered.

After the meal Annabelle, together with Miss Beryl and Miss Florence, walked in the gardens for a while, as they did on most days. Despite the protestations of Miss Florence, who liked to stop at the window and exchange waved greetings with her father, Annabelle took a path which would keep them well clear of Reverend Thornton's study window. Miss Florence was so visibly unhappy about this deviation from the norm Miss Beryl felt obliged to remind her of how unfitting it was for a young lady to show her displeasure so openly.

'We have only to do this because Miss Collett has taken a dislike to Father,' Miss Florence protested.

Annabelle felt such a display of rudeness and lack of manners should not go unremarked but could not find the right words and so pretended she had not heard Miss Florence's comments. Instead, she declared it was surely about to rain and they would return at once to the schoolroom, whilst there was still sufficient daylight for them to work on their embroidery samplers for an hour or two.

Miss Florence groaned audibly. This was punishment enough, for she heartily detested any form of needlework.

The quiet hours of needlework, with no visit from Reverend Thornton, calmed Annabelle somewhat. The gentle movements of needle and thread, the growing beauty of the picture emerging, eased her mind and allowed rational thoughts to linger long enough for her to begin planning for the future. This evening, she decided, she would write a letter to Miss Nightingale. Perhaps, whilst she awaited a response she might return to the Forest of Dean, to her aunt's house where her mother now lived. Surely, they would not turn her away – surely. She jumped as the needle pricked her finger and a small, perfectly formed, bobble of blood eased out. She held her finger suspended from her work to prevent the blood staining it while she sought her handkerchief with which to soak away the blood.

'Shall I open the door, Miss Collett?' Beryl asked, her voice lulled to quietness by the hours of sewing.

Annabelle looked up from her examination of her finger, 'The door Miss Beryl, has there been a knock?'

'Yes, I am certain whoever is without has knocked at least twice, although so softly I barely heard the sound and I fear you have heard it not at all.' Beryl left her seat and moved to the door.

Hands shaking and heart racing Annabelle turned her head towards the door, Reverend Thornton would be standing there when it opened, of this she was certain.

Beryl pulled open the door. Florence squealed loudly and covered her eyes with her hands. Beryl released her hold on the door handle and lifted her hands skywards, 'Good heavens, whatever has happened, who has done this.' Her hands sprang to her mouth to suppress the words of the question to which she already knew the answer.

'Master Miles…' Annabelle struggled to find further words, 'come, sit, come, sit here.'

Recovering a little, Annabelle commanded Beryl to close up the door once more but Miles lifted his hand to contradict her, 'No Beryl, first go with

Florence and spend some time with Nanny and the babies. I must speak alone with Miss Collett. Close up the door behind you as you leave.'

'Come, Miss Collett, Annabelle, sit alongside, there is room for two and you will be able to make a more thorough examination if you are closer.' Miles reached out a hand which shook and took into it the quivering of Annabelle's hand. Without thought, each held tightly to the other.

Annabelle reached out her free hand, her tender touch traced the bruised cheeks, the swollen lips, the blackened eyes, closely. 'Your father has done this.' she said, more as a statement than as a question, 'Because you pulled him from me?' This time it was a question, although she knew the answer.

Miles raised his own free hand, gently wiping away the tears beginning to fall from Annabelle's eyes.

'I could not let him hurt you, be close to you. I had hoped, when this learning of Latin and Greek had been achieved to his satisfaction, I had hoped to leave here, to make a way for myself in the world. I have a small inheritance from my Maternal grandfather. I had hoped, foolishly perhaps, you would leave here with me, as my wife. Hoped we might make our way in the world together. For I love you Miss Annabelle Collett and I believe some at least of my feelings may be returned.'

As Annabelle attempted to speak Miles saw his feelings were indeed returned, wished he had spoken sooner, taken her from here sooner. Now it might be too late.

'Miles, I will go with you into the world, although I have little but my knowledge of languages and my skills with needlework to bring with me.'

'Alas, Annabelle, I fear it may be too late. My father sent my sister and brother-in-law to China as missionaries and now he has decreed I must follow them. Annabelle, he wishes me to go as a missionary to China. He is making the arrangements as we speak. I could not ask you to accompany me there. My sister has gone because she had as little choice as I, bearing as she was our father's child. He had swiftly married her to a man too dull of brain to realise the child was not his. Likely they will never return. Most missionaries die young in China.'

Annabelle rose and paced the room, hoping to hide her tears of despair from Miles but he rose too and followed her. She turned to meet him, to walk into the offered embrace, hold the bruised face, kiss the swollen lips, as tears fell from his eyes also.

'We cannot allow this to happen, we cannot,' Annabelle clasped her hands firmly on his shoulders. 'We cannot allow this to happen. Miles, I love you as you love me. We must keep together. We belong together. We must not let despair and hopelessness stifle us, prevent our future. There is light in every darkness, we just have to find it.'

Roughly Miles wiped his hands across his eyes, ignoring the pain his action brought to the dark spongy bruises. He laughed, more loudly than he had intended, 'Annabelle, I declare you are a wonder. I came to you in despair, and you have found hope. With you by my side we will find a way. I must go now. Father must not know I have been here. Do not be afraid - he will make no further move in your direction until I am gone from the house. We have a reprieve of time in which to make our plans. I will return tomorrow whilst Father is gone to talk with the bishop about my future.'

Miles reached the door. Returned to kiss Annabelle. Reached the door once more. His hand on the doorknob, his head twisted back over his shoulder, he whispered so only she might hear, 'Miss Annabelle Collett, will you marry me?'

How my heart races now with joy. Miles is to be mine. None must know our intentions. Not Miss Beryl, nor Florence, not Nanny, nor Tessa. Miles returned to me once the young ladies were abed. We spoke long into the night. Now we have made our plans which are joyful and terrifying in equal measure. I am not able to take actions myself, confined as I am to the house and gardens with the young ladies. But we are agreed, Miles is to obtain a special license for us to marry because we cannot have the banns read in church by Reverend Thornton himself. Miles is to arrange my transportation to the Forest of Dean where we will marry.

I have persuaded Miles to agree to my staying for a day or two in the caves near my aunt's home - those caves where I played in my childhood days. For Mother and Aunt must not know of our plans until we are married, lest they stand against it and return me to Reverend Thornton. If I go to the caves Miles and I need not leave this house on the same day. Then, perhaps, none will suspect we have fled to be together.

Despite the anxieties of her impending departure there was a lightness to Annabelle in the following days. Nanny remarked upon it more than once, 'Someone's happy since Master's last visit to the schoolroom, happen he'll be back soon to check on progress.'

Beryl and Florence made no comment. They found their governess easily persuaded to move to pleasant subjects, such as studying the globe and reading histories more suited to younger children, when they quickly tired of Latin or Greek. They found she paid little attention to their needlework and less to her own. Beryl devoured novels as surreptitiously as she felt was needed. Florence gazed frequently from the window and told stories in her head to the toys she had left behind in the nursery.

Under the guise of preparing for departure to China, Miles was able to make the necessary arrangements to secure a marriage license.

Today Miles came with the news of an increased urgency to our plans. His father has identified a ship sailing for China in just four days' time. We must, therefore, leave this house with all possible haste lest Reverend Thornton decide on some drastic measure to detain Miles before the sailing. Miles has gone now to seek transport for me back to the Forest of Dean. I must leave tomorrow or the day following.

***

Late in the evening of the following day, when he knew all but Annabelle would be gone to their beds, Miles climbed the stairs to the schoolroom to give Annabelle the news he knew she so anxiously awaited. As he closed the door quietly behind him, she rose to meet his silent embrace.

'Tomorrow, dearest Annabelle - you leave tomorrow. I have arranged for you to travel on a carrier's cart. I fear it is not so dignified a mode of transport as you deserve but it will not draw undue attention to you.'

'And you?' Annabelle asked, 'What of you?'

'I will follow you in two days. Then we will be married quietly in the church of your childhood worship. It is arranged and the Rector sworn to secrecy with a bigger bribe than I had anticipated.'

Annabelle reached to stroke the fading bruises on Miles' face as his left arm snaked around her shoulders, pulling her closer to him so he might slide his right arm around her waist. She drew his head gently towards her.

With a crash which set more than one of the babies in the nursery to screaming for Nanny, the door flew open, banged against the wall, crashed again as a kick from Reverend Thornton's boot hit it.

Along the corridor Miss Beryl and Miss Florence quivered in their beds and buried their heads under the bedclothes, hiding from the wrath of their father.

'What do you think you are doing sullying the good name of my household - enticing and bewitching my son, you filthy little whore. Release him at once, do not think you can get your claws into him and destroy my family, you are wicked, wicked. You reject my kind offer to befriend you, an orphan girl in need of assistance, when I wanted nothing more than to be your friend and yet here you are throwing your modesty, your virtue, your body at my son, who is too young and inexperienced to know what you are about. You are indeed a wicked and ungodly woman and will surely burn in hell for all eternity for your sins. You leave my house tomorrow morning. And you, boy, you leave this room now! It is fortunate for you tis but four days until you leave for China, a journey for which you must at least look respectable.'

***

Annabelle spent a sleepless night curled in the blankets from her bed against the door of her bedchamber, which had no key to otherwise secure it. With every creak of the house, she tensed. She imagined heavy footsteps on the stairs, her brain convincing her the footsteps were real. She prayed for the lighter footsteps of Miles but knew they wouldn't come. Even her beloved Miles could not come to protect her this night. She knew not that he spent the night resting in an armchair beside the open door of his own bedchamber, listening, as Annabelle was, for his father's footsteps.

As the soft light of dawn began to creep through the window, Annabelle swiftly packed her few worldly possessions into the small wooden trunk she had brought with her from her childhood home.

Miss Beryl and Miss Florence did not appear in the schoolroom for breakfast. Annabelle heard their falsely bright voices echoing from the nursery. She opened the door, thinking to join them, but her exit was barred by the smirking presence of the butler who had, almost a lifetime ago, refused her admission at the front door of the house.

'You're to stay in the room – Miss – until the cart arrives to transport you.' He offered no further explanation, merely taking hold of the door handle and pulling it closed as he muttered, 'And a cart is more than you deserve, you …,' Annabelle did not hear his final words. Clearly, her reputation in the household had been sullied by Reverand Thornton, even before her departure.

Annabelle was saddened to realise she was not to be allowed to say her goodbyes to the young ladies, nor to Nanny and the babies. She knew not if Miles was similarly kept prisoner. Knew not if their plans could be enacted or if they would lose the beautiful future they had planned. Would she never more have sight of him? She stood silently, looking from the window, willing her tears not to fall, determined to leave the house with as much dignity as possible. She stared from the window until she saw a cart trundle slowly to the servants' entrance. With a deep sigh she turned, moved to the door, waited to be summoned to take her place in the cart.

At last, I am here, safe for now in the cave with my gallery of ladies. I have my small trunk, hastily packed, with all my worldly belongings. I have also the bows and arrows given to myself and Miles by Mr Ashworth. Miles must have loaded them on the carrier's cart. It gave me great pleasure to see them, not least because it reassured me Miles will join me and I had almost given up any hope of our reunion. Their presence reassured me also Reverend Thornton has not imprisoned Miles, for he was able to load them on the cart. But I did not see him before I departed and still I fear I will not see him again. Reverend Thornton is an evil man who does not like to be crossed. He may yet manage to detain Miles until he is escorted to the ship and left to sail alone for China. If he does not come in two, or perhaps three days I will be obliged to seek my aunt's hospitality. I fear I will receive little welcome and will rapidly be dispatched to who knows what future.

I experienced some difficulty in persuading the carrier to put me down at a distance from any dwelling. He had been instructed to on no account deliver me anywhere but my aunt's house. I recalled how Miles has paid the Rector for his silence and so offered the carrier what little money I had. It seems his silence and cooperation are as easily bought as was the Rector's.

I pray Miles joins me two days hence, which should be my wedding day. I mind not the lack of a wedding gown or flowers, only I pray for us to be joined in marriage, free from the terror of Reverend Thornton.

The first day, Annabelle rested quietly in the cave. She was surprised at how comfortable it felt, the cave almost seeming to embrace her and draw her into its soul. She found Miles had packed a little food alongside the bows and arrows, together with a flagon of water. She stayed within the cave, her few belongings hidden behind an outcrop of rock, anxious none should think anything amiss if they ventured nearby.

As evening drew in, Annabelle found herself restless for some activity. She braced her bow, it felt good to have the bow once more in her hands. She ran her hand along its length, warming the wood as if preparing to shoot. She laid the bow to one side and picked up her bundle of arrows. 'I will shoot just one arrow,' she said aloud, glancing around to make certain none had heard her. Yes, she thought, just one arrow, there is no one about. She picked up the bow from where it lay thinking, now I have the bow in my hand I find I really must shoot an arrow. I do not believe I will be able to sleep at all this night if I do not shoot just one arrow.

Annabelle looked around her in every direction. She saw no signs of movement, heard no sound except for those of the birds coming home to roost. She climbed above the cave entrance. Shielding her eyes against the brightness of the setting sun, she scanned the surrounding land as far as her eyes could see. She saw no one, heard no one. Yes, she decided there could be no harm in shooting just one arrow before she settled for the long, lonely night beyond which she prayed Miles would come for their wedding.

The bow rested easily in Annabelle's hand. She felt the warmth of the leather grip in her palm. I will shoot down the hill, she thought as she nocked the arrow to the bow. Downhill there was less chance of losing the arrow, as she had no target to aim for. Annabelle eased back the string until the bow was at full draw and then as her hand continued its backwards movement her fingers released their grip on the string. With the faintest swish the arrow left the bow and flew in a smooth arc through the air. It landed with rather more of a thud than Annabelle had expected but she gave the sound little thought as she relished the familiar thrill racing through her. She let down the bow, secured the string and placed the bow gently back behind the boulder.

Returning to the cave entrance she saw a head appear above the undergrowth, she would have to leave the arrow until this person had passed by. She melted back into the darkness of the cave.

'Well, Miss Annabelle Collett, what a very good shot you have turned out to be. You have secured for us a rabbit for our wedding feast whilst narrowly avoiding an arrow through your husband to be.'

Annabelle let out a gasped squeal of delight. Miles stood before her holding her arrow on which was impaled a rabbit. 'Miles you are here and a day early, my heart is full of joy to see you.'

'Mine also to see you but come we must hurry while there is still daylight for the Rector to see you. I have spoken with him. He has agreed to marry us at once.'

'At once, Miles! Not tomorrow?'

'No Annabelle, at once, if not sooner. My father pursues me, he discovered by bribery, where I was travelling to. He must have guessed our plans. Immediately I had left his house he set off in rapid pursuit. Only by devious means of travelling hither and thither around the countryside have I managed to outwit him so far and keep him from you. Come,' he reached out to take Annabelle's hand in his own, 'We must make all haste to the Rector who has delayed his dinner in order to join us in holy matrimony before my father finds us.'

***

Annabelle felt the anxiety and fear emanating from Miles, knew it to be the same anxiety and fear which caused the slight shaking of her hands and the swift glances which she cast over her shoulder towards the heavy oak door of the church. She was aware of how Miles shifted restlessly next to her as they each fought to suppress their own impatience, whilst the Rector took them slowly and ponderously through the marriage service. Annabelle felt Miles tense beside her. Knew he was listening, waiting for the crash of the door.

When it came, as Miles had known it would, both of the Rector's sisters, whom he had enticed to be witnesses to this hasty marriage, screamed in alarm and then faltered to have made such an unseemly sound in the house of God presided over by their own brother.

The Rector, absorbed in the long familiar marriage service, completed the blessing. He confirmed Annabelle and Miles as wed whilst looking with contempt, at Reverend Thornton who stood in the doorway, red in the face and flustered shouting the marriage was not to take place.

'Too late', Miles declared, 'Annabelle is now my wife.'

How wonderful those words sounded to me.

Following their marriage, Annabelle and Miles returned to the caves. Darkness had begun to fall. They would spend this night here, relishing their newfound freedom together. On the morrow they would visit Annabelle's mother, tell the world their news. Then they would make their plans for the future.

'Annabelle,' Miles whispered in the darkness, 'now we are married I should like to be known by your name, I should like to be Miles Collett. I do not wish you or our children to carry the name of my father.'

How wonderful to wake this morning with my beloved Miles lying in my arms, the grass outside our bridal chamber damp and sweet smelling with the early dew, the sun rising to warm the first day of our life together with the promise of beauty and joy to come.

I showed to Miles the gallery of ladies from whom I am surely descended. Miles persuaded me I am now an archer and have shown every bit as much courage as they might surely have shown. He persuaded me to add my own portrait to the gallery and I have done so. I have added flowers, alongside my bow and arrow to show those who come after this is my wedding portrait.

Soon, I feel certain, I will bear a daughter. She, too, will be strong, as will her daughter and her daughter's daughter, ever forwards through the family which begins here with Miles and myself. I have added the smallest, faintest of outline pictures of my future daughter in expectation she too will find joy and fulfilment through archery when she is strong enough to draw back a bow.

But this is my secret I did not tell Miles what the picture of a small bundle besides my own portrait represents. When our daughter is born, I will tell him.

But this is for later. Just now we know not what our future might hold. Whatever it holds we will face it together. At last, we are married. I am married to Miles, and he is wed to me, for ever and all eternity. We have not yet determined where or how we shall live but I know we will be always together. I know we will be happy.

....

Annie

2039

Annie stood behind the armchair in which James was slouched with eyes perilously close to the screen. 'Come on, lazy legs, put your phone in your pocket and your boots on your feet and get some fresh air with me.'

James mumbled.

'Sorry James - can't hear you. You'll have to lift your head off your chest, which, of course, will have the added benefit of enabling you to actually take oxygen into your lungs so your brain starts to function.' She placed a kiss on the top of his head and ruffled his hair.

James smoothed his hair, 'Don't mess my hair up. Why do we need to get fresh air? Surely, you've been outside all day at work?'

'Indeed I have. Today we were building shelters with the kids in the woods and teaching them some whittling skills with carrots and potato peelers. You, I suspect, have not so much as opened a window all day.'

James positioned his legs, placed his hands on the arms of the chair and, with a deep sigh, heaved his long body from its recumbent position to upright in one slow push. Three long strides took him to the door. 'Where do you want to go, Annie Collett?'

'Look at you,' Annie's hand reached up to stroke his face, 'you're so pale. You need fresh air. We're going into the woods, along the ridge, down past the pond, up to the far path and then back along the main path. I want to see if the elderflowers are getting ready for picking to make some more wine.'

'It's miles,' James mumbled into his chest as he struggled into his walking boots.

Annie ignored him as she updated her friend Olivia via text.

O Finally got J out the door don't think he's left house in a week A

The fresh evening air felt good. Surreptitiously James took deep breaths, hoping Annie wouldn't notice how glad he really was for the enforced outdoor activity.

'See, James, it's so beautiful at this time of day, we can almost hear the world getting ready to go to sleep. You really do miss so much by not coming out here every day. Listen to the birds, all on their final flights before the darkness falls.' Annie slowed her progress, waiting for James to match her step and slow also. She stopped, raising her face to study the tops of the trees. James stopped also, he reached out to stroke her long hair as it tumbled over her shoulders and down her back. Annie laughed, 'You're supposed to be watching the birds and the trees, not my hair.' She took his hand as they began the descent to the pond. On the far side a pair of ducks quacked quietly to each other. 'I think they're talking about what a lovely day they've had swimming on the pond in the sunshine. They get to spend all their time outdoors. They don't complain about a bit of fresh air, do they?' She punched James playfully on the shoulder.

James wrapped his arm around her, 'It's alright for them, they don't have anything to worry about, except finding food. They don't have to spend hours every day earning a living by staring at a computer screen.'

'Neither do you, James,' Annie said as she snuggled further into his embrace, 'If you weren't fixated on earning as much money as possible, you could work outside, run a forest school like me or do woodworking or gardening or forestry or, well, all sorts. You just need to learn the skills.'

James held her close. She was right, but he was frightened of change, reluctant to lose the familiar, to launch into the unknown, to risk security for the chance of adventure. In his heart he wanted to be as free from these constraints as Annie was. Perhaps, he thought, if he trusted her with his career as he trusted her with his heart, he too might experience the joy, freedom, and zest for life which she exuded each day. Maybe he would give it some thought, make a plan, something definite, before he abandoned the security of his computer.

'Come,' Annie took his hand from her waist and held it as she led him away from the water towards the path. 'If we climb very quietly up this path we might see some deer, I often see deer around here, sometimes a fox as well, especially as evening falls.'

A rustling, grunting in the undergrowth nearby reminded James there were wild boar in the forest. He clung to her hand, pulling her to a stop, pointing in the direction of the sounds, 'Annie, I think there's boar here, I mean right here, like we might meet them.'

Annie hid herself in the undergrowth, she didn't want James to see her laughing. She also didn't want him to see her check the message which had just arrived on her phone. She tried to create the impression she didn't use her phone in the forest.

A how's your walk O

O J scared to meet boar A

A find a big one to meet ha ha O

'It's gone,' Annie said turning and reaching out her hand for James to help her negotiate the steep incline. 'But you don't have to worry too much about the boar – they can't see very well. It's because their food is on the ground. They forage, they're not hunters, they don't need good eyesight. And they grunt very loudly, so you usually hear them before they get close.'

By the time they had negotiated the steep climb to the main path, James could feel the muscles in his legs complaining at the unaccustomed exercise. Annie was right, he reluctantly admitted to himself. He really needed to do more physical stuff if he was going to live beyond the age of thirty, well, maybe forty.

The sun was beginning to set as they emerged from the forest, still hand in hand.

'Annie, we didn't see the elderflower trees, did we?' James tried to stifle the feeling he'd been taken on the walk under false pretences. After all it had made him resolve to think about maybe trying to change his life so it must have been a good thing.

'I saw them, James, but I think I forgot to point them out to you. The trees are elders - I mean they're not elderflower trees, they're elder trees which grow flowers from which I make very special wine. If you can wait two years for it to be properly mature. If you promise to walk in the forest every day, I'll let you have some of my elderflower wine in two years' time.'

***

'Annie, what's all this on the calendar? I can't work out your scribblings,' James called, head buried in his first coffee of the morning. He wandered into the hall, took his head away from the coffee and directed his voice up the stairs. 'Annie, what's all this on this stupid calendar? I can't work out your scribblings.'

Footsteps overhead told him Annie was on her way. James returned to the kitchen, positioned himself beside the wall calendar, ready to indicate the scribblings to which he referred.

Annie was running late. A glance at the kitchen counter told her James had not made up the promised lunch. She looked briefly at James as she hunted for the bread knife.

'What's all these scribblings on the calendar? And why do we have to have this stupid wall calendar? Nobody's used an actual calendar for, like, centuries, why do we have to?' James persisted.

'James, James, my love, where have you been hiding? Everyone has a retro calendar this year. It's fun and actually very easy to keep track of things without having to get your phone out all the time.'

'Huh,' James grunted, 'well it's stupid anyway, but what about the scribblings?'

'For goodness' sake James, they're not scribblings, they're my life mapped out. Just so you don't book anything in when I'm already booked up. They're just in code. You should be able to deal with a simple code, after all that's what you do all day for work.'

Simultaneously, James puzzled over the codes on the calendar and marvelled at the speed with which Annie had constructed her lunch and put it safely in her backpack.

'Can you explain the codes? Then I'll know where you are because it doesn't look as if you'll be here much.'

'OK, quickly now James - I'm late. retain the information.' Annie stood beside him, resting one hand on his arm, pointing with the other hand to the calendar. 'This is an arrow. An arrow means archery practice. Two arrows together, like here,' Annie's finger stabbed a Sunday, 'means an archery tournament. This is a mushroom, meaning Olivia is leading a mushroom forage, which I might or might not go along to. This is a leaf. A leaf means Olivia and

Beth are leading a general food foraging walk, which I probably will go on. A big O means outlaws, those are the days your parents are visiting to continue their reminders we haven't yet provided grandchildren. This,' her finger stabbed again, 'is a fork. A fork means someone is coming round, the initials tell you who. Today it says O C B, so we know Olivia, Chris and Beth are coming for food tonight. If it were to say @OC B, we would be going there for food. Got to go,' she landed a kiss on his cheek and disappeared in a whirl of bag and jacket, reaching for her phone as she climbed into her car.

O had to explain code to J can you believe? A

As she pulled away from the house her phone pinged a reply.

A J's brain fuddled lack of oxygen see you tonight O

Before she exited the car, she reached for her phone.

J get food for tonight xx A

***

James saw the message just as he was finishing his second cup of coffee and switching on his computers for the day. Food, when was he going to get food? What food was he supposed to get? No point texting Annie, she didn't take her personal phone to forest School sessions. He wondered if they'd agreed on a menu. He stared out of the window, no memory of a menu came to mind, 'just have to wing it,' he muttered.

At 2pm James returned to the kitchen, torn between the need to go and buy food and the fact he had not yet had lunch. An online meeting loomed at 3pm. James placed the bread on the bread board, reached for the bread knife, sighed, returned the bread knife to the drawer, picked up a shopping bag and left the house.

As James was paying at the supermarket, he realised he could have ordered a menu box online, then he would have had time for lunch.

Back home, James put the leg of lamb in the oven to slow roast. He put the cheesecake in the fridge. No point hiding the packaging, Annie would know that if dessert wasn't a fruit crumble, then he hadn't made it. As he stuffed a bag of peas into the overfull freezer his eyes caught sight of frozen mixed berries. 'Oh, fancy dessert,' he mumbled, putting the berries to defrost. As he logged on again James noted, with relief, he was only five minutes late for his meeting. Fifteen minutes into the two-hour meeting he remembered he had still not had lunch.

At five, just as James was closing down his computers, Annie arrived home to the aroma of roasting lamb. She opened the fridge, saw cheesecake and berries. You've excelled yourself she thought as James entered the kitchen and they exchanged an end-of-working-day hug. James' stomach rumbled loudly. Annie patted it, 'Oh James, did you forget to have lunch again? Maybe you should have a biscuit to keep you going, Olivia and co won't be here until seven.'

James thought a whole packet of biscuits might be more the thing. He surreptitiously managed several while Annie's back was turned. Suitably fortified he set about preparing vegetables. Annie went to the supermarket for the drinks James had forgotten.

***

Nobody except the parties involved was entirely sure of the exact nature of the relationship between the three guests. Olivia, Chris and Beth shared a house. A house with two bedrooms, owned by Beth. Olivia and Chris had taken up residence in the house at different times but, James observed, they often behaved like a couple. Chris and Beth also often behaved like a couple, Annie sagely pointed out. When Annie and James stopped to think about it, they realised Beth and Olivia often behaved like a couple. James thought Annie could just ask Olivia. 'After all, she's your friend, isn't she?' he asked.

'She might be my friend, James,' Annie replied, as the doorbell rang to announce the arrival of their guests, 'But I'm not asking who has sex with who. If they are a threesome, they might think we're interested in joining in.' She glanced at James, looking for signs of interest or disinterest. His face was averted. 'And I can tell you James, so long as you and I are a couple, neither of us is having sex with anyone else. Besides, I'm not interested in what other people get up to, are you?'

James choked on the piece of tomato he had stolen from the salad, as he sought to stifle his amusement, of course he was interested in what other people were up to, but Annie didn't need to know.

'Oh, and James,' Annie prodded James in the ribs, 'Whatever you do, don't mention the conflict, I want a nice peaceful evening.'

***

'Tried it once. Didn't suit me. Too much repetition. Stand on the line, put the arrow on the string, draw up, fire.'

'It's shoot or loose, Chris.'

Chris looked puzzled by Annie's words. 'Sorry?' he said enquiringly.

'I mean, Chris, we say shoot or loose, or release the arrow, not fire because there's no fire involved. It's a bow, not a musket.'

Beth helped herself to more lamb, 'I was thinking I might come along and try out archery next time you have a beginner's course. I don't mind a bit of repetition, at least you know where you are with repetition. Have you got one of those bows, you know, like they shoot in the Olympics?'

'No, I've got a good old-fashioned longbow, but you would start with one of the lighter training bows and then decide which route you want to go down once you know what you're doing.'

Chris placed his knife and fork neatly on his plate, 'I guess you've heard about how the medieval archers ended up with one shoulder bigger than the other because of the weight of their bows and their regular practice?'

Annie nodded, 'I don't know if it happens to the same extent these days. Modern longbows are much lighter than the old war bows.'

'But some of you do practice quite a lot, don't you?' Olivia emerged from her enjoyment of the food to join the conversation, 'You seem to go to the club quite often.'

'Doesn't she ever?' James mumbled as he gathered plates and cutlery.

Chris turned to Annie, 'Seriously Annie, from a professional, physiotherapist point of view I'd be really interested in examining your shoulders one day.'

Annie left the table to help James clear away, 'Tell you what Chris, when I injure myself and need a good physio I'll come to you. I'm not keen on being examined unnecessarily by any sort of medical practitioner really, no offence intended. Would anyone like coffee with desert.'

'Depends what sort of crumble James has made.' Olivia looked expectantly across the kitchen at James while Beth surreptitiously stroked Chris' arm, soothing his ruffled feathers and hurt feelings.

James laughed, 'Crumble, my signature dish, no, today I've made a cheesecake.' James held the cheesecake aloft with a flourish before lowering it to the kitchen counter and removing the packaging.

Chris laughed, 'That's my kind of baking.'

'Mine too,' said Annie, 'I'm not big on making puds. They really are James' department in this house, but he's cheated today.'

As they finished their cheesecake Chris turned the conversation to the conflict, the topic Annie and James had been carefully avoiding.

'For goodness' sake, Chris,' Beth said with a sigh, 'we don't need to talk about the conflict tonight. Let's just enjoy the evening.'

But Chris had mentioned the conflict and once mentioned it could not be let go. Suddenly they were all speaking in voices quiet with awe and horror. The images which passed through their minds were of devastation, death, starvation, disease, destruction, while the words which came from their mouths turned less hopeful than they had anticipated when their phrases and sentences had formed in their brains.

Dreadful. Did you see what they did to Paris yesterday? And Copenhagen. It's all gone. What's happening to the people. Probably none left. All dead? Most likely - hard to see how they would survive such an attack. But Paris, that's getting a bit close. Didn't seem so bad when it was all up in Scandinavia. Well, it was still bad for the Scandinavians, wasn't it? Just it didn't seem so bad because it was further away, you know, what the eye doesn't see and all that. But Paris! Paris is just like, next door. All those beautiful old buildings, they can't ever be replaced. What about all those beautiful people? They can't be replaced. Did you see how

Sweden is practically obliterated? Nothing left. I heard the government here are going to start a call-up very soon. Won't do any good, troops on the ground are never going to match the weapons we're seeing now. Pity they've closed the borders otherwise we could all just pack up and move to Africa. I think that's what they're trying to stop so they can keep a fighting force here. Won't do any good. They had a fighting force in Paris and where are they now? Obliterated, that's where they are now, gone, annihilated - nothing left for their parents to bury, even if there were any parents left to bury them, but they've been obliterated as well. Will we be obliterated soon? No, they wouldn't bother with a small place like Britain. Would they?

Would they?

'Shall we watch the news?' Annie asked, trepidation in her trembling voice.

'Forewarned is forearmed,' said James as he stretched his arm for the remote.

Vivid red warning messages flashed across fleeting pictures of grey. Grey smoke, grey dust as buildings descended to rubble, bodies lying on the ground coated in the grey dust and smoke of destruction. The messages came and went too quickly. They couldn't read them. Thought them to be in a different language. The horror of what they were seeing rested uncomfortably on them. But they had seen such images for months now as northern and eastern parts of Europe and Russia fell to the ongoing destruction. The crises of refugees and displaced persons were small because few survived.

'Do you really think they'll leave us alone?' Beth asked.

'It's Big Ben,' Chris fell from his chair, trying to get closer to the flickering images on the screen.

Someone screamed.

The ground shook. They thought they had imagined the shaking of the ground. Thought it was the shock they were feeling. The ground shook again. The antique glass vases which had belonged to Annie's great-grandmother lay in tiny fragments on the floor in front of the television.

'Big Ben's gone.'

'That's London.'

'London's gone.'

Someone screamed.

Someone sobbed, gasping to regain their breath.

The television flicked into darkness and silence.

***

Nobody moved, nobody spoke, they barely breathed. In the quiet stillness of the room, they all heard rumbling explosions, implosions.

Chris was the first to speak. 'Well, at least the sound's working on your telly.' His glance swept over his friends, a faint, nervous laugh emerged from his throat. He knew what they knew.

Olivia's voice quivered as her words stumbled out, 'There's no sound from the telly, it's all outside.'

'Not right outside, but close,' Annie said moving through the hallway to the door, 'I'm going to see.'

'Wait,' called James, his voice lost in panic. He tried again, he thought he was shouting but little more than a squeak came out, 'Wait, I'll go with you.'

In a stumbling rush they all struggled into shoes as they pushed through the doorway, stood on the drive in a bewildered tangle. The thundering sounds of destruction louder now they were outside. Which way?

James grabbed Annie's arm, 'This way, over to the play area, we're on the top of the hill here so we'll see all the town from there.'

They ran the short distance, knowing speed would change nothing, caught up in panic and the hopeless thought, perhaps they were wrong, perhaps the town still stood.

Someone screamed.

The town was gone. Descended into a dusty smoking heap of grey.

The rumbling stopped. Silent stillness filled the air.

The rumbling sounds of destruction started up again, but quieter this time. In the distance they saw towns and villages on the far side of the river descend into grey, plumes of dust rising above them.

Almost without movement they huddled closer together, wordless in the horror of what they had witnessed.

Behind them the trees of the Forest rustled and swayed. The swirling waves of wind created by the destruction slowed, reaching the trees as increasingly gentle breezes. But for the mangled heap of the town before them and the dust settling on and around them, it could have been any warm evening in late spring.

Annie held Olivia close to still the shaking which overwhelmed her. 'Everything is gone, your home is gone. Come we'll go back to the house. You must all stay with us until this is over and everything gets back to normal.'

For long, silent minutes, nobody spoke.

Someone sobbed.

Finally, James opened his long arms wide, trying to take each of his friends into a comforting embrace as he spoke the words which were in all their minds. 'It won't get back to normal, Annie. It's probably not even going to be safe to stay in our house. The structure might be damaged, it might collapse. They might see our house still standing on the top of the hill and come back to destroy it. I don't think we can stay in the house.'

'But James,' Beth's voice emerged more calmly than it left her mind, 'James, you're being unreasonable. Of course we must go back to the house, where else can we go? There's nothing else left, look,' her arms swept across the view of destruction, and look over there, the bridge is also gone, we cannot even cross the bridge to escape.'

Annie released Olivia from her embrace and gently took Beth in her place, 'Beth, I think James may be right. Even if the bridge was there everything on the other side has been destroyed as well. In other countries we have seen them return to destroy a single building. They will come for the house, if not tonight then tomorrow.'

'But where is there left to go?' Chris spun around as he spoke, searching for signs of a safe place, 'it's all gone, it's all gone.' His head sank into his hands in despair as Olivia held him close.

For long, silent minutes nobody spoke.

A sharp intake of breath from Annie broke the silence, 'We'll go into the forest.'

'But Annie, said James, 'what if they return to destroy the entire Forest of Dean?'

'If they destroy the Forest, we will all be finished but if they don't see any buildings standing, they may not bother to destroy the Forest.'

Beth stifled a sob. 'But if they do destroy it, we'll all be dead. We can't take the risk Annie. Can we?' Beth's enquiring eyes met the eyes of each of her friends in turn.

Annie spoke quietly the truth which they all knew, 'There is nowhere else. We must go into the Forest, it's our only hope. There is nowhere else left to go.'

Silent acknowledgement reached her. Annie thought quickly. 'We must take food from the house, tools we might need, my forest school stuff.'

'And our skills.' Olivia said. 'Our skills will be with us. Beth and I can forage for edible plants and mushrooms. We have a lot of skills between us to help us survive if they leave the Forest standing.'

Caught up in the adrenaline rush of preparation their minds told them they were embarking on a planned adventure, not trying to escape from the certain death which awaited them if they remained. Returning to the house they gathered food, tools, quilts, warm clothing, confused as to what would be useful and what would be useless and a burden to them.

Reality seemed far away.

Finally, bags and bundles were ready. They stood once more on the drive going through routines of normal life as if they were embarking on a weekend camping trip.

'I'll take the car keys,' James said, 'don't want anyone taking the car while we're away.'

‘I don’t have my phone charger.’

Nobody responded.

Carefully Annie checked the back door. She put the key in the front door lock and turned it to secure the house.

‘Why are you taking those?’ James asked as Annie picked up two longbows and several tubes of arrows, ‘They’re just going to get in the way, aren’t they?’ his eyes appealed to Chris, Olivia and Beth, ‘Surely we’ve got enough to carry?’

With practised ease Annie rested the longbows over her shoulder. She looked at James, her voice solemn and scared, ‘We might need these. James, this is real. It isn’t a game.’

***

In the gathering dusk they walked into the Forest of Dean, just as they had done many times before. This time it felt the same and yet it felt so different, knowing the world they had always known was no longer there. There would be no return this evening, no glass of wine on the patio, no fond farewells at the end of the evening and promises to meet up again very soon. As the world they had known closed down behind them the Forest seemed almost to open its paths. It welcomed them into its somewhat haphazard embrace. It offered them no certainties, no familiar comforts.

Darkness descended early under the canopy of the trees. They tripped and stumbled on rocks and tree roots. They had no plan beyond going into the

Forest, putting distance between themselves and the destruction they had witnessed. Silently they each acknowledged everyone else whom they knew and loved was gone. Everything which had made their lives safe and fun was gone. They had nothing beyond each other and the few possessions they had carried with them. They needed to rest, sleep, wait for daylight to return. Descending darkness, returning daylight and the turning of the seasons - these were the only normalities left from their old world.

Annie halted them, 'I don't think we can go any further this evening. It's way too dark to move on safely.'

'We don't want any broken bones, do we?' Beth's voice shook slightly, 'Chris might be a good physio, but his knowledge is really not going to help us much with broken bones.' Beth shuddered as the reality of their situation gripped her. She felt the shudder reverberate through the group. She heard groans and gasps of realisation and despair. Who they came from she couldn't tell - maybe from herself, maybe from others. Whoever they came from they were all sharing the feelings of despair and realisation.

This was their new reality. None of them wanted it.

Neither Annie nor Olivia mentioned their first-aid training. First-aid training wouldn't set broken bones. First-aid was what you did while you waited for medical help to arrive. No medical help would be reaching them.

'Well, nothing for it but to hunker down and wait for daylight,' James' voice carried more optimism than either his heart or his head.

'Good job we brought duvets,' the enforced brightness led Olivia's voice to emerge as a high-pitched squeak.

Huddled close for warmth, they tried to force the spirit of adventure to the surface.

'Annie,' James whispered, as he stroked the chillness of her cheeks, 'remember the caves you showed me? Where you used to play as a child.'

Annie struggled back to the present. Her thoughts had been deep elsewhere. James was talking of caves, why was James talking of caves?

Caves! Remembrance dawned slowly, 'Oh yes James, fancy you remembering those now. I took you there and you complained about it being a long walk.' She snuggled into his embrace, 'It's only three miles from here, but I guess that's a long walk for you, Lazy Legs.'

They both laughed, it seemed so long ago, so far back into their old familiar life since she had called him Lazy Legs.

'James.'

'Yes, Annie.'

Annie held her breath. She realised the others were probably still awake, now was not the time to share her own news with James. Instead, she forced her mind back to the caves, 'Do you remember the pictures on the wall of the cave? All the lady archers? That's why I took up archery, wasn't it?'

James squeezed her too tightly, but she didn't complain, she needed to feel his warmth and strength, 'I'd forgotten,' he laughed, 'you said you were going to take up archery so you could add your picture to the gallery. And because you're a very determined woman, you did. Clever you.'

Annie felt tiredness overwhelming her, 'I haven't added my picture yet, but one day I'll take you there and you can help me draw my portrait,' she mumbled sleepily.

'Actually, Annie, I was thinking you could take us to the caves tomorrow. We could use them as a sort of base camp.'

Olivia sat bolt upright. Her movement pulled the duvet up with her, sent a cold wave of night air over Beth and Chris. 'Of course,' she shouted, the squeak gone now from her voice, 'I haven't seen the caves, but Annie has told me about them. If they are really only three miles away, we can easily reach them tomorrow. Sheltering in caves would feel safer than being here under the trees. James you really are a genius.'

Annie riled inwardly at Olivia's praise of James. While she agreed James had done well to think of them, they were still her caves, none of the others had seen them. She felt some of the praise was due her way.

'My caves,' she said, 'yes, we'll go to my caves. They always felt like a safe haven when I was a child. I used to go and play there when there was no one else around to play with, so I was usually there on my own, but I wasn't ever afraid when I was there. I used to talk to the archer ladies etched onto the wall and make up life stories for them.' Annie laughed, 'Better than imaginary friends because I could see from the pictures they must all have had exciting lives and adventures.'

Beth stroked Annie's arm, 'I think we should try to sleep a little now,' she said. 'I, for one, feel ever so slightly happier knowing we have some shelter to go to, a base where we can plan for the future of all five of us.'

Six, thought Annie, nestling into James' shoulder. She would find a private time tomorrow to tell him her news.

***

Just as the first flickering of dawn could be seen through the emerging spring foliage on the trees above them, a soft, gentle rain began to fall. Annie felt the damp seeping slowly about her. Her hand reached all around her, confirming what her body had suspected, James was no longer beside her. 'Where's James? James where are you?' Her voice quivered in panic, 'Where's James, who knows where James is?'

Olivia reached to reassure Annie, 'James and Chris went back to your house to get more tinned food and stuff. Now we know where we're going and we'll have a dry place to store it we might as well take as much as possible, even if we have to make two trips from here to the caves.'

'It's raining, it's raining - we're going to get soaked. I want to go home,' Beth's voice floated small, thin and fragile. She held her face to the rain. 'Why us, why did this happen to us?'

'I guess we're the lucky ones, because we survived. Or maybe we're the unlucky ones because we survived,' Annie shuddered as they started to pack into bundles the already dampening bedding. Alerted by deep rustling in the undergrowth, she stopped her task and looked warily around, this wouldn't be a good time to encounter a large boar. The rustling turned into James and Chris.

'Where's the food?' Beth looked at them askance, 'Where's the food? You were supposed to bring more food from the house. We aren't going to survive long on what we brought with us last night.' Desperation echoed through her voice, 'Where's the food?'

'The house is gone, there's nothing left.'

'Nothing?'

'No, nothing,' James swept his hand over the few possessions remaining to them, 'this is all we have. Nothing else is left.'

Olivia, still desperately trying to convince at least herself this was just an adventure, a camping trip, self-inflicted privation for the weekend before the joy of a Sunday evening return to a hot bubbly bath and a cold bubbly drink, called brightly, 'Let's go on to the caves at once then we can have breakfast in the dry.'

Without speaking the words, however, they all knew this no longer had a feel of adventure. This would be their life from now on.

Annie knew she did not want this new life. She wanted the comfort, security and fun of her old life back. She wanted to snuggle on the sofa with James, tell him their baby would be joining them in a few months, share a glass of wine to celebrate the news, before abstaining through her pregnancy, 'for the good of the baby'. Later another glass of wine, or two, to celebrate the birth.

***

The walk to the caves was slow, wet and dismal. Annie led them at a pace she hoped they could all manage comfortably. She knew Chris and James were unused to walking. In gestures of chivalry more suited to a long ago age the two men had insisted on carrying the bulk of the bundles, which made them ungainly and created logistical difficulties when the paths were narrow. When she judged the struggling to be at its peak and their will power and chivalrous thoughts to have been sufficiently compromised, Annie called a halt. Loads were redistributed between all five of the friends. Nobody spoke.

They continued their journey in silence, each lost in their own thoughts. Each summoning from within themselves the previously dormant strengths their new life would demand of them. The journey took longer than even Annie had anticipated. For the others, who did not know the way or the length of their path, the walk seemed never-ending, as if this walk was their new life, as if they had been condemned to walk for eternity.

Perhaps we actually died, thought Beth, perhaps this is what happens after you die, you just walk and walk and walk and walk.

***

'Here we are,' Annie called loudly and brightly.

The caves were before them, on the edge of the trees, looking out across a hillside on which sheep grazed, oblivious to the destruction of the world of people.

'Be careful with this first cave. It seems big, actually it is big, but it has an abyss further back. As far as I know nobody has been to explore it, so I don't know how deep it is. We should use this cave instead. It's quite big and it's dry, I played here often as a child, even camped out a couple of times,' she laughed, 'I had to promise not to go into the other cave. I never did because I was frightened of falling down into the abyss, but I still had to promise anyway to my mum.'

Annie stood at the entrance to the cave, lost in happy childhood memories, as the others staggered wearily in, putting down the weight of their damp bundles. Someone suggested food. Someone else suggested finding a way to hang the wet bedding in the hope it would dry before nightfall. Once more the precariousness and desperation of their situation overwhelmed them, but the horror of what they had witnessed was suppressed within them as the cave filled with a flurry of activity.

James reached for Annie's hand, 'Thanks Annie, this will be so much more comfortable than we were last night.'

'Yes, thanks, Annie.'

'Well done, Annie.'

'Don't know where the five of us would be without you Annie.'

Annie felt the warmth emanating from her friends, they were all one family now.

'Six,' she said, 'soon we will be six.'

Immediately she had spoken Annie regretted letting James hear the news of his impending fatherhood so publicly. She hid her regret in a close embrace which momentarily excluded all others.

Amidst a flurry of congratulations Olivia's words echoed through the trees, 'Oh my God Annie, how are we going to manage a pregnancy and birth if things don't get back to normal very soon?'

All eyes moved from Annie to Olivia. 'Olivia, things aren't getting back to normal ever again.' Nobody could say for certain who had spoken those words. Everyone knew the words echoed their own thoughts.

As the others set up camp Annie sank into silent thought, only these friends would be here to deliver her baby. Her baby would know nothing but this new life they were forging deep in the Forest.

***

Annie had brought her forest school supplies, including an old wok and a kettle. Forest streams provided water. Still in shock, each individually processing the meaning of their new life and the loss of their old life, their families, friends, and communities, they sank into a stupor which lasted as long as their food supplies.

The food they had brought with them lasted two days.

The third day brought a breakfast of two teabags and half a packet of biscuits shared between them, dry weather, warm sun, and dawning realisation of the need to find more food.

Beth stood at the cave entrance, her voice emerged high and thin, 'Olivia, come we must go on a foraging walk.'

Olivia knew the meaning of the squeak in Beth's voice, Beth was frightened. Olivia guessed they were all frightened, they just showed it in different ways.

'Good idea, Beth, there will certainly be new nettles, wild garlic and young dandelion leaves - who knows what else we might find.' Olivia smiled the smile of false happiness as she gathered basket and knife. 'Annie, get a fire ready we'll be having a lovely big veggie stew when me and Beth get back.'

Chris wanted to go with them, worried they would wander far, be unable to find their way back to camp.

'Chris, you are more than welcome to come with us, might be a good thing for you to start learning about the plants we're probably going to be depending on for evermore.'

Chris shuddered at Olivia's words, 'for evermore.' Evermore was always, the rest of their lives, never ending. He felt his carefully constructed belief they were camping for fun jolted from him, felt his feet stumble and his head spin. This was what forever felt like.

'Come with us Chris,' Olivia's voice was gentler, she saw his distress, 'but you being with us won't stop us getting lost.' She looked to Annie. Annie knew the Forest best of all of them. 'Annie, how do we not get lost, how do we find our way back?'

'Until you get to know the paths you have to leave a trail to follow back,' Annie nudged James who was deep in his own despairing thoughts, 'James, make a code, you're good at codes, it's what you do… what you did all day every day in your fusty office. Make a code we can carve on trees. A code they can follow in reverse to get back. And we can follow if we need to find them. It's got to be simple though - they won't have time to carve elaborate pictures, they need to find food.'

Finding the skills of his old life had a use in the wild unfamiliarity of the dense trees, James put aside worries about their survival, about Annie and their unborn baby. The sun rose higher, darkened from time to time by passing clouds, as James spent a frustratingly long time constructing the simplest of codes showing direction and date.

A light drizzle fell as Olivia, Beth and Chris finally set out. Determination gripped Annie. It was time to get organised. She gathered dry wood to make fires for cooking and warmth in the evenings. Carefully she stacked it far enough inside the second cave to keep it dry, taking care not to put it far enough back to risk anyone falling into the abyss. She organised the few tools and utensils they had brought from their old life. Gathering flat stones she created shelves.

Accustomed as he was to Annie's busyness James was worried, 'Annie, what are you doing? You should rest, for the baby you know. What's all this pointless activity for? You look as if you're settling in, you know, making yourself at home.' He laughed, 'Are you nesting, ready for the baby coming?'

'Yes, James, I am settling in, I am making a home ready for the baby, although the baby won't be here until autumn. James, you need to wake up, this is it now. This is what we have. This is forever. This is probably the only life our baby will know.' She took him into a warm embrace, feeling the wetness of his tears on her face, holding him for a long time as acceptance crept into him.

Later, they sat watching the sun begin its descent, waiting for the others to return. Annie felt the reassurance of her fire lighting flint in her pocket. The fire waited to be lit. She and James had collected water ready for cooking.

A small, resigned voice emerged from James, 'Annie, how do we know the water is safe to drink? How do we know the plants are not poisoned in the attacks? How do we know the water, or the plants aren't going to kill us?'

Annie's voice shook slightly. She spoke quietly as she reached for James' hand, 'The truth is we don't know these things, but this is all we have. All we can do is trust all the goodness of our Forest has not also been destroyed. We must make use of the different skills and knowledge we all have so we can survive here amongst the trees. Certainly, there are still birds, you must have heard them singing and we have seen squirrels, so they have survived. Perhaps tomorrow we should see if we can find any of the boar, or sheep, or find signs of, well, you know, rabbits, badgers. We could go back to the pond, see if the ducks have survived. If the trees, land and water are still providing for them, it will provide for us also.'

Annie knew none of these signs of survival would change their situation, but she saw her reassurances lift James' spirit, take him from the depths of his despair to a place where he could begin to have hope.

Guessing the others would not be much longer in returning, and needing some activity for herself, Annie rose and lit the prepared kindling. Slowly she fed wood to the fire, trying to keep her thoughts positive for the sake of her baby. She placed large stones around the fire, containing it, keeping it safe.

Rustling footsteps and voices announced the return of the foragers. Olivia's basket overflowed with green leaves. Chris carried more.

'Look,' Beth cried triumphantly, showing handfuls of wild mint and blackberry leaves, 'We can have tea to aid our digestion, almost like being at home and buying mint tea from the supermarket. Come to think of it I don't know why we didn't always just make our own.'

'Well, it would certainly have saved us some money, the amount of mint tea you used to drink.' Chris laughed without mirth. The foraging trip had not enamoured him further of forest life in. The thought of vegetable stew, followed by mint tea and another night in the cave did nothing to persuade him this new life would become bearable.

'Look,' Olivia's voice bubbled with enthusiasm as she flourished the spoils of their forage, 'we've got sorrel and garlic mustard.' She tossed the sorrel into the cooking pot, 'here Annie, hold the garlic mustard back, it's going to be very bitter if we cook it too much, we'll put it in at the end. Look we've also got ground-elder, goosegrass, dandelion, nettle and good old wild garlic, even Chris likes wild garlic, even though he doesn't really eat vegetables, do you Chris?'

Chris grunted and pushed thoughts of bread, potatoes, oranges aside, 'Could do with some meat,' he mumbled. He sat despondently on a low, hard stone, 'and a sofa.'

'And a telly,' James muttered, hoping Annie wouldn't hear him, hoping Chris would.

Beth heard him, 'Honestly you two, you're just going to have to get used to not having all those creature comforts.' There was a catch in her voice. Now their coffee supply was gone her head had ached all day. What she really wanted was cake and caffeine as well as the veggie stew Annie was cooking. She wanted to be able to regret the irritation in her voice but found it served well as an expression to herself of her own discomfort, her own wish to have their old life back.

'This stew is delicious. It's got a real garlic taste from the wild garlic and the jack-by-the-hedge.' Annie's enthusiasm was not contagious.

James grunted in response, 'Yeah, delicious, just not very filling, could do with some pasta to go with it, not very sustaining on its own.'

'James is right,' Chris spoke quietly, sadly, 'hard to know how long we can survive on just this.'

They all detected the false brightness in Olivia's voice, 'Don't worry chaps, when the weather conditions are right, I'll be able to find us loads of mushrooms, you know, edible fungus, they'll be much more filling.'

'And roots,' Beth's brightness was even less convincing than Olivia's, 'there's loads of edible roots. After all, aren't carrots and parsnips and potatoes just edible roots.'

As spring drifted into summer they sought damp spots for occasional mushroom finds. Leaves and roots continued plentiful. They knew, when autumn arrived there would be an abundance of chestnuts, hazel nuts, mushrooms and edible berries.

***

By the time summer was well under way Olivia declared James and Chris to have become sufficiently knowledgeable in plant identification to be trusted alone on a foraging walk. 'Perhaps,' she said to Beth and Annie once the two men had departed, 'it might lift their spirits a little. They have so little resilience and I for one find their gloom very suffocating. Maybe spending some time together just the two of them will, you know, perk them up a bit.'

James and Chris reluctantly marked their trail as they left the caves, 'I suppose we'd better, just in case one of us falls and breaks a leg.'

Chris laughed at James' remark, 'More likely they'll just take it into their heads to follow us, you know, check up on us following the rules and all that,'

Slowly their basket filled with edible plants, 'Better leave the mushrooms, don't want to poison anyone, Olivia can collect those, at least she knows what she's doing with them.' James kicked a fungus and watched as a cloud of grey spores puffed out of it.

'This is crazy.' Chris said, 'We won't be able to live like this through the winter, maybe we should try for squirrels.'

Chris' words jolted James. So much had he sunk into a depressed acceptance over the past few weeks, he had ceased to consider how their situation might be improved. Their foraging search had taken them to the very edge of the Forest. They paused to watch a small flock of sheep grazing. The scene unchanged forever, unless they raised their eyes to the grey devastation far in the distance, the open river a bridge had once crossed, the heaps of rubble where a town had once stood. They kept their gaze on the sheep.

'The sheep!' James almost screamed. 'The sheep,' he repeated in more moderated tones, embarrassed at the screeching voice which had emerged in front of Chris. 'If we get a sheep, you know, like, kill it, the sheep I mean, if we kill a sheep, there'll be loads of meat. Roast lamb and lamb stew. Oh, my mouth is watering just at the thought of eating lamb. Look, it's right there in front of us. Just think how pleased the ladies will be, you know when we take back meat, when they get a change from veg stuff.' James turned to face Chris.

Chris wanted to hold back his enthusiasm, sorry the idea had not been his, but the thought of lamb roasted over the fire prevented him. Drooling was all he managed to hold back. 'You're right James, let's go for it. We'll get a big one then, ha, added bonus, we'll have a good-sized fleece to keep your baby warm after it's born.'

Carefully they studied the sheep.

‘There, he’s a big one, got a good fleece on it too,’ Chris pointed.

James nodded, ‘Got the knife?’

Chris nodded.

‘Right, let’s go, I’ll pounce on it, grab its head, pull it back and you cut its throat with the knife.’

Chris nodded.

Slowly, cautiously, they crept around the flock, edging almost silently towards their target sheep. From too far away James launched himself headlong onto the sheep. He clung tightly to the thick fleece as the startled sheep, bleating noisily, dragged him with it in a wild attempt to rejoin the flock which had surged away, terrified by the commotion.

‘Chris, Chris,’ James screamed, stones and brambles tearing at his legs, ‘come on Chris, I’ve almost got him.’

The fleeting thought, her not him, passed through Chris’ mind. He refused to let it linger, this was not the time to be pedantic. He ran, stumblingly, trying to put himself between the sheep and whatever safety it saw in the distance. Stop the sheep, was the only thought he allowed to linger.

‘Chris, Chris,’ James’ screams were becoming fainter and more desperate as he felt his strength begin to leave him. He buried his face in the fleece, just clung on, tried to ignore the pain in his legs.

Seeing Chris ahead, the desperate sheep turned back on itself dragging James under her, his body crushed and trampled. James struggled to breathe. From beneath the sheep he heard Chris call, 'Don't let go James, I've got it now, just got to get the knife out.'

Chris held the head of the sheep, pulled it backwards, trying to get the knife to its throat. In terror the sheep thrashed, letting out long screaming bleats as she struggled in vain to regain her feet. Chris had never used a knife for anything beyond cooked meat. In his old life he had even found the cutting of raw meat rather more than he could easily tolerate and so the task of basic food preparation had always fallen to Olivia or Beth. Chris felt his stomach heave forth the remains of his last meal as he drew the knife, with what he hoped was sufficient force, across the sheep's throat.

Strangled, screaming, guttural, bleats still echoed, started anew. Without conscious thought Chris knew the force of his knife had been insufficient. He would have to cut again. Loudly he cursed the now unconscious James for leaving the butchery to him. Everything slipped in the warm coursing blood of the sheep, his hands slipped, his feet slipped. The sheep slipped as she continued her fight for life all the way to death. Even James slipped. As the sheep rolled off him his limp body slithered slowly down the incline of the hill. Time passed in slow motion for Chris as he took in all the happenings around him before pulling the knife once more across the throat of the sheep.

The sheep lay still, its fleece slowly staining red with its own blood.

Chris lay still, apart from the heaving of his chest as he fought the panic and terror which had engulfed him. Desperately he tried to breathe, to calm himself, to restore some feeling of normality. Slowly the sheep's blood he lay in stained his clothes red.

James lay still, his clothing stained with the sheep's blood, with his own blood.

'Bloody hell James, that was,' Chris gasped, still fighting for breath, 'that was… I don't know. I don't know what it was, do you? But we won in the end. Sheep's dead alright. Didn't know sheep had so much blood in them. It's everywhere, oh God, I'm covered in it…and it smells and, oh God, we've still got to cut the bloody thing up. And take the fleece off. Well, I'll tell you what, I'm not washing the fleece, you and Annie are going to have to do it, it's for your baby.' Chris tried to laugh, 'Unless you want a smelly red fleece to wrap your baby in?'

Chris stood, shoulders hunched, breathing as gently as possible through his mouth, trying to avoid taking into his lungs or his brain, the dead sheep smell. He felt his body swaying, his head heavy on his neck. He felt a fierce aching in his arms and shoulders. He leant against a tree, determined to keep upright, move on, get the job done before darkness came. He experimented with cautious arm movements. They still worked, but slowly, weakly, painfully. He looked for the knife. Saw it embedded in the neck of the sheep. The knife looked small beside the size of the sheep. The size of the task it still needed to perform.

Slowly he lifted his body from the support of the tree. He stayed upright. The swaying became less. He walked, experimentally, a few steps. His legs ached almost as much as his arms. But they held him upright. A few more steps took him to the sheep. Slowly, feeling revulsion within himself, he reached for the knife handle. His other hand he placed on the bloodied fleece covering the shoulder of the lifeless sheep. The knife slipped out more easily than he had anticipated and so the force of his pull sent him flying backwards, one arm held aloft, desperately trying to keep the knife secure in his hand and out of his own body. A loud grunt escaped from his throat as he landed heavily in brambles. Blood oozed slowly from the deep scratches and crept down his face to mingle with the drying blood of the sheep.

Chris called to James, exasperation in his voice, 'James, come on, you going to lie there all day? We've got work to do. A bloody great sheep to cut up in case you hadn't noticed.'

For the first time since the killing, he looked towards James. The images seeped slowly into his brain. James lay still. James lay crumpled. James' legs were covered only by a few remaining tatters of his trousers. A broken bone protruded from one of James' legs. The angle of a shoulder told Chris it had dislocated from its socket. Chris felt everything inside him lurch and sink, felt the world erupt in a crazy spinning. Was James dead?

'James,' he called. 'James, are you okay? Don't try and move, I'll get help. No, I need to make sure you're okay first.' He knelt beside his friend, trying to contain the lurching in his stomach. From this vantage position he saw James' chest rise and fall in shallow, heaving breaths. A wave of relief passed through him. 'Well James, you're alive and breathing. I'll get help, I'll fetch Olivia or Beth, better not let Annie see you like this, you know, with the baby nearly due and stuff. No, I can't leave you here alone. Bloody hell, of course I can't leave you alone, what am I thinking, you're not even conscious, are you. And all this blood and the dead meat, God no, I can't leave you alone. It's almost dark. Wouldn't even find the way back in the dark, would I? And what about the foxes? I bet they won't be long coming after the meat. Oh my God, and the boar, they're basically pigs, aren't they. They'd probably eat you as well.'

'Shut up.'

Chris stared at his friend's face, 'Bloody hell, did you speak James? Did you speak? Well of course it was you, there's no one else around. Oh my God James, I thought you were dead.'

Chris saw James' eyes were open and full of pain.

'Help me, Chris.'

Chris moved his friend as gently as he could find the strength to do.

'You've got two dislocated shoulders James. So long as nothing's broken I can put those back, although your arms will be pretty much out of action for a while so everything around can heal.' Slowly Chris explored the damaged shoulders, better to put them back into place now while James was semi-conscious and already in so much pain a little more would make no difference.

James screamed as the first shoulder regained its socket and again with the second but they both felt better for being where they belonged. He tried hard to hold onto the knowledge Chris was helping him, tried not to blame Chris for the pain.

Chris felt calmer now he could direct his attention to helping James. He looked into James' eyes. They focussed on him, moved on request. No bleeding from the ears. When James spoke, his words were coherent. 'Well, James, the good news is you don't seem to have any brain damage.' They both managed a smile. Chris moved his hands along James' spine. 'Can't find any damage to your spine either.' He moved his hands to James' chest, 'Okay James, you've got some broken ribs. They'll just have to mend themselves, can't do much else with broken ribs except try not to move too much until they start to heal.'

Hands continuing to move over his friend Chris confirmed he could find no damage to James' pelvis, 'But your left leg is obviously broken.'

'Is it?' muttered James, struggling to focus beyond the pain on what Chris was saying, desperately trying not to slip back into oblivion. He needed to know what was happening to him.

A dry, choking laugh emerged from Chris' throat, 'Yeah James, it certainly is, I can see the bone.' He continued rapidly, not wanting questions from James. 'I can fix it together if we can make a splint. I can't x-ray so it might turn out crazy, but you'll be able to walk.' I hope, he muttered to himself.

'Your other leg looks fine, well I mean not broken, obviously you've got a ton of cuts and bruises, and it looks bad. Don't know what to do now. I can't leave you alone through the dark so I can get help from the others. Probably I need to try and fix your leg up. Sooner the leg is in a splint the better, I suppose. Not much light left though,' Chris sighed deeply, 'we'd better get on with it then. You ready? It's going to hurt.' He wished Annie, Beth and Olivia were there - he didn't want this responsibility to himself.

Chris was used to feeling tension in his physiotherapy patients, used it to help him assess their pain level and the exact location of their physical problem. He was used to sensing his patients mentally pulling away from him as he got close to their pain. This was different, 'another level', flashed through his mind. James was clearly in agony. Everything Chris did increased James' suffering. 'Hold on James, hold on, won't be long, I'm trying to be as gentle as I can, trying not to hurt you. Once I get the bone back in position and some kind of splint in place then at least you won't have me fiddling around with it.' Chris wished James was unconscious so he wouldn't feel the pain.

James prayed to the God of his childhood for the agony to be over, intermittently wishing he was dead, remembering Annie, the baby, regaining the will to live for them.

The splint was makeshift in the extreme, but it served its purpose in preventing James from moving his leg. As darkness fell, the two friends settled to a night filled with cold, pain and fear, the smell of the dead sheep all around them, sounds of foxes feasting on it. Chris heard boar as well but thought he'd better not let the immobile James know. Neither slept much beyond a few moments of exhaustion before a jolt back to reality. Chris listened through the night for the groaning, grunting, mumblings of pain which told him James was alive and conscious.

***

Night faded. Light crept back. The blood-dried clothes, the knife, lying where Chris had abandoned it, groans of pain from James, his leg in a splint, the cuts and bruises covering both men, the mangled carcass of the sheep, all told Annie the story of the night as she emerged from the trees.

She stood looking over them, 'Why oh, why, are you two men just so stupid?' All her fear from the night of worry, when James and Chris had not returned from their foraging, exploded in the words. 'Is his leg broken?' She looked to Chris for an answer.

'Wow, Annie, am I pleased to see you. However, did you find us?'

'Chris, in what way have you answered my question? I found you by following the code you marked on the trees. Just as well you managed to remember to mark the code, isn't it?'

Chris opened his mouth. A squeak came out.

'Don't bother answering the question about his leg. I, at least have enough common sense to see it's broken. Good heavens, look at the state of the pair of you. I can't believe you tried to kill a sheep with the foraging knife. What the hell did you think we were going to do with all the meat? Do you have any idea how much meat is on a fully grown sheep? Looks like you've probably provided food for all the boar in the entire Forest of Dean. It's fortunate they found the sheep I suppose, or they might have eaten you.'

Annie paused, looked from one to the other, shook her head, resumed, 'Why did you do anything so stupid? Now I'm going to have to sort out this mess you've made. We won't be able to move James for weeks. We're going to have to build some kind of camp right here. I'll have to go back and fetch Olivia and Beth, they'll have a better idea than me of what plants, herbs we're going to need for your wounds and for any infection. I can't believe you've been so stupid.' She knelt by James, gently stroked his face, watched the lines of pain ease at the touch of her fingers, placed a kiss on his blood-free cheek, rose, looked down at him, 'Good grief James, you smell disgusting.'

Annie walked to Chris, who had risen to his feet trying to block out the screams of protest which seemed to come from every muscle in his body. 'Right Chris, I'm going back to get the others, it's only a couple of miles. We'll be back as soon as possible.' Annie pulled a stronger knife from the bag she carried, 'Here, while I'm gone and you're still filthy, find some clean meat on the poor dead animal and see if you can do anything to save the fleece. Then you're going to have to move the carcass as far away from James and our new camp as possible. There's a stream quite close so when I get back with the others, you'll be able to get cleaned up.'

As Annie moved away Chris called, 'But Annie, you can't walk back to the caves and back to here, you're like seriously pregnant, you need to rest.'

'Chris, I'm pregnant not an invalid. If you hadn't been so stupid I'd be able to rest all day, wouldn't I?' She turned away.

Chris called again, 'Annie, have you got, you know, any food with you? Me and James are starving.'

'No Chris, I don't have any food with me. If you remember, it was your job to collect food yesterday. Get the meat sorted from the sheep and some dry wood collected then when we get back, we'll cook some lamb. James is going to need all the nutrients we can give him.'

***

Beth and Olivia stared at Annie, both struggling to make sense of her words, both wondering how James and Chris could have made the mistakes which left them all now in such a dire situation. 'As if things weren't bad enough already,' said Beth, 'but at least we were coping and had the cave for shelter.'

'And your baby nearly due, Annie you can't give birth under a tree.' Olivia tried unsuccessfully to keep the tears from her eyes, they had already lost so much, almost everything. Now the actions of James and Chris threatened to take away the little they had left.

'Nonsense,' Annie said, her voice emerging louder and more strident than she had intended, 'My baby isn't due to be born for at least a couple of months. With luck we'll be back here in the caves. If James still can't make it back by then, we'll come here for the birth and the boys will just have to look out for themselves. But they want meat. I don't think their foolishness will stop without it. Soon enough it will be winter. There will be little enough fresh vegetation available in the winter.'

'But Annie,' Olivia's voice was calmer now, 'you told us what a mess they made of the sheep. And what a waste, they must have known we can't possibly eat all the meat from a sheep before it goes off.'

Annie added her bows and arrows to the bundles they would take with them.

'Look, my bows have just been here in the cave since we arrived. I was beginning to wonder if bringing them had been a mistake. Now I know it wasn't a mistake. I've only shot at target bosses before, but I'm sure with practice, I could shoot a rabbit or deer. You wanted to have a go at archery Olivia, I can teach you. And you too Beth. You can learn to shoot and we can hunt for meat sometimes - you know, to like supplement the foraged food.'

Beth smiled, the first real smile they had seen from her during the months of their new life, 'Wow, sounds great Annie, if we shoot the rabbits or whatever, can we get James and Chris to, you know, skin them, cut them up, all the gory stuff?'

Suddenly all three of them were laughing together and the future seemed brighter.

Beth lifted the cooking pot from the fire and poured dry earth over the fire to extinguish it. 'Won't need a fire here for a while, will we. Here Annie, you should eat the mushroom stew we made this morning.' She sensed Annie's reluctance to delay their departure longer, 'Annie, you have to eat, you've already walked a long way today. You must eat, if not for you then for your baby. He or she isn't going to thank you for starving them.'

Annie ate quickly, anxious to be back with James but grateful for the food her friends had saved for her. 'Olivia,' she asked, 'Have you got the small whittling knife packed?'

Olivia nodded, anxious not to distract Annie from the food, 'It's right here.'

'We're going to need it, as soon as James can sit up and not be in too much pain, he can be put to useful employment making more arrows for us,' Annie laughed. James had never wanted to shoot a bow but he had enjoyed helping with her arrows and had many times told her he could make them from scratch more cheaply than she bought them. Now was his time to do so.

***

Their new camp lacked the security of the caves. Shelter had to be built around James. They could not risk moving him before the bones in his leg and ribs began to set. Chris engaged in an almost continual battle to keep the wet out and the warmth in as James' body struggled to overcome the constant pain and the infections from the open wounds on his legs. The pain from his dislocated shoulders eased as muscles and tendons slowly repaired themselves, aided by the enforced inactivity in the rest of his body.

Beth and Olivia foraged for plants and fungus - yarrow and self-heal to stem James' bleeding, ground elder to ease the burning bruises and, at the edge of the Forest, the rare find of feverfew to soothe the pounding in James' head. They sought the most nutritious leaves, mushrooms, roots, nuts and berries to build strength in his body and so aid his recovery.

'You need to eat as well as possible also, Annie,' Beth looked to her friend with concern, 'You'll need strength and resilience for the birth. You'll need to feed the baby.'

Annie laughed, trying to hide her fear, 'I guess there'll be no going to the supermarket for formula milk, will there?'

At Annie's words a wave of longing for their old life passed through James, 'Oh, my God, remember supermarkets? I remember thinking, I don't know how we'd manage without supermarkets, when I dashed out to get cheesecake, you know the night you came round, the night of the, well, the devastation. Now I know. Now I know how we'd manage without supermarkets.' He sighed deeply from his bed in the bracken and turned his face away from the others.

For a long while nobody spoke as their memories jostled for space in their minds with the everyday concerns of this new life.

'Well James,' Annie's voice emerged a pitch higher than she had expected a reaction to the optimism she had forced into her thoughts. 'Just as soon as your shoulders let you sit up and make yourself useful,' her smile belied the harshness in her voice, 'you can fulfil your long-held ambition to make my arrows. I am going to teach Beth and Olivia to shoot my longbows then we can hunt for, well, you know, rabbits and squirrels - lots of iron and stuff to make you strong again.'

'And for you and the baby Annie, you really need to start thinking about yourself now,' Olivia stretched her arms around Annie's increased girth, 'this baby represents a future for us all. We might have lost our old life, but we haven't lost everything, so long as there is life and birth there is hope.'

***

In the days following Chris was left to care for James, to keep the fire lit and to forage in the area close to the camp for nuts and berries, having received careful instruction from both Olivia and Beth on which they could eat, and which would likely kill them all. He cleaned the fleece, recovered from their ill-fated first hunt. He spent silent hours, while James' body sank into exhausted sleep, looking deep into his memory, recalling the survival skills and knowledge he had learnt as a child with the Woodcraft Folk and the Scouts. With no paper or pen to record these he persuaded James to create a code of symbols which would prompt his memory and keep the knowledge alive in their growing community.

'I'm going to etch it onto the wall of the cave when we go back for the winter, James, so it's always there, you know if…' his voice faded, Chris didn't want to finish the sentence.

James groaned as he experimented with movement of his lower torso to ease the threatening cramp, 'Good idea Chris, but I think you'd better use the wall of the second cave, the one we use for storage, the one with the abyss at the back. Annie won't be too happy if you start putting code all over those drawings of lady archers, will she?'

Laughing hurt his ribs, but it felt good.

***

Olivia took the bow from Annie, her left hand wrapping tensely around it, she felt her arm shaking slightly as, under Annie's instruction she raised it to shoulder height. An arrow, nocked firmly to the string, rested lightly across her glove-covered bow hand.

'One finger above the arrow and two fingers below it on the string.' Annie instructed, 'Now turn your head towards the direction the arrow is pointing in.'

Annie paused her instruction as the baby inside her changed position.

'Ok, now as you're pulling up the bow you're trying to get a straight line from your bow hand, across your shoulders to the elbow of the other arm. Tuck your fingers on the string under your chin and keep your hand, your arm, moving backwards as you release your fingers from the string and let the arrow go.'

The arrow released from the bow and Olivia's body collapsed into itself again. She took in a deep gasping breath. 'Bloody hell, Annie, archery is so much harder than I thought it would be. You make it look so easy.'

'Sorry Beth, hope we haven't put you off,' Annie laughed. 'You'll be good, Olivia, you just need some practice. Of course, beginners don't usually start with such a heavy draw weight, but my bows are all we have so it's in at the deep end I'm afraid ladies. You'll both have to shoot just a few arrows every day, to build your strength over time. Oh, and Olivia, remember to breathe, if you breathe out gently with the arrow release, you're much less likely to asphyxiate.'

'Sounds good,' said Beth with a laugh. She took the bow from Olivia and followed Annie's instructions. 'Wow, feels good,' she said as the arrow landed thirty yards in front of them, 'but you're right Olivia, it's much harder than it looks when you watch someone else do it.'

Beth and Olivia took turns to shoot a few more arrows until Annie announced, 'Ok enough for today, we don't want either of you to injure yourselves, do we? I'm not sure Chris could cope with looking after another injured person. Let's go to where we saw the rabbits grazing and see what I can do. I've never shot an animal before, not even a pretend animal. It's going to be trickier than shooting at a static target.'

Annie, Beth and Olivia watched the rabbits feeding. Annie's heart raced. For today, she thought, I have only one chance. She looked to Olivia and Beth, 'When I release the arrow from the bow it must find its mark if we are to have meat for James. No doubt the rabbits will sense their danger and run away for today.'

Annie raised her arm, clutching the bow, too tightly, aware of her arm shaking as she had seen Olivia's arm shake. Thoughts raced through her mind as she struggled to put all her training and skill into the shot. I need to keep the bow steady, I'm holding it too tightly, I can feel my heart lurching and the baby as well. The baby seems restless and anxious, maybe she knows how important this is. I wish the baby would lie quietly for a while. Lie quiet little baby,' she whispered, 'I need to get meat for everyone.'

Annie drew back the string of the bow but quickly, too quickly. With a sigh she brought the arrow down, releasing her draw on the bow. 'Start again,' she whispered to herself. She could feel tension coming from Olivia and Beth, knew they were willing her on. She must start again.

Slowly Annie raised her bow arm, hand lightly steadying the bow at the leather grip, arrow securely nocked on the string, bow arm still. Steadily she pulled back the arrow, easing it to full draw, aiming at the stillest of the rabbits. This time her heart did not pound. She drew her breath in deep as she drew back the arrow. Her breath exhaled smoothly as she gently released the arrow. It felt almost as if she was breathing the arrow from the bow to the rabbit.

'I think it died instantly,' Olivia said quietly, examining the rabbit. 'I don't think it had time to suffer. You did a good job Annie.'

Annie, who had never before killed anything beyond a fly or a slug, breathed slowly, carefully, stilling the disquiet in her body. She knew she would have to do this again. 'Do you think a rabbit has a soul?' she asked.

Beth nodded, 'Yes, I'm sure they have souls. This one died a good death, no suffering, its soul will float away easily, soon it will live on in another rabbit.'

Annie did not stop to think how astonished she was by Beth's words. She thought only of how grateful she was for the reassurance they gave her.

'Come on,' Olivia picked the rabbit up by its back legs, 'let's take it back and cook it. Build James up a bit, he'll be getting weak just lying there waiting for his leg to mend.'

***

In time the warm summer gave way to a gentle golden autumn. Olivia and Beth became stronger and more skilled with the bow. James' shoulders mended well. His ribs healed. The bones in his leg knitted together. He experimented with bearing his weight on the leg. Slowly he regained his former strength. His leg would never again be as straight and true as it had been, he would walk always with a limp. When the danger to his life had passed, he spent his healing days making arrows for Annie, Beth and Olivia.

Once caring for James no longer took all his time, Chris took to watching Beth and Olivia as they practised archery. Late one warm autumn afternoon he stood beside Annie as she too watched them. 'I think, looking from my physio knowledge, the bows are too heavy for Beth.'

'Yes,' said Annie, 'see how she bends her body to accommodate the weight of the bow. Really, she shouldn't shoot it, but she is so keen to learn and to help feed everyone, especially when the baby is born and I might be out of action for a while. I only have two bows. My lighter bow is fine for Olivia and the heavier one is the one I usually shoot.' Annie paused as memories of tournaments and practice sessions on green fields surrounded by other archers drifted through her mind. 'I don't have a bow light enough for Beth. I'm worried she might do herself some permanent damage.'

Chris rested a reassuring hand on Annie's shoulder, 'If there's one thing I do know a lot about,' he said, 'it's the way bodies are formed and the ways they work. I'd like to have a go at making a bow for Beth.'

'Oh Chris, what a great idea,' Annie reached to hug him, 'we don't have anything to lose. There's no other way to get a lighter bow for her. If you do a good job, I'll let you make a bow for my daughter just as soon as she's big enough to shoot.'

'Might be a son,' Chris reminded her.

'No, I feel she's going to be a daughter, an archer. When she's born, I'm going to etch a picture of her alongside a picture of me on the cave wall, with the gallery of ladies already there. Once Beth and Olivia shoot a rabbit or a squirrel, I'll let them have pictures on the wall as well.' Annie laughed. The happiest, most unrestricted laughter Chris had heard from any of them since they had come into the Forest.

***

As autumn drifted lazily along Beth declared it was time to return to the caves.

'I know it's only a couple of miles,' James protested, 'but I can't even manage a couple of miles just yet, we'll have to wait longer, and I'll work at getting my leg stronger. We have to think about everyone's needs, not just if it's going to be a bit cold and damp for a couple of weeks while I get stronger.'

Beth looked towards James, she almost laughed but realised just in time he was serious. 'For goodness' sake, Chris, have a word with James would you, I can't believe what I'm hearing.'

Chris looked up from the length of wood which was slowly emerging into a longbow in his hands, 'Well, he's got a point, Beth. It's a couple of miles of pretty tough walking for someone not long back on a broken leg, especially as it's not mended too straight so he's going to limp and put extra pressure on his spine and his other leg, not to mention his ribs might still be a bit tender.'

Beth's mouth opened but only vague spluttering came from it. Tears of frustration appeared in her eyes.

'For heaven's sake Chris and you James, in fact you especially James,' Olivia had no trouble finding her words, 'whatever are you two thinking of? You're so wrapped up in how 'poor James' is going to manage you seem to have completely forgotten Annie. Annie isn't usually the size and shape we see her today you know. You've just come to rely on her providing for you. You seem to have both forgotten Annie's baby,' she paused with a piercing glare, which shot deep into James, 'your baby James. Your baby will be born any day now. It's already cold and damp at night. We've spent weeks camping out here because you two boys were so bloody stupid, trying to kill a full-grown sheep with a foraging knife. Well, we've waited for you, looked after you, kept you in food, kept you alive. Now it's time for us to think of Annie and her baby.'

Annie felt a twinge within her, she had been feeling them all day, had ignored them. Listening to Olivia she knew Olivia was right. She had no wish to give birth in this exposed camp, possibly in rain, when the relative comfort of a dry cave was just two miles away. She put out of her mind the crestfallen look of defeat on James' face. His needs had seemed paramount for so long but now she knew it was time for her baby's needs to take precedence.

'Beth and Olivia are right James. I really need to go to the caves right now, this evening. It's scary enough knowing there's no professional help for this birth but at least in the cave I can be as comfortable as possible. Then our baby will have the best chance we can give her.'

'Olivia and I will go with Annie,' Beth's firm decisive voice took them all by surprise. It left no room for further negotiation. 'Right away, we will go right away. You two,' she waved towards Chris and James, 'can come in your own time. Maybe by the time you get there you'll have a son or a daughter, James. Being a father will wake you up a bit.'

***

Baby Flora wasted no time in making her appearance in the world once they reached the caves. Named in honour of the forest plants which had sustained them all when everything else was lost to them, she would grow up knowing no other life but the nurturing life of the Forest of Dean and her small community.

In time, other children arrived. Beth kept careful family trees, coded onto the walls of the cave so future generations could arrange their children's pairings to avoid any close family ties.

Soon after Flora's birth Annie added pictures to the gallery of archers on the cave wall. She added Beth and Olivia, who were both becoming competent archers able to provide for the community. She added herself and her daughter. She depicted Flora as grown somewhat. Flora with a bow of her own, about to embark on a hunt with the women of her community so they might provide for everyone whilst the men stayed near the camp, busy with the making of bows and arrows.

In her seventh summer, Flora received her first longbow from Chris, her first arrows from her father James. Overjoyed she took them everywhere with her. Thus it was, Flora had her longbow in her hand one day as she ventured to the edge of the Forest. She looked out across the devastation over which the trees and undergrowth were slowly encroaching.

Flora stood, the tip of her bow resting on her foot, watching a woman walking towards her, a longbow in her hand, a lamb close beside her.

....

....

Also by Tricia Davies

Harold: A Wise but Unpretentious Man

Harold was born in 1920, the world changed a lot before his death in 2018. Harold was not an extraordinary person, except, perhaps, in living a longer life than many. Like all of us he was a victim of circumstances, a man of his era, and a product of a less than perfect education system. Harold was keenly interested in the world around him. He cared about humanity. He knew that some struggles are worthwhile and some are not; some things are worth a battle, some are not.

Harold was a wise but unpretentious man who lived a long life and left the world no worse for his having been here. Here are some of the stories from his life.

....

Any Port in a Storm

A novel of historical fiction

Late in the 19th century, in south-west England, a long-lasting feud between the villages of Entney and Newlyd continues almost silently. Will the inhabitants of the two villages ever see themselves as part of the same fishing and farming community?

Moving gently through the lives of the villagers, Any Port in a Storm explores some of the ways in which lives are subject to the vagaries of fate. The story tells of the ways in which some of the villagers, from both Newlyd and Entney, have sought their own 'ports' in their times of need, the storms of their lives; until the day a storm at sea threatens the lives of those out in the fishing boats of both villages.

How will the villagers respond to this crisis? What will be the legacies for their communities?

....

William Fitzhenry 1649

Historical fiction

William Fitzhenry, an extraordinary man.

He thinks.

Your opinions may differ from others who know him.

Are you right, are you wrong?

Who can tell?

Do you see what he sees? Do you know what he knows?

People around him, do they know him well?

Does he hope, does he dream? Does he love, does he scream?

Does he take, does he give? Does he live and let live?

Meet him and judge for yourself.

Here are some tales of his life.

Some of pleasure, mostly strife.

....

Printed in Great Britain
by Amazon

54961136R00156